Stars of the Milky Way

Patricia A. Brahm

Winston-Derek Publishers, Inc.
Pennywell Drive—P.O. Box 90883
Nashville, TN 37209

Copyright 1991 by Patricia A. Brahm

All rights reserved. No part of this book may be reproduced in any form without written permission from the publishers, except by a reviewer who may quote brief passages in a review to be printed in a newspaper or magazine.

First Printing

PUBLISHED BY WINSTON-DEREK PUBLISHERS, INC.
Nashville, Tennessee 37205

Library of Congress Catalog Card No: 89-51295
ISBN: 1-55523- 261-2

Printed in the United States of America

*This is for Matilda, my maid,
who fed me emotionally, as well as physically,
while I worked on this novel.*

PROLOGUE

John W. Tillman had never looked more docile. For once, his eyes were closed in peaceful sleep. Yet, knowing Dad like I did, I had to wonder if my wise old man wasn't just playing possum . . . lying perfectly still, watching and counting every last one of his callers as they paraded by his grave, listening intently for any negative comments. I just knew he was *dying* for the chance to pounce on one of them, if they as much as *contemplated* an evil thought over his bloodless corpse. He was a proud man and hated to die. If there had been a way for him to ensure his mortality, I guarantee he would have found it. My dad fought death bravely, fighting all the odds and hanging in there until he was very confident that his last will and testament was securely in place. He would have been sixty-two next month, in April.

I have always believed that wills and last testaments were made for our government's purpose of securing their fair share of the money, the lawyer's guarantee of more than their rightful share, and finally for children of the deceased to squabble over and challenge once their parent's are peacefully disposed of; out of sight, out of mind!

Battle rockets can be launched in certain families when a will is probated, and the parents who built that rocket, unknowingly, have provided us heirs with the booster's fuel and igniter. Such was true of my family. Since birth, we Tillman heirs were taught to be aggressive . . . be alert to one's own needs . . . stand up for your rights . . . fight for your place in life and what's rightfully yours . . . nothing will be handed to you, work for it . . . stand on your own two feet: our *past legacy*! Sometimes, when conflicting past and present legacies come together, it can be quite a display of fire power!

Before my dad's will was probated, I never really gave the contents a second thought. My mom was still living, and I assumed what they had worked so hard for would rightfully be left to her. But, as you will see, some men don't play by the rules of death according to Hoyle!

Dad was a strong-willed, fast-tempered, shrewd, brute of an Irishman that used his cunning, inherited traits to build upon his father's legacy, massing a fortune by the time of his death. Unlike Grandpa Tillman, who found his will only a paper necessity, we third generation Tillmans didn't provide my dad with such an easy guarantee after death. For John W. Tillman's strongest and most capable child was not his eldest and only son—it was his middle child: a female rebel-rousing product of the sixties, the spunky, black sheep of the family—Patricia Anne Tillman, alias: Patricia Tillman Sawyer, divorced; Patricia Tillman Pollack, divorced; and finally, born again Patricia Anne Tillman. I'm all of those Patricias.

The thirty-eight years I shared with Dad on earth never gave me a clue to the real way he felt about me, not until the day his will was probated. Our family's day in court: the day he withdrew his protection that two of his children had sheltered themselves so comfortably in for years, the day one's past rides forward and takes hold, challenging your sanity and purpose here on earth, the day some families are divided forever, or, linked to immortality through a new awakening!

Things happen to families. This is a story of such happenings that shook my being with such force that I crawled into a hole. It wasn't until after I peeked my head up like a ground hog in search of fresh spring air, and smelled the arrival of the first early spring in four years, that I was able to chase my winter shadows away! First, I was forced to look back, then forced to look forward and carry the Tillman crest on my shoulders.

I'm going to report flashbacks of my childhood history that led me to my ground hog hole. I'm going to tell you why, for thirty years I had been carrying a shovel in my hand, digging with little scoops, one at a time, until I was ready to jump into the four-by-six hole I had prepared.

For so many years, I had successfully buried my childhood. I buried the bad memories, lying to myself so convincingly that I no longer could tell truth from fiction. I had taken a hurt heart and darned it with with threads of woven lies.

I had needed to love my parents without reproach, placing the blame for my family's evil and horrid ways on certain siblings; infrequently on myself, never on my dad. As a child, I always felt I wouldn't grow without my parent's love, needing them like a plant needs fertilizer. But no matter how many times I desperately tried to sever that needed love, I failed. For some strange reason, my draw always came up one card short of a flush, or a straight, or even two-of-a-kind. I barely survived the deals dealt me as a child. But things changed when the last family game I joined in on had a new dealer and a fresh new deck of cards, and my final hand would prove to be a winner.

At first, the other family players in the game sat smirking in delight at their dealt hands, while I sat frowning in fright at mine. I knew I was ready to fold, no bluff would work this time. I was ready to drop out. Then, the wise dealer dealt the hand, giving me a final draw that I could stand. Fresh cards from the bottom of the deck seeped into my dark hole, letting me inhale long, deep breaths of luck, chance, and some fresh air—for my dealer, Dad, had dealt me a royal flush!

After my big win, I was ready to play again. After sucking up the pot from the win, I wagered a large investment, my family's future, and offered anyone of the five players the right to cut. I dealt from the top of the deck, but still, two of the players wanted a new deal. It was too late, Dad had stacked the deck his family would use for the next ten years, and I would give them the choice to draw, stand, or fold!

I've shuffled the deck, ready to deal . . . are you ready to play?

PART ONE
BRIDGING THE GAP

CHAPTER ONE

The limousines lined the last road Dad was to travel here on earth. Money reeked throughout the crowd, minks and sables adorning the beauties that were fortunate enough to be friends with the great man. Women certainly outnumbered the men, as the family found it difficult to sum up enough pall bearers to carry the large man to his final resting place. He had been a man of women.

It was mid-winter in Nashville, as the Tillman family progression filled the front row of seats that sided the large hole in the frozen ground. The wind whistled, producing sounds of flapping tent doors and forcing a dreary feeling over the already large gathered crowd. The grave site had been prepared months ago when the ground was still soft under summer feet, calling out for him to fill it before the first freeze. To the hole's satisfaction, that day had finally come.

First came his ailing wife, Amanda, pushed in her wheel chair by her lifelong companion and our family priest, Daniel. Mom was still very lovely, capitalizing on every youth cream since she ripened to forty. She was alert, quite sneaky at times, and sometimes even witty. She was crafty as a fox, one not to be underestimated. Her mind had stayed in tact, but her body paid the price of severe arthritis and chained her to her mechanical wheels.

Next came the only son, William (Bill). Rightfully so, he didn't have the tag of John Junior. He was an overly dependent child, clinging to Mom's chair for a free ride through life. I never thought of him as being handsome, but my opinion is somewhat clouded by his weak personality and our tarnished relationship. With his head hung low, in what would look like a remorseful pose to anyone who wasn't well acquainted with the son, he carried his slumping body to the first chair and took his seat. His wife of ten years, Mary, and their two children obediently took their place behind their only link to the famed Tillman name.

Bill was followed by the oldest daughter of Amanda and John, Matilda; Tilly the Hun to daring minds . . . especially to my younger sister's and mine. Tilly was overly tall, overly fat, overly homely, single and sour at thirty-six. To be around Tilly invited hurt.

The family procession continued, paving my way next. I was the third child, and was the beauty of the family to nonmembers only. As usual, eyes raised and mouths watered as I eloquently stepped my way to the seat next to my older sister. Flanked on both sides by my three children, we made quite a picture; two generations of beauty and brains. My children took their seats directly behind me, not quite ready to spread their wings yet. Soon, when their time came to fly, all three would soar with the Tillman name crested on their lappets.

Meekly, Angelica trailed me like a dog trails its master, and took her seat with poise. Angelica was my shadow. I was her coat of armor. A similarity existed between us, but only one of looks, not personalities. Angelica was the soft and most caring daughter, the baby of the family, who was known to nurse swatted flies back to health, setting them free when she healed their wounded wings. Angelica was truly a beautiful cherub and was meant to be adored by the whole world.

All four children came to their father's grave out of love, not duty. Some regrets, but no debilitating feelings of hurt from past wrongs dealt by our dad's large firm hand kept any of us from his side on that day. Each child held their own memories, and each handled them privately. We all had loved him, knowing him for who he was, and accepting him with all his faults and wild hairs.

Mom and Dad had been an undivided team in parenting, and only together did they cause the pain and suffering each child has somehow survived. Separated, John and Amanda would have been completely different parents, and

I often wondered what my life would have been like if I had been raised by one or the other, not both. I know if I had been given a choice, I would have picked my dad to raise me.

I sat patiently waiting for Dad's final bow in life, thinking that if Mom and Dad had been buried together on this day, as a team, some of us children would never have shown.

As the wind whipped at the tent, Father Daniel made the final sign of the cross, and made his way to Amanda's side. "Let us all go and leave John in peace," were the last fitting words heard in the cemetery on March 4, 1976.

• • •

The smell of life and its abundant harvest filled the Tillman mansion as the mourners called and shared their condolences with the family. The day's ordeal was almost over, and soon the family friends would leave their sorrow behind and go about their lives as usual. A few of us Tillman's would continue to mourn Dad's death for a long period, but not I. He wasn't really gone, I just couldn't see and touch him. He would always be next to me in thought, and if I needed him, he'd be there to guide me; somehow I believed this to be true. Heaven was always some place high up, out of reach to me, until Dad's leaving brought heaven and earth together. That magical place was now in my reach, not further than Dad's continuing voice of strength as I questioned his wisdom and sought his guidance. I just couldn't touch his materialistic body. . . .

"It's about time they stopped coming, Mom, so why don't you let me get you settled for the evening," Bill said, meekly offering his aid.

"Don't patronize me, Bill. Tilly will see to me when she's ready," retorted the elderly lady of sixty-one, whisking Bill's hand from the arm of her precious wheel-of-fortune chair. "Aren't you leaving for your place, or do you plan on sticking around to see how much your father left you?" She spun her wheels around, moving her eyes to Dad's portrait that hung above the mantel. Bill was alerted to her indifference; it being one of the rare occasions when she snapped angrily at him.

"I know when the will is supposed to be read, Mom, I'll be back then." Bill's sad, untrusting eyes took a quick glimpse in Dad's painted direction. Now that he's gone, maybe the time's right to ask what she knows of the will, he thought to himself. "Do you know the way he left us all, Mom?"

"No . . . you'll just have to wait until Monday." Amanda's quick mind drifted to the conclusion she had long ago derived at concerning last wishes and wills, "Why should one get a say after death anyway?"

She never did like hearing from the dead, and dreaded the reading of the will terribly. She often spoke of how her grandfather's final act in life had destroyed and dismantled her family's future—instead of a large undivided family, her's became a vengeful, hating one. Man and money can do that, she thought. It's a legal combination and all it takes is one stroke of a pen.

• • •

The last act of John Tillman's would be his wildest. Not one of us offspring, not even Mom, would have been able to see it coming, or speculated that his final wishes would talk like they did.

As the lawyer inserted the video tape, I watched as we all tried to cope with Dad's final display of style. I sat confident in my individual thoughts relating to what dear old Dad had bequeathed to each. Surely he had seen fit to leave his fortune to Mom, his team partner of forty years. Possibly he'd provide some little token to each child, I assured myself.

The tape began to revolve soundlessly, and after advancing beyond the black and white streaks which were the overture to Dad's ninety minute resurrection, we all listened as his voice and image echoed from his grave.

"Being of sound mind, I, John W. Tillman, will proceed to lay out for my family, summoned here today to the office of my best friend and legal advisor, Brad Sawyer, my last wishes. Take one good last look at your dear father, children, because when this tape is finished, I have instructed Brad to erase the contents. I was afraid some of you would replay the thing until my facial features became garbled, which would displease me greatly. If needed, a legal written copy will be on record at the courthouse for your use, although Brad has ensured me there is no legal way to change my last will and testament."

Dad was reciting from memory, sitting tall in his favorite black leather chair in his very private study. This was a rare occasion for me, because no one, myself included, was ever allowed to enter his study. I remembered his habit of locking the door whenever he left the room, leaving me even more curious each time about its contents and secrecy. Finally, via camera, I was allowed to enter his sanctuary.

I listened as Dad directed his words to Mom. "Amanda, my true love, you never did get to host our fifty-fifth anniversary bash, the one you started planning on our fortieth, so, I've set aside an ample amount of fun money for just that purpose. Celebrate our day in your usual grand manner, knowing I'll be by your side."

He took a pause, flicked his tongue over his lips and smiled at us all before he continued. "See my dear, I didn't cheat you out of your party . . . , even in my comatose state I heard you curse me for dying before our fiftieth!"

I knew that was a dig, he didn't smile before he got his last word in.

"Also dear, I'm sure the money I've left will carry you through old age to your deathbed in style. I've seen to it that you have no dependencies on anyone, only the ones you may choose to implement yourself. I'll be waiting somewhere for you, eager to discuss all the future happenings regarding our family. Please take good notes."

Then, he hesitated, and added, "Remember, I love you."

Bleep . . . bleep . . . then, "The Sound of Music" melody was heard as a picture of blue sky, pieced with moving clouds of pure white, scrolled across the large screen. I remember wondering if that was the end of Dad's bequeath, until suddenly . . . the sounds of thunder and dark grey clouds replaced the last fluffy white one as it slowly edged off the screen. A bolt of lightning flashed, striking a weeping willow tree to the earth. My heart pounded to the beat of the storm. The base of the tree lay smoldering, its branches ripped off and scattered around the base of the trunk. With the image still fresh in my mind, Dad's angry voice alerted his family to attention.

"I remember well the day my first child was born, bringing the sound of music to my ears and heart. I had many dreams for you and I to fulfill, William." The curves of his mouth turned down, the cancerous portion of his lower lip reflecting pain. "I needn't go into detail explaining the years you will spend on earth without me."

Inwardly, I could feel a big slam coming. Dad's voice was one of anger and vengeance, and I knew that tone so well.

"You're on your own, William!" His eyes were shooting red darts!

I couldn't believe what I had heard. Dad thought about Bill exactly like I did . . . my eyes surveyed both Bill and Mom. Their expressions were identical, exchanging looks of hurt, pity, and then almost simultaneously, a paired look of mutual understanding came across their faces—Mom would bail her wounded son out, once again, I thought.

It was a shocking bequeath that literally amounted to nothing, but perhaps one that would prove to be perfectly suited for Bill. I felt it was something both my parents should have done years ago; force their overly-dependent son to stand on his own merits. But why did Dad wait until now?

A well-timed intermission, accompanied with soothing music heralding from the screen's speakers. Tilly, Bill, and Mom huddled together like lost sheep, obviously deep in conversation about the spectacular way Dad chose to emote his dying thoughts. I supposed that somewhere in their conversation Bill tried to secure his future with Mom, and Tilly was babbling her assurance that he needn't worry about his future. She'd say anything to please Mom.

Angel had moved to my side, wearing a shitty grin of approval over what she had heard. Angel was always at my side.

Coffee and Danish were served, and after the allotted fifteen minute break, which I felt was too long of an intermission because the anxiety of what was to come was arousing my ulcer, we all were finally seated and ready for Dad to begin again.

The tape produced a poster reading, "Intermission Over, Ready Or Not!," which was held by a shapely blond clad in a mini-french maid's uniform. As she pranced her bountiful wares across the screen, I thought about Dad enjoying one last look at young flesh: a look I was sure still brought an erection to the one part of him that would never die. God save the angels!

The tape rolled a chubby, brunette ballerina onto the screen, high on her toes, gracefully stretching in her pink tutu in front of us, replacing the card-holding blond. The color of her tutu was symbolic, telling all that his next child to enter the world was a girl: Matilda.

Before Dad appeared back on the screen, we were shocked when the tall dancing ballerina's right ankle gave way and she clumsily tumbled to the floor with a loud thud. She tried to stand, but realizing she couldn't use the wounded limb, she succumbed to the floor in tears and crawled mercifully off the screen.

I thought of Tilly, sneaking a glimpse down and across two chairs to where she sat. Her crossed, lumpy leg was bobbing as if her ankle was really broken.

Dad's voice broke my thought. "Hello daughter Tilly, my first pink bundle handed to me by your loving mother. Like the frame of Bill's, at first your birth delighted me."

At first were his key words . . . don't tell me he's unhappy with her, too, I thought, as I continued to listen to his husky legacy.

"In my arms I held an image of a daughter that should have turned out to be a mold of her mother, but somehow your mother's genes, mixed with mine, exploded together to produce a 'mold-spore'."

I didn't mean to laugh out loud, it just happened. A mold-spore, ha! I've called her many things, but none quite so creative.

Dad continued, "After a visit to my allergist, I found out I was allergic to molds of all kinds. I tried desperately to rid our home of the dark, damp places that molds thrive on, but you grew anyhow, thriving on such conditions to no avail of mine. Every time I thought I had 'X-14d' the mildew," (Dad gave us a squirt from the bottle that he was handed by his blond aid), "your Mother turned on the shower, dampening my efforts. I've been assured that no 'mold spores' grow where I'm going."

He drew in his stomach, filling his expanding chest with needed air. "So, my message to you, Tilly, is to prepare yourself for a change and accept it. The world you have created for yourself will no longer exist after today. I want you to learn to enjoy your remaining years, to smell the dry, fresh, sunshiny days ahead of you." His voice dipped lower, becoming threatening. "If you don't my most brilliant chemist has developed a new compound called, 'Trish-Away'—a very powerful antidote that once unleashed, will destroy any mold fermenting from this day forward."

'Trish-Away' . . . me! What is Dad trying to say?

"You'll have to be patient and wait to find out the details of my bequeath to you, which I'm sure will become clear after the tape has played itself out. Although you won't comprehend the entire consequences of my final actions at first, I'm sure in time you'll learn my purpose."

Dad always did like cliff hangers, I thought. I now mused over the memory of his rushing home to catch Alfred Hitchcock's weekly thrillers; it was the only night of the week that you could set the clock by the time he arrived home.

Me next . . . my turn, entered my mind. After seeing what he had so cleverly put together to depict his feelings for his first two children, which I thought were his favorites, I was scared as hell in anticipation of my frame. Both Mom and Dad had told me many times that if birth control pills were available then, as today, they certainly would have stopped after Bill and Tilly. My heart sank, and I decided that if my legacy from him was as bad as I expected, I'd leave—grab my children and leave Nashville for good. I held too much pride to sit there and take any more crap from my family, especially since the one person I cherished the most was now gone. I prayed he wouldn't hurt me.

But the preluding music was soft, and at first, just for a quick second, mind you, I found myself tempted to relax some, but I came to my senses because I knew better than to trust my so unpredictable dad. Any minute now I expected a hell of a storm to blow in. The soft music was just a bluff—some fraudulent ply to keep me there, I thought. I knew my untrusting instincts were right, when he announced that he was postponing my frame until after Angelica's. I was left sitting in anticipation again.

Now his face was soft and his smile was kind. I also knew that mood of his, but it didn't surface as frequently as his gruff one did during the years we had shared together. But knowing and loving Angel like we all did, I couldn't imagine any other tempo sounding from Dad as he sweetly started reading to Angelica:

> "Angelica, Angelica . . . so tiny at birth,
> You'll never be shadowed
> By the ups and downs on earth.
> Never once in twenty years
> Have I shed over you a tarnished tear.
> You're my daughter of beauty,
> Both inside and out,
> Your future is paved without any doubt.
> An angel of life is what you're all about."

I proudly heard sniffles next to me. I joined those whimpers and softly our tears flowed.

"Angel, I wrote this poem when you were only twelve, and I never shared it with you before this day. I now know it was meant to be saved for our final moment." His face, now drawn and pale, remained kind. His eyes reflected the softness of their shared love. "I loved you easily, and will rest in peace that someday you will join me, still as pure as you are today. I'm sure after the next and final frame, Trish's, you'll agree with my bequeath. I'll miss you."

Dad's hands closed the book he was reading from, and his head slowly bowed as the next intermission maid slinked across the screen. This time the maid was a redhead. Variety, Dad did like variety. God pardon the devils!

Confusion, tears, snickering, many dirtied tissues, toilet breaks, and the clink of glasses followed. Our refreshments during the final intermission had changed to something more suitable for the occasion, red wine. I secretly hoped the red wine wasn't some symbolic point that he was trying to get across to me—blood!

God, how I wanted a sneak preview of the conclusion, but knew I had to be strong on the outside and take my frame in stride.

Dad's lawyer gave Angel the book that he had read her poem from, and Angel was crying as she thumbed through the pages. I never knew Dad as a poet, never suspected he penned anything but business contracts. I wondered if there was even one in the book about me, and if that's what he did in his secret hideaway, write poems?

Tilly, Bill and Mom remained glued together like the three musketeers, swords drawn from their sheaths ready to slice the tape into shreds.

I refreshed my lipstick and then adjusted my suit, crossing my legs as nonchalantly as possible, considering my legs felt like limbs blowing out of control by the wind, and my hands were ice cold. I never was one to show fright to anyone, especially not to my family. My mind told me to take a deep breath, because ready or not girl, here it comes. My spotted past was about to be played in living color, and the audience was smirking in anticipation.

A scene from the Civil War paced the screen in brilliant color. Soldiers uniformed in gray were keeping step to "When Johnny Comes Marching Home Again, Whorah! Whorah!" Clips of burial sites, cannons, smoldering smoke, tattered rebel flags being carried proudly, and wounded soldiers being helped by nurses in gray, hailed in front of me for the next few moments.

Then came pictures of beautiful southern plantations, including our homestead in Nashville. A picture of a slave shack appeared next, . . . no, it was our old cabin in the Adirondack Mountains, except black slaves sat on the front porch.

I mentally tried to comprehend the double meaning Dad had wanted to get across to us from the previous pictures, but didn't have enough time to formulate a final theory before the next scene flashed on the screen. I almost asked Brad to push pause, but then I was glad I didn't, because I really got the shock of my life. As I sat watching, I could feel heavenly relief rejuvenate my frazzled nerves and calm my active ulcer.

A remake of pictures of Dad and I flashed, one after another, each reflecting my growth from around four until my present age, thirty-six.

The picture of me trying to build my first bird house, wearing Dad's carpenter belt like a shoulder holster, hammer in hand and teeth gritting nails, captured back a memory long forgotten. It was a pleasant memory, one that I hadn't completely erased or buried, and at least it was one I could recall with pride. My build was small but firm. My black pigtails hung down my back, reaching my bottom. I noticed the tip of my tongue was showing between my lips, a habit I had if I was deep in concentration. My eyes glistened deep blue, reflecting the four naive years I had lived as a Tillman.

Certain pictures I could relate to as if they had just been taken, like the one he took the night I was chosen "Prom Queen," with my sweetheart, "The King," at my side. Another good memory, and I found myself sighing in relief.

We all wormed through my athletic accomplishments being boasted in front of us, including every trophy I had ever brought home to him. It seemed like ages since I had seen those things, and wondered where he had kept them hidden all this time. I recalled what it was like to give Dad one of those trophies....

I remember I couldn't wait to get home, trophy under my arm and smile of victory written over my face. "Wait until Dad gets a look at this one." My bubbles were still rounded, flying higher and higher in anticipation of relating how I had received this statue of bronze, with my name etched clearly in capitals across the front. "Is Dad home?" I asked Mom, eagerly stepping into the kitchen.

"He's in his study." She looked at my ego tucked under my arm and asked, "Where are your books, Trish?" I never answered her, knowing she'd rather see books in tote, and it was her deliberate way to shun my achievement. I didn't want to let her pop my floating bubbles, so I hurriedly exited toward the study.

"Dad, can I come in? I've got something for you." I stood meekly waiting for his answer—always the same, as if he had a tape recorder and played the reply every time anyone of us tried to interrupt whatever he was doing behind those closed doors.

"I'll be out in a few minutes. Wait for me in the living room." I knew better than ask if I could go in his study, but I kept trying anyhow, hoping that this would be the time that he'd change his mind and let me in.

I dusted off my smudged prints, absorbing the last bit of self-praise I could from the statue as I backed away from the door. Soon, the trophy would disappear as all the others had. I often wondered if my mom had them melted down for her jewelry.

Dad entered the living room, and I could see pride swell up in him. I'd start to relate my detailed victory, shot for shot, basket to hoop, more points, and then the usual happened, someone, more often Mom than anyone else, interrupted my glory story and Dad left with my trophy. No matter how fast I tried to tell my story, always speeding it up as I went on, I never got to finish it. Gone was my trophy, short-finished was my story!

As a child, I wondered why Mom and Dad made so little of my accomplishments, down-playing them and sometimes just plain ignoring the honors I had won. They never displayed one trophy or clipped one newspaper story of my triumphs, and always changed the subject if I brought up how I felt about my latest win. They never took into consideration how pleased and proud I was of those fetes and of how hard I had worked to be the best—probably afraid it would hurt their clumsy, poor excuse of an unathletic son. They just ignored me and my bronze trophies, hoping both of us would just go away. . . .

I glanced at the screen, as the tape kept flashing my victories, and took a quick peek at Bill. Too bad the athletic traits had been saved for my birth, I thought. They should have gone to Dad's only son. I found out later that it wasn't easy for brother Bill to watch this section of the tape, because my being such a good athlete really bugged him.

Lord, brother Bill was terrible at sports! He actually embarrassed me when we were in school, and more than once I prayed he would give up trying to be good at any sport. I giggled to myself as I thought about the time he went out for high school football, spring practice no less, and he stepped into a gopher hole and broke his leg. That was the longest he ever lasted in football. Oh, but he carried around his cast and wore the team uniform proudly, like he had been injured in a real game or something. It was the only year he ever made the team. He wasn't a pansy, but he definitely didn't have any natural ability for athletics either. How I wished Mom or Dad had spared him the anguish and had just leveled with him—just told him the truth for once.

So far, I was pleased with Dad's walk down memory lane, and again had to warn myself that his moods could change more quickly than any man I knew, so I took another deep breath and got ready for the expected change.

Yes, the good pictures had played themselves out. I found the picture of the state trooper arresting me very embarrassing, as I always thought everyone made more of the incident than it warranted.

My venture as Huck Finn riding the stolen boat down the river at age nine was just a tomboyish-girl, living out a fantasy in a very realistic manner. How did I know that dowdy Chris Weeks would call the cops and report me for stealing his boat! I can still remember how my arms and legs ached for days after being forced to return his boat to his dock, upstream five miles against the driving current.

I had no idea how long a VCR tape could play, but by now I knew Dad had saved half of it for this climax. God save me!

He seemed to be flip-flopping between good pictures and not so good pictures, so I gave up anticipating which type would come next. I decided I'd close my eyes if the next one was bad.

To this day I still favor the next picture of Dad and I fishing on First Lake. I was so proud that I was his only child that qualified for a seat in his boat. He had no patience for frilly, whining, talkative fishing mates. When Dad fished, he treated the sport like man against beast, counting on man to strike down the trophy with every cast. Well, my competitive nature matched his skill, cast and catch!

I even recalled irritating the hell out of him on one excursion, when I was the lucky one to land "Ol' Grandad."

Usually, we kept our stringer's quota for the day, but not on that day. He made me release "Ol' Grandad." I always figured I had to do it just so he could possibly revel in the same catch on his lucky day. He actually made me feel like I had done something sacrilegious!

The last picture came into view. I was standing on the courthouse steps, flanked on both sides by my children. Divorce number two was final. I was so surprised to find out someone had captured one of my more vulnerable days on film that I forgot to close my eyes.

There we were, the children and I, saluting our past, our four middle fingers freely shoved in the direction of the above; embarrassing, but a justified gesture!

Next, Dad appeared wearing a tuxedo, holding a magician's wand and top hat, sided by the blond on his right and the redhead on his left. After slyly glancing at both of their paired puffs, which were highly exposed, he flashed a wink and tapped his wand on the floor several times, again snapping us to full attention, (as if he had to), before he announced, "The finale will begin." A planned pause came, one I was sure he planted so I could take a deep breath, followed by a loud, and needed sigh of relief.

"I'm not going to spend time and words justifying my actions. I never did in the past and I'm not about to now. Search deep and you'll understand them all."

The big moment was about to un-scroll. "Trish, my third child, born female gender . . . , you know that you tricked your mom and I. We didn't want anymore children, and definitely not another girl. You were supposed to be my next son. . . ." His expressionless face took on a new look. He slowly began to smile, and then spoke, "I compliment you on being both a son and a daughter to me. I look at you, knowing that if I had been born a girl, I would have been just like you. I'm glad you tricked us. . . ."

   Thank you, Dad, thank you, I murmured to myself in relief. He didn't hate me, he understood. . . . Angel reached across and placed her warm hand over mine.

His face and eyes turned sad with regret, and I remembered that look also. After a brawling battle of fists flying and cursing words flinging back and forth between us, the fight would end in exhaustion and regret. I was sorry and so was he. For a couple of days after one of our bouts, our regretful eyes would meet, but no words of apology were ever spoken.

I can't tell you that he beat me, I fought back as hard as I could. Yes, I did swing and land a few good, shocking blows during our three-year period as sparring buddies. I'll admit he abused me, but he never beat me!

"Because of our likeness, you have suffered through many ordeals that your brother and sisters never had to. But, through the school of hard knocks and with my rough riding hands, you have learned the most. And you are still growing stronger and wiser as you age. Some people learn by being told, and some learn by doing; you're a doer. No one could ever tell you anything . . . you always demanded proof."

Cigarette break. After a long inhale and exhale, he began again. "At times I felt like I hated you, but it wasn't really you that I hated, it was myself. When I liked myself, I was capable of bestowing a great, strong love on you. You gave me bushels of love back. When I disliked myself, I was capable of destroying you, and you gave me bushels of hate back."

He was right about that, I never did take his crap sitting down. I'd fight him every inch of the way, blow for blow.

"I'm sorry for all the dislikable times! When I look back, as I hope you can and will do, I think our likable times far out-shined our dislikable ones. I'm glad you have returned home, once again."

The trio, (Blond, Redde, and Dad), sang out with "who-rah, whorah!" Now I understood the opening Civil War scene, the symbolism . . . the pain-stricken scenes . . . the battles we had . . . the mending of wounds and the scars.

His next words I'd never forget! "You are my chosen link to the family's future. If you need *revenge*, get it! If you want *forgiveness*, seek it! If you bestow *love*, demand its return in a gentle way. If you think you need *guidance*, search only within. Trust your *instincts* by peering into your eyes which hold the *future*. Use your *powers* to continue to read your *foe's* minds, and take the hand I have dealt you and play it! You're me, and you will be me to the family. I need you now to care for them."

I could see his tear-stained cheeks . . . the hurt in his eyes. He didn't know it, but he had just conquered immortality through me!

I keyed on nine words: *revenge, forgiveness, love, trust, instincts, guidance, future, powers,* and *foes*. I didn't know it then, but those nine words I'd replay again and again over the next ten years, ranking them to suit myself, sometimes someone else, or him.

Abruptly, he tapped his wand on the top of the magician's hat, turned it over and retrieved a scroll which he rolled out in length. For the first time in my life, I saw my dad's hands shake as he held the parchment open.

Blond and Redde used all the wind they had stored in their chest to blow those damn trumpets as loud as they could, announcing Dad's closing words with a blast! "Now here this! This is an amazing trick! What you see and hear before your very own eyes today will astonish you all."

I sat marveling at him, very impressed with his choice of exiting, so anti-normal, I thought. I knew I had inherited his lust for change and the constant need to test the unknown. I had learned my *past legacy* well, and finally was dealt a winning hand, my *future legacy*.

Basically, he left control of his mass fortune to me. I was directed to handle Bill as I saw fit. Same orders for Tilly, except I was to incorporate her into any future investment plans. (She never did work a day in her life!) Angelica shared capitol control with me, but not directive control. Dad had said this would allow his Angel the freedom to fly around earth like she was born to do.

When Brad handed me the deed to the Galaxy Farm located in Pulaski, Tennessee, the one Dad had purchased for me two months prior to his death, I was so proud, but also very shaken. Clipped to the deed was a letter explaining his thoughts on the purpose of the acquisition, and his inspiring ideas on how to use the place as an investment. The last line of the letter, situated between the family seal and his signature, read, "*Do as I would, or as you see fit.*"

The tape finished, and my family sat stunned, pondering what they had heard. It was one hell of a way to probate a will! I hated to see the tape erased. For a brief moment, silence took over the office, then the quiet was interrupted by the noise of Mother's traveling wheelchair.

"I completely agree with what your father has done, and I sincerely hope you all can comprehend what he hopes to achieve by it. I suggest we leave Brad to his other business," and turning her chair to face him, she reached out her wrinkled palm and with a very alert mind, thanked him for his time and help. I thought how nicely she covered her real feelings in front of Brad, and listened as she ordered her family to leave. "It's time to leave, children, will you get the door, Tilly?"

"Certainly, Mother," Tilly complied obediently as ever, jumping like a scared rabbit to open the door, assisting the elderly Tillman and her flock forward into a new reality.

CHAPTER TWO

As Angel and I sped off toward our home, I theorized in confidence with my younger sister my first reactive thoughts of Dad's bequeath. "I can't help but feel a little sorry for Bill. But honestly, Angel, I think I know why Dad did what he did. He knew Bill would always be living off of one of us, and by not giving him any special funds now, he forced Bill to continue to live that way. Why give him money just to squander it all away? It's sort of like he figured Bill would never change and why pretend he would."

Angel and I were closest of sisters, trusting our deepest thoughts to one another for over twenty years. Not once had either of us betrayed that trust, even when we got caught snickering together and Tilly and Bill had demanded to know what our topic was, and why it was so funny. We'd wait in silence for their invasion to leave, and start up where we had left off . . . leaving our sister and brother thinking they were our main topic of delightful conversation.

Angel piped in, "I guess he knew what he was doing . . . and you're probably right, Bill will never be a responsible person. You can't change someone at his age . . . but I wonder what he's feeling and thinking right now. I can't help but feel sorry for him."

"Cursing, you mean, not thinking. He never thinks, he's a dimwit," I quipped. "Everyone always feels sorry for Bill, that's part of his problem. Don't worry Sis, I imagine Mom is trying to soothe him like she's done for forty years."

"I'm glad Dad had the tape erased. I hate looking at someone who's supposed to be dead, although he did have that twinkle in his eye, the one that always preceeded one of his wild hair actions. I used to love that look." Angel smiled a little, and then added, "I bet Tilly would have killed him if he hadn't died naturally."

"Yup, she's got a lot to think about. I guess Dad knew all along how we felt about her, but do you think he really knew what she has been like all these years?" I asked, wondering what made him finally see the light.

"Obviously he did, but he took the coward's way out by forcing you to handle her."

I thought about what Angel had just said. Maybe she's right, maybe he did know all along what it's been like to be a child in his household. No, he would have stopped it, changed things. Dad was no coward . . . was he? Why did he leave all of his and Mom's problems behind? He couldn't have known everything that went on . . . he just couldn't have! I pushed the thought of him being a coward from my mind.

I kept driving in a trance, not paying much attention to the road and cars around me. The speed of the car reflected my racing mind, which for the first time in months was excited with thoughts of how my life was about to change, again.

"I'd better slow down, or we'll end up next to Dad," I reflected to Angel. "I'm just so excited and anxious for us all. I can't wait to finish this mourning act and get on with our newly inherited venture."

I could tell by Angel's expression that she thought I was being somewhat cold and calculating in regards to Dad's death. But she knew I was speaking the too honest truth out loud like I always did, something that she had actually grown to expect of me until late. Angel had noticed that I no longer tried to tell it like it was, even accusing me of mellowing. I told her I was tired of forcing the truth upon people who didn't want to hear it, and that no one listened anyhow, and it would never change anything or anyone, so why bother. I was tired of being hurt. I was finally learning to play the game of "hide and forget."

My mind drifted in thought to the future, imagining what the old vacated Galaxy Farm looked like. I had never been there with Dad when he visited his old business friend, but I had heard all the stories he related about the huge farm when he returned after weekend hunting trips. I knew he kept a few prize horses in the Galaxy Stables, before King Candy died and his family let the place go down. My father's smile came into my vision, remembering his wide beam whenever he spoke of the little man who compounded a chewy candy bar and became fabulously rich on nickels.

"Well, little one," I turned to Angel, "Dad certainly fooled us all." Reaching for my sister's small hand, I clasped hers to mine and squeezed it in optimistic delight. "Just hang in there with me, little Sis, and I guarantee you that we'll have some good times ahead. Little, sleepy Pulaski is about to meet the three most prospecting sisters they have ever known."

"It makes sense now, why Daddy suggested I go to Martin College. I only applied there," Angel confessed, "to keep him happy, hoping he knew what was best for me. I wanted to go to a large school, like you did. But, I'll follow his wishes and spend two boring years there." Her eyes drifted out the window, obviously deep in thought. "I guess I'm not getting any younger. I need to do something besides hang around the house. I miss the Peace Corps."

"All the pieces do come together, don't they? With you attending Martin, you can live at Galaxy with me and the kids, and commute. It won't be boring, we'll be together." No one had ever accused me of living a boring life.

As my red sports car pulled up the long winding drive to my soon-to-be old home, I wondered what would become of the beautiful mansion. Dad's idea of turning the farm into a bed and breakfast inn in Pulaski, demanded my full attention and my live-in occupancy. I wasn't sure I would miss the old homestead in Nashville. I looked forward to my new venture and fresh faces that I wasn't tired of seeing every day and people's smiles that didn't hold double meanings.

Yes, I thought to myself as I climbed the steps of the old homestead, my dad had remained shrewd right up to his death. I felt a form of elation that only I could understand: one that gave me great optimism toward the changing future. Just knowing how he really felt about me gave me birth again.

Five times in my past I had left the security of the homestead to dare on my own into the future. Each departure had been memorial, with myself braining with optimism or steaming with despair.

My first departure/return, which I refer to as D&R, was college and four years later, my graduation. My second D&R was marriage, and five years later, with two children by my side and divorce number one final, I returned. My third D&R was for career advancement, and early retirement due to boredom and lack of challenge. My fourth was because of a family feud over my single-life behavior, and my return came about after a two-year cooling off period. My fifth D&R was marriage again, followed by divorce number two and one more child. I was ready for departure number six, once again full of excitement and cheer, although I hoped this departure didn't end with a return like the other five; more husbands and children I didn't need. . . .

As Angel and I approached the library, we could hear the piercing voice of our older sister, trying to cut through all the red tape and take control of the situation. Tilly's voice always sounded like her nose needed blowing. She was surely twanging a plot, laying a path that all family members were supposed to take, crowning herself God of the clan, ensuring she was boss, as so often she had done during our childhood days.

As kids, my folks went out a lot and traveled constantly, depriving us of their much-needed attention on a regular basis. Before they returned from one of their so-called rejuvenating side trips, I can remember Tilly ordering Angel and I to clean the entire house. We had to push and pull the furniture out, rearranging the rooms the way she liked them, after we cleaned and scrubbed every crevice. My mom wasn't much of a house cleaner, she could have cared less where one chair was from day to day, as long as someone else moved it to a clean spot. Angel and I were so young, and played right into Tilly's hands more than once. After doing all the work she ordered done, we'd anxiously await my parent's arrival, standing in line for our praise and thank-you's for a job well done! But, sly Tilly made sure she was the first child to open the door to them . . . the only child they listened to and praised before the reality that they were home again sank in, which depressed them into boredom, and they'd push us all aside, seeking their paired solitude once again. Consequently, Tilly always managed to get all the praise and applause, while we tended to our blisters and aches and pains from all the work we had done. Thank God Dad finally hired a cleaning lady to replace Angel and I as Tilly's slaves. Slaves . . . my mind clicked back to the video-will . . . was that Angel and I? Were we the blacks on the front porch of the cabin? Did Dad know how she slaved us? Did he regret not bestowing praise where it really belonged?

Boldly, I interrupted Tilly the Hun. "Can't wait to take control and undo everything Dad planned for us, huh, Tilly?" Mom's mouth fell open in a gap of surprise at my question, and Angel linked arms with me, waiting to hear what response our older sister had to my confrontation.

"Certainly took the two of you long enough to get back from the lawyers," Tilly squinted her eyes and met my challenge with an observation dealing in no way with the subject proposed by my accusing question. Whenever she disliked something said or asked of her, she cleverly averted the topic, and usually got away with the planned aversion. But not this time. . . .

"Mom, would you like to rest for a while, or would you like to stay around and watch me de-feather the oldest daughter of your flock," I asked in a confident, more forceful than ever, shocking tone. Pluck her!

Mom panicked, knowing that a family feud was about to break out any moment. "Please, let's not argue and say things we'll regret . . . not on this day of all days. Please," Mom pleaded with daring eyes at me. I was used to that look. But I knew that if I was going to attack, take control that so surprisingly had been delegated to me, then I needed the element of surprise on my side.

Tilly rushed to Mom's invalid side, grabbing her hand in an attempt to coax her into protecting and siding with her. Tilly was clever, and if she had only used her brains in life to better herself instead of strategically scheming and causing everyone around her pain, she could have been a brilliant scholar, or anything she wanted in the line of professions available to women today. But she only saw as far as her pointed nose reached: a foot ahead of her.

I spoke my thoughts. "Not this time, Tilly! Never again will you influence everyone's life like you've done in the past." The battle lines were clearly defined! "Dad has made sure of that for us, and before we join him, you'll learn to get along with us all . . . as an equal . . . not as our Lord and self-appointed master, but as an equal!" My determinate thoughts added confidence to my will, and I found myself continuing to speak with authority like never before. Was Dad speaking for me?

"We need a family meeting, now . . .," and turning to Angel, I asked, "You find Bill, Angel, and have Sarah put the tea on, because this could last for hours."

Angel hustled, smiling her way out the library double doors. "Forgive me Daddy," she shared her inner thoughts with him above and us that were close enough to hear, "if I had know Trish was going to take control around here, I might have wanted you to die sooner."

"Bill, Trish has called a meeting, in the library. Better hurry down, and for God's sake, stop drinking," Angel demanded. "It's not the end of the world, you now . . .actually, it might be your beginning." Her quick little feet could be heard exiting Bill's alcoholic, reeking room as fast as they had entered.

Bill joined us all in his usual, uncaring, teetering manner, bottle and refreshed glass in hand.

Once again, I checked with Mom to see if she wanted to stay, and getting the agreeable nod from the stately lady, acknowledged the time was right to start the meeting. Everyone that mattered, including my three children from two previous marriages and Bill's family, was there.

I felt like I looked good, my clear blue eyes sparkling with sharpness. My perfect ten figure, which I worked hard at keeping, added to my overall package, giving me power from both inside and out. I was ready, but the question remained, were they?

"I've made some decisions regarding our futures, and I think the sooner we bridge the gap between the *past* and the *present*, the better for us all. I refuse to recognize any one of you until I've finished with my say, so don't open your mouths until I'm done. I hate being interrupted!"

I shot a quick challenging glance at Mom, as my mind flashed trophies. "Possibly I've waited too long before setting the record clear, but better now than never. When I'm done, if any of you have anything to say, I'll return the courtesy of listening to you."

I was brilliant, the words flowing from my cage with conviction, words flowing out loud that I had recited quietly to myself for many years. How many times had I rehearsed these words, I painfully counted to myself. I was ready to deal out our future, after I buried our past.

It felt good, unleashing all the bitterness I held toward my older sister and brother . . . divulging happenings that the accused knew were words of truth.

Mom looked shocked by the stories I blurted out, more shocked than she looked when she heard Dad's will played out. She questioned my every sentence aloud. "Did Tilly really make all those lies up? John and I were wrong. We never believed you. You never stole Tilly's beau's heart, never seduced him into an affair with you? You never pawned my jewelry? Then where did it go?" Her eyes quickly turned to Tilly. It wasn't you that set her bedroom curtains on fire; a stunt she said you pulled to get her into trouble, rushing to tell us that you were smoking in her room and set the house of fire. Oh dear God, all the beatings you took for someone else. . . ."

As I continued, unfolding terrible but truthful accusations at my older sister, my family sat astonished. I was just waiting for Mom to put a stop to my ranting, but for some reason she let me continue. I thought of Dad's words, "If you need *revenge*, get it," and then I called on additional *power* and rang out loud and clear with the choking facts about my brother raping me when I was twelve!

I was crying, slow deliberate tears. Tears for peace that come when a woman can finally speak the wrong done to her. It no longer was just my secret, or just my shame. It now belonged to the whole family.

Mom sat at the head of the table just staring at her hands. I was shaking, but she wasn't. How I hated to hurt her, but at the same time I had a need to survive. I felt both sorry and happy that finally, all the truths and untruths had been unveiled . . . even at the expense of everyone in the room. I was thinking of only my own salvation, my own sanity was in the truth surfacing. Out of love for life and with a need to survive, I had to take control and march forward, even if it meant I walked the future alone. Since the age of twelve, I had been alone anyhow, alone with the terrible memories. My time had come to be free; Dad's passing had paved the way. I couldn't hurt my dad or myself now, only my *foes*. The nagging pain and hurt I had suffered as a child had come out. My wounds were deep cuts, and highly infected. They required stitches, one at a time, pulling the opening together, ceasing the flow of old blood. Only the scars would remain, and I prayed they'd fade in time.

I peered around the table, wondering what each person was thinking. I had forgiven myself, but would they forgive me for needing my salvation?

Rebecca, my only daughter, age twenty, sat perfectly still, staring at me. Her eyes reflected a sadness as she mumbled a prayer, thanking the Lord that I had found my tongue and the courage to face my enemies of youth. She glared at Uncle Bill, and said, "Mom made it, she'll be just fine from now on." Then, in a much lower, temperate sounding voice, said, "No wonder I've had so many fathers."

Angel had an expression that I couldn't read anything from. A silly grin framed whatever thoughts she was having. Then, just like a planned sequence, each person rounding the table took their turn saying something. The next few minutes were awkward for all.

"Trish, I didn't know. You should have told Dad, but maybe it was for the best you didn't." Her angel-like eyes cut in the direction of Bill.

My oldest son's analytical mind spoke next. "I'm going to like you in control, Mama," he announced. "And Mama, I'll see that Bill gets his!" A threat from my overly protective son of nineteen was no threat to ignore. I should have warned him about violence, but didn't.

I assumed John Jr., my third child by my second husband, now seventeen, was wondering what all of this meant to him. "I wonder if this means we're leaving, again? I like living here with Grandma and the rest of them. Maybe I can get a new car. . . ."

Teenage trivia, I thought.

The sequence picked up pace, moving on to dear sister Tilly's reaction. I anticipated furor was about to invade, and being as predictable as ever, listened to her attempt to discredit everything I had divulged. In a loud counter-attacking voice that seemed to bounce off the book filled shelves in the room, Tilly said, "It's too late little Trish, Dad can't hear you now! You can never change the way it's been, and Mom will make sure you never change our future. You're crazy and flipped your wig over Dad's death. Mom will never believe all of that garbage . . . we'll challenge the will . . . I'll make sure of that!"

I dreaded hearing the next voice, that of Bill's. I secretly hoped is mind would be in its usual state, null and void. After all these years of not confronting him, I felt queasy about having done it now. It's a feeling I've tried to explain to my psychiatrist, Doctor Barrett, but I always come up short in my reasoning. It's almost like guilt for not having told on him, like I was afraid I would have lost what love my parents had for me. I was ashamed, and thought everyone would blame me. He knew the fears of a very young and vulnerable little girl, and capitalized on them. Christ, I was so young I didn't even know what he was doing to me . . . at first.

I was still in my tomboy-stage, hadn't even reached my budding stage yet. I was happy playing Huck Finn! He took my fantasy world, my youth from me! The best theory I can come up with is, that for no other reason than fear, I chose to keep it a secret, staying clean and pure in my parents eyes.

My secret wish came true, his mind was tied up in swollen, alcoholic, filled knots; not a coherent sound to be heard! He broke the sequence.

My eyes, the eyes that were bleary and in reddened pain moved on to Bill's wife, Mary, and their children. I prayed she would understand my need of divulging the past wrongs, and hoped this opened her eyes regarding the safety of her own daughter. I wouldn't put anything past my sick brother! I watched as Mary and her children exited promptly, not sticking around for my finale. I felt pain for them.

"So, I've decided to make Dad's dream come true. Some of us will work hard at turning the farm into a very lucrative business. All business decisions will be handled by all three daughters . . . well, sort of . . .," and turning to glare at Tilly, I continued to format the working relationship we all would have. "Tilly, your primary function will be to watch and care for mother, after all, that's the reason you did all those things to us . . . your constant need to be number one in her and Dad's life. Well, you can and will be number one in her life now, comforting her through all the sorrow she has just acquired."

Sharply, and without hesitation, I turned to older brother, acknowledging by my stern look the disgust I held for him. As expected, he didn't meet my eyes. "When it comes to you Bill, it's a loosing battle. The best we can do for you is to continue to care for you . . . handing everything to you and your family . . . everything you'll need to remain solvent until you go to heaven and answer to Dad yourself. He's watching and waiting!" With a threatening and revengeful voice, I stripped him of what pride he had left. "I will never let you handle any business affairs, or acknowledge you in any way publicly. You can stay on in Dad's house, but you won be joining us in Pulaski. An ample check will be mailed to Mary once a month. I sincerely hope you find some way in life to make amends to your mother, because you have wronged her more than me."

I didn't adhere to Dad's, "you're on your own now" philosophy toward Bill for two reasons: first, I knew Bill would bilk Mom of her security that Dad had guaranteed her, and, secondly, his wife and children were not responsible for his attitude in life or his past actions. I would deliberately see to their care by endorsing a monthly check to Mary, not him. I would never pay my rapist, my childhood robber!

I reached for my cold cup of tea, pulling up the massive chair that used to be Dad's, and took a seat next to my daughter. Beck took my hand into hers. Silence prevailed. No more rebuttal, just the cold hard silence that my ugly truth and Dad's knowing pen had brought!

• • •

Totally exhausted, I folded my last item of clothing and clasped my suitcase, almost ready to depart the old homestead. I was ready, but this time, somehow I knew I would never be returning to my place of birth, the home of my parents, brother and sisters. It felt *good.*

Good was putting it mildly! Exhilarating and free were possibly a better way to explain my feelings. With Dad gone, I no longer had a binding feeling to this cold, memory filled mansion. I inwardly prayed that once I was settled at Galaxy, once I was gone from here, all the ugly memories would vanish also. Oh, I loved some of the memories that this house held of Dad, Angel and I, but I didn't love the recurring flashbacks that I suffered from when something or someone forced my mind to click backwards, re-living a thousand times the many disgraceful things that had taken place in this house so well suited for secrets.

I stood by the window, saying a final farewell to my hidden past. The memory of being twelve, full of life and eager to learn all about it flashed through my mind. I blinked back my tears. From those first young memories, I saw it again, in my mind's eye. I recalled being told I was beautiful, different, full of spunk, and very much a tomboy. I was a natural to steal my Dad's heart; the female son my Dad wished he had seeded. Normal little girls didn't play hockey, especially the position of goalie, nor did they mess with mechanical things, or fish as well as I did. Angel and Tilly were normal daughters to John and Amanda, not I.

As I watched a robin dip for a worm in the emerald green, well manicured grass, I thought about my mom and our so-called relationship.

A mother-daughter relationship never existed between Mom and I. I always wrote off my mother's lack of attention, assuming she didn't know how to handle a girl with such boyish traits. I continued to reflect, thinking hard for any good, happy memories that had revolved around Mom and I when I was a child; none came readily to mind. But, my head was filled to capacity with the great memories of the times Dad and I shared, especially when I was young and stood tall, still undefined physically; sexless.

Mom and I had very little in common when I was young. She was sickly, frail, and spent most of her able time doting on Bill or Tilly. Bill clung to her skirt. Tilly was a mother's daughter; a quiet, room hibernator that dreamt of fairy tales and Elvis. She always managed to have her own room, her own clothes, and her own private conversations with Mom. I think Mom got tired after raising her first two children, and quit on her next two obligations.

As another memory flashed, I recalled one incident Mom and I shared. . . .

I know my older sister heard the facts of life first hand, from Mom. Angel and I had to ask our gym teacher to fill us in. Even back then, Tilly played games and capitalized on Mom's weakness as a mother to me, to serve her own purposes. I know for a fact Tilly was supposed to tell Mom, if she found out before her, when I started my period. Well, Tilly did find out about it soon after I was cursed, but, so true to Tilly's behavior, she didn't tell Mom. She kept it a secret because she hated to include me in on their common little circle . . . she wanted to remain the only other woman in the house who had periods. She needed to keep her "something in common" with Mom just between the two of them.

Consequently I used paper towels and washcloths for protection for over six months, hiding my period from everyone and sneaking pads because I was too embarrassed to tell anyone, or, ask for the money to purchase my first soft blue box of protection.

Finally, someone noticed my soiled sheets, probably our live-in maid, and Mom instructed Tilly to give me my own personal arsenal of pads. "I know you already know how to use them," Tilly said as she threw the box on my bed and left. I just knew that she knew, all along she had known that I had started my period! So much for the binding mother-daughter beauty of becoming a woman! Why hadn't Mom just sat me down and told me, like a mother should have?

Yes, things certainly did change when I was twelve, and now I knew many of the reasons why. Twenty five years of searching for the answers to why it all had happened, along with aging and two years of therapy, had enlightened me with some answers. Although I understood most of the reasons, I still couldn't find enough justification for their actions.

I shook off a sudden chill, taking one last glance out the window from my room on the second floor. The room my brother used to invade, seeking out his innocent victim whom he used to satisfy his roaring young hormones and pent-up anger. I could still remember with pain the threats he made . . . over and over again I played the words trying to answer the one question I still groped with; why didn't I tell my parents? Why did they leave and go on so many trips? The dresser I moved against the door isn't holding him back. . . .

As the details of his incestuous acts became clearer in my mind's memory bank, I shook myself and corked off the tap to the barrel. I still refused to let my mind recall certain details.

I told myself that it didn't matter, they wouldn't have believed me anyway, for I was the family devil, the one with all the crazy imaginative stories. How clever he had been, telling me they would never believe me and that they would hate me for causing trouble again. "They'll hate you even more!" I could see him flash that dirty grin as he tried to convince my youthful mind into believing him.

For a period of time that I can't recall, because I have mentally blocked it out, I put up with his abuse, first feeling shame and guilt, dirty and bad, followed by what turned into hate for him and distrust for all men. I no longer remained close to Dad, resenting both parents because I should have been able to go to them, to tell them what he was doing to me. I had no one to tell, no way to stop it, because I was so afraid they'd dislike me even more than they did. I was so afraid that they would choose him over me!

But, just maybe, if I had told them, even if they didn't believe it, it would have been enough to stop him. At least they might have watched him more closely, possibly scaring him off. My mind continued to skim the surface of that terrible part of my past.

Then, God interrupted my thoughts and saved me. I thought about all of my trips to church and my private conversations with the Lord, the ones that finally were answered. As fast as his abuse started, it stopped. God sent me Jimmy!

My first true love took over and he helped me. I clung to my first love for protection. We spent every waking moment together. There was no time for abuse. No time for anyone else, just Jimmy. Someone loved me, and Bill knew I meant it when I said I'd tell if he ever touched me again. I had stopped trying to win my parents' love. I no longer needed it for the next four years, because I had my own personal protector who loved me! I had found love and was different. Jimmy's love gave me an arm of strength. It scared dirty Bill off! Physically, he would never hurt me again, but emotionally, he had scarred me for life.

Incest is ugly and dirty; carrying the terrible facts of it around for so many years just added to the soiled pile! For so long I had pushed all the ugly memories far back in my mind; pushed them behind the "Tillman family's honor screen." Finally, I had told my world . . . freed my mind of the anger I held inside. Whether or not they believed me, didn't matter. Bill has to live with the truth the rest of his pitiful life. When he looks at his mother, wife and children, the guilt of the shameful acts will haunt him, torture him, and I hoped cause his death some day. I realized I hated my brother. I wasn't capable of killing, but I sure as hell could wish him dead!

I looked out over the grounds of the homestead, and marveled again at the perfectly manicured shrubbery. The pool glistened with the sun's rays, and one delightful thought brought a revengeful grin and gleam to my face as I wrapped up my thoughts of the past; I'm glad for small favors, glad I was the victim, not the victimizer. I'm free! He's *caged* with guilt, and every monthly check from me will be a kindly reminder as it passes from Mary's hands to his. I vowed to myself, as long as I hold the keys, he'll remain locked in the cage he built for himself!

I'm free!

PART TWO
<u>CROSSING THE BRIDGE</u>

CHAPTER THREE

"Mom, do you need any help today?" Becky asked as she pulled her ponytail up high in the back, forcing the rubber band to tighten and hold.

"Help? Why do you ask?" I joked back. The entire Galaxy Farm was a shambles, unpacked boxes all over the place, holes in the roof that caused drip, drip, drip in the strategically placed coffee cans, driving me bonkers, and my daughter dare ask such a question!

"I wanted to go to town and see what it's got to offer, but I guess I need to buckle down and help you out around here, huh?" Becky tested.

"Go along, one more pair of hands isn't the answer anyhow," I quickly handed Becky a list of things to be done in town, and asked her to handle as many as she could for me, hoping to capitalize on her youthful bounce. "Just be sure to stop off at the paper and get that ad placed as soon as possible," I added as I watched my girl fast step out the door.

What I'd give to be young and fresh like that again, I ruminated. Becky was a grand star, illuminating everything around her for miles. Her hair was pitch black, as dark as coal, with natural waves that flowed over her shoulders. Her radient smile could generate instant steam from any man, as it widened and reflected the deep dimples in her cheeks. Becky had not inherited my tomboyish tendencies, and always represented her sex in a grand feline manner—she'd spend hours primping and fixing her appearance until it was as perfect as she could get it. My dad used to look at her and tell me, "Trish, you're going to have your hands full with her."

"Hello, anyone home?" came a masculine and unfamiliar voice from the half-opened front door.

"In here," I replied, looking up from the aged-pine hardwood floor where I was seated next to one of the many boxes which still needed unpacking.

"Telephone company, Ma'am. Came to give you service."

I thought I was much too tired for service! "Good timing young man. I could use that phone to call the National Guard—maybe they have some able-bodied men willing to help a lady in a declared disaster area," I suggested, flashing a big welcome smile at an extremely handsome, but much too young of a man for me.

"Moving is hell, isn't it?" the telephone jock sympathized with the cause.

"The only thing good about it is the exercise and maybe the novelty of it all. At least I can see a little progress being made." I picked myself up from the hard floor and motioned for the kid to follow me, hoping to show him where I wanted all the phones. I tucked my dust rag into my jeans pocket, and started toward the kitchen.

"Ma'am, I only have an order for one phone, not twenty."

I stopped in my tracks, turned to his bewildered face, and challenged his comment. "Well, I told them twenty-six. Call in and tell them they blew it," I ordered. I pulled down my blouse, ridding it of the pucker that opened by the force of my penned up heavy breasts. "You do have a truck radio, don't you?"

"You aren't kidding, are you?" The telephone jock was amazed. Twenty-six telephones is more than the main branch of the largest bank in Pulaski has.

"No, young man, I'm not kidding. When the rooms are refurbished, each one will need a phone, plus two in the main lounge, one in the kitchen, one in each barn, and so on." I sighed with disgust, throwing my arms up over my head; how I hated businesses making mistakes. No room in my busy schedule for someone else's goofs.

I clarified further, "I stopped in the office three weeks ago, gave them a copy of the main house floor plan, and practically did their job for them in determining where and how to put the damn things in."

"Sorry lady, I never got those orders. Besides, what you need is a telephone crew, not just one man." He was trying to cover up for his company's error, but knew by the look on my face that it was impossible.

I don't know what he thought I was thinking, but I found myself musing over his comment about needing a crew . . . I was thinking what fun it would be to have a whole crew around here, especially if they were molded like him and I was well rested.

"Got a problem, Sis?" interrupted Angel who came out of nowhere. Angels have that habit.

"Oh, nothing that I'm sure this young man can't handle." I glanced at the man who was now mesmerized in admiration for my younger sister.

"Did you hear me, either of you?" I had to ask, because the two young people stood staring at each other, like they were both angels whose halos got tangled when they accidentally flew into each other.

"Yeah, Sis. I heard." Angel was wearing the family heirloom smile.

Guess I'm not needed here any longer, I confided to myself. "Why don't you take this master plan for phones, and escort him around. Maybe he can make sure everything I ordered will cover it all," I handed the plan to Angel, knowing that they would enjoy getting better acquainted without my presence.

I remember when men looked at me like that. Oh well, everyone ages, at least all's equal for mankind in that area. I went about unpacking, putting what things I had either purchased new or took from the mansion in Nashville where I thought they best fit.

After hours of physical labor, I plopped down on the only couch in the great room, analyzing my day's efforts. The room was huge, quite suited for a bed and breakfast inn's main lounge area. I had a wide open, massive, interior look, with a cathedral ceiling, plant ledges, two bay windows, a stone fireplace, and was approximately twenty-six feet long. It held almost limitless possibilities in furnishings and accessories. It would make an impressive main room for the inn.

I relaxed, closed my eyes and fantasized my way into

dream land, visualizing the future as I hoped it would turn out. Different people were roaming around, gabbing with one another about their travels, puffing on cigars and cigarettes, enjoying their lodging as the room filled with exhaled smoke. The six large paddle fans swirled the haze, and added the right amount of nostalgia to the post-bellum era I hoped we had captured in the decor. I even imagined whiffing the smell of a pipe, the one that the handsome man in the corner was enjoying.

David Hunk was the name he registered under. I checked which room the clerk had given him, and forced his radiant smile by asking him (all two hundred pounds of mean, solid man) if he needed any help with his bags. His muscles flexed as he picked up his two suitcases with one arm and paraded to the elevator and out of my fantasy.

Oh well, another vision, one of different people roaming around replaced my tall, dark hunk. Breakfast was over, and soon all of our one-night-stands would be gone, with fresher faces replacing the already stale ones. I teased myself, thinking about what a great occupation this was going to be, wondering how many of the faces were hiding some secret about last night's lustful pleasure. Wouldn't it be fun to have a camera in each room? I devilishly thought. I wouldn't have to rent those movies anymore. . . .

As usual, when my dreams were just starting to get good, changing from black and white to bold color, both of my "embedded" characters and I were interrupted by a knock on the front door.

I reminded myself to add the broken doorbell to our growing "needs-fixing" list, and tiredly ambled over to the door. I took the outstretched warm hand of the man standing at the door, looking up into the face of a farmer. He had to be a farmer, his manure spotted coveralls gave him away, and the fresh smell added to my conviction.

"Hi, Donald Beacher, your neighbor on the south side."

"Howdy . . .," I said with a shitty grin as I caught myself mocking his down to earth appearance. "Come on in, new neighbor, I'm Trish Tillman, owner of this big monster."

"We, Meg and I, saw all the commotion around the old farm, and guessed someone had bought the place." He helped himself to a seat, and took out a cigar that was half-chewed and ragged looking. I wished I'd had a fresh new one to offer the poor guy, and added cigars to "needs-fixing."

"Can I get you something to drink? Tea, coffee, or a shot of some home brewed stuff I found in the basement yesterday?" I remained standing, waiting for the farmer to answer.

"That stuff in the cellar must be pretty ripe. Don't mind if I do test it out for you. It might be poison by now." Donald followed me to the kitchen. I could feel his eyes sizing my bottom as it swayed left and right. At least this caller is more my age, I thought. But he did say something about a Meg. . . .

"Pull up a stool, and let's both try some of this overfermented stuff. I could use a good kick about now," I said, handing over the unopened bottle to the strong hands of my new friendly neighbor. Two hours and one empty bottle later, I led the to way the front door, giggling and waving as Judge Donald Beacher went home, a hell of a lot happier and sweeter smelling than the so-called farmer he was when he came calling.

Angel and the telephone jock, now Peter to her, came bounding in the room with smiles that gave away their new found happiness in meeting one another. "Sis, your drunk!" exclaimed Angel, "and you didn't call us to join you!"

"Sorry, but Judge Beacher and I didn't want to share any of the good stuff with anyone." I smirked as I openly admitted my happy state to Angel. "You two will excuse me, I'm sure. I need a shower and some fresh coffee." I started to the stairs, tired and happy, giddy and high.

"See you at din, Sis," ended Angel laughing. I could hear her being overjoyed with my unwound state, letting her new friend share in her delight. "I haven't seen Trish like that in years. Good for her, she's too much business all the time."

Pete spoke knowingly of Judge Beacher. "She picked a good drinking buddy, one of the town drunks, but somehow he still manages to hold his chair." Then came a pause, as if Pete was thinking about what he had said . . . afraid it would get out that he called Judge Beacher a town drunk. "I don't know that first hand, about his drinking that is, but some of my friends have told me a few hair-raising stories about the old man. You'd better forget I said that about him." Pete was clenching his fist, a habit we all came to know.

"Don't worry, Pete. I judge people for themselves, not on gossip," Angel stated. "I take it he's a local we don't want to irritate, huh?"

"Let's just say he has pull around this town! I'd better get back to the shop. See you Friday at seven, right?" Pete checked to be sure their date was still on.

"Can hardly wait. I haven't been dancing since Dad passed away," Angel delightfully confirmed their date.

• • •

Life moved at a fast pace as Angel and I made some headway with the Galaxy Inn. It was beginning to look like a resting place for harried travelers, and within the month, we would hold an open house for the entire populous. Angel and Pete became a thing, and yes, the thirty-six phones finally got installed. Nashville telephone men had to be called in to help out the small Pulaski crew, and the event was the subject of local gossip. Even the newspaper printed a front page story about the three Tillman Sisters inheriting the Galaxy Farm and turning it into the Milky Way Bed and Breakfast Inn.

At least one of the thirty-six phones kept ringing, day and night; bankers, contractors, prospective guests hoping to reserve a room,, wage hopefuls, neighbors, and just plain town folk, curious to see the place and meet the so talked about Tillman sisters.

The clouds moved slowly overhead, as I walked from the stables to the back door of the main house. The work in the old, stone-walled stables was progressing slowly. I promised myself that as soon as the open house was over, I'd put my full attention on them; speed up the workers. But tomorrow is our big day, the day our hard work and brains go on display. I felt elated inside, exhilarated by the excitement of the upcoming event, and rejuvenated by the smooth hands of the local chiropractor.

I was never a believer in bone-crushers, all that snapping and popping of joints that for thirty years had settled, crooked or straight, into their chosen place. I always figured my body adjusted quite well to my own pushing and pulling, and a chiropractor was the last type of doctor I needed. My grandma told me that chiropractors were just students that ran out of energy and patience while attending medical school, opting for a lesser degree in order to recoup their investment in education. Her opinion did make sense to me.

I remember very vividly the one lady I knew that visited such a doctor every week, Mrs. Gullicky. She was crippled all over and very crooked, looking like the perfect mate for "The crooked Little Man That Lived In The Crooked Little House." Her hands were so badly deformed that they looked like claws, ready to grab me every time she caught me stealing her grapes, hiding under the leaf covered arbor, getting my fill of the purple, pearl shaped, juicy fruits. If a chiropractor helped her to look like she did, I knew I'd never go to one of them. Besides, Grandpa said they practiced snapping your brain.

With my deep-seated fears of chiropractors, I couldn't believe I took Angel up on her suggestion and visited the local "magic-hand-man." I fell prey after two weeks of Angel's prodding—she even went as far as leaving positive magazine propaganda in my personal reading room.

So, two weeks later, I made my first visit to the great doctor, and met Nathan. He was of medium height and frame, more solid than most of the irritating, dusty county dirt roads around Pulaski, and more fun to be with than anyone I had ever met. He made me feel like I was sixteen (sexteen as he called it), and life suddenly had new meaning for me. We laughed constantly.

Nathan H. Brawn was a gift I knew Dad had picked out for me, scouring the earth for the perfect match, the man his daughter would love until death, our death. I could envision Dad looking down, testing different males, watching them and waiting for the right match for me, finally giving the good doctor a nudge in my direction. Dad probably put a spell over him, too, one that for some strange reason made me trust my new friend more than anyone. It just seemed so unnatural and very different for me; trusting any man ever again was not something I thought I was capable of. Dad must have kept his magic wand and waved a nice trick on us both!

I opened the back door and smelled the great cooking in the kitchen. I thought about the other accidental meeting, the two cooks and mine. Last Tuesday, Angel and I ate at Martin College cafeteria, after Angel registered for classes. The food was superb, far outshining anything I had eaten in the small town before.

Pulaski was sorely lacking in good restaurants, with all the prime corner lots being developed around town by mini-marts. Grab a hot dog, a cup of coffee, and eat in your car was the town's speed. One could go to the few well-known fast food places scattered around the sleepy little town, but most of the teenagers had cornered that market. The so-called restaurants that housed a slot on the town square were old and dingy looking—dingy like dirty; plastic coffee cups minus a saucer, plastic table cloths, and plastic water glasses that never looked clean, the free type from the soap boxes. The family waitresses, dressed in tee shirts and jeans, made me wonder if they had just dropped their pitchforks and fled in from the fields.

So, like a good business person and one in need of a good cook, I wormed my way into the kitchen at Martin and bettered their salaries, engaging two new cooks for the inn. Angel's dust was on my side that day!

"Smells darn good, Tom. Want a tester?" I asked.

"Afternoon, Ma'am. Does set your mouth to waterin', don't it? Gladys always did say nothin' like pinto beans cookin' to spike your hunger."

"Everything ready for tomorrow, Tom?" I checked, although I knew his answer would be yes. He was a picture of Uncle Tom, and I say that out of respect for all Uncle Toms.

"Ready for them all, Ma'am." Tom went back to his job, dropping a few extra onions in the beans. I wondered if any of his color ran off and into his culinary delights, adding some secret spice that us whites could never duplicate.

I decided to call the homestead and check on Mom and

Tilly. They were probably at each other's throat by this time, but better theirs than mine!

I hadn't missed having Tilly and her bossy ways around for the last month, not one bit. Angel and I had snickered more than a few times to each other, wondering and imagining what was going on at the old house in Nashville. After my explosion of the past, we wondered what Mom and Tilly were doing with Bill, and if their nightly discussions were about their absence in Pulaski. But, we had decided to halt our refreshing break from our sister Tilly and invite her and Mom to the open house. After all, Angel might be right, we had pushed Tilly to the background long enough, and we owed Mom a visit. Not that we had completely left Tilly out on the redecorating of the farm; she had to sign off when we paid the help and all the contractors. I set it up that way, so there wouldn't be any squabbles over where the money went. I was hoping that Tilly had learned some lesson, now that my display of truth was out in the open, and leaving her in Nashville to care for Mom should have been enough to straighten her up. In a funny sort of way, maybe I had missed the old hun.

• • •

"It's remarkable, I can hardly tell the old place," Mr. Lilly said while taking in every nook and cranny as his head turned at an amazing speed, almost in a complete circle, admiring what we had done with the old farm. "I imagine this set you girls back a ways?" questioned the envious bank president, wondering where we had obtained financing. His beady eyes flicked each time he summed up the amount we had spent on redoing this and that.

It was a well-known fact that people didn't like to borrow money from old man Lilly because he wasn't very cooperative when you hit a snag and had some difficulty with your payment; he'd rather foreclose and obtain more property, adding it to his personal portfolio as planned at the time he approved the loan.

Some people would call his motives shrewd, capitalizing

on poor country farmers who didn't know enough about finances to tell if they could afford such big loans. I call it ruthless, and was damn glad we didn't have to float a loan with the likes of him. I had decided if this venture, the inn, made good, my next one was a consulting and loan firm for the local farmers in need of capital. Someday, I might just undermine old shrewd Lilly.

Tilly was slow to answer the banker, because she hadn't seen the books. At first, she attempted to mentally keep a running total, but let it slip and discontinued checking as she knew she had missed totaling a few debit checks along the way. She'd get her chance to scrutinize the totals as soon as I had hired an accountant. "You're asking the wrong sister, Sir. I've been in Nashville, caring over Mother while Trish and Angelica coordinated all of this," Tilly enviously and truthfully spoke. "Someone has to keep the homestead running, and Mother prefers *me* to care for her," she martyred. We all know Mom didn't have a choice.

"Well, they did a superb job," lowering his eyes to his glass to tell Tilly that the emptiness was the reason he was through talking wit her. "Guess it's refill time, dear . . . nice chatting with you," and he disappeared, just like all the men in her life. Five minutes later, you could find the prominent banker in deep conversation with Angel.

The crowds came, and kept coming long after the open house hours had expired. People never seemed to want to leave, and the hired crew was getting tired. Angelica nudged my arm, interrupting and dragging me off to the kitchen. The punch was gone, the dishes wiped clean from the tasting crowd, and the help looked irritated and about ready to exit. One thing about us "Northern-Southerners," when quitting time comes, we quit. Overtime pay means nothing to us, but our leisure time certainly does. How did we ever get the name "volunteers," I wondered.

"How are we going to get the last of them out of here, Sis?" Angel quizzed.

"Tell them the open house is now closed. No, I know, why don't you go bang on the piano, something catchy and befitting the situation. Something rude, like them. Try, "The Party's Over," that ought to tell them something!"

The piano played, and the guests left.

Tilly and Mom were still sitting in the main room when I fixed myself a nightcap and joined them. I proudly sashayed my hard earned firm bottom over to the piano bench and sat down next to Angel. I purposely waited for Tilly or Mom to speak first, wanting Tilly to swallow some pride and force out some kind of compliment for Angel and me. At least this time she can't take credit for something she had no part in.

Mom spoke first, just like I had guessed she would. But, I didn't like, or expect, what I heard.

"It wasn't right, Bill not here. Trish we need to talk in private. Do you girls mind?" Mom questioned Tilly and Angel with a look that said, "please leave."

"I'm exhausted, and really am glad to call it a night, how about you Tilly?" Angel asked. With a sweep of her hand she caught Tilly's arm and nudged her to leave.

"Sure, let's go. But, are you sure you'll be alright, Mother?" Tilly questioned Mom with a fake caring look thrown at her. But I knew she was thinking, *Damn, I want to hear what they're going to talk about.*

"No, Tilly, she'll curl up and die without you!" I remarked while contorting a nasty face for her benefit. "Maybe Mom and I will get roaring drunk together!" I said, just to irk her.

"Your idea might not be so bad, dear. Got anything stronger than that punchless-punch you served tonight?" Mom requested something with a kick in her own witty way.

"Sure," and I secured the new bottle of scotch that Judge Beacher had dropped off last week, repayment for the stronger stuff we had killed together from the cellar. Two ladies, mother and daughter, sat waiting for the other one to start their talk. It was unusual for Mom to ask the other's to leave, and I found myself wondering why she wanted to take her chances with me alone; normally she liked to rip me apart with as large an audience as she could gather by her side.

Out of due respect to her, I broke the ice after I slurped a big gulp of scotch, swallowing both the drink and my fear of the subject she wanted to approach. "Is it really necessary to discuss Bill, Mom?" I was praying she would postpone the talk.

"Yes. And if I was strong enough to hear your out, then you're capable of hearing me out now," spoke the determined woman. Mom's voice was sad, but demandingly determined. "Bill hasn't said one word to me since you told us all what he did to you. All he does is stay in his room, drinking. Even Mary can't get him to leave and go home with her."

Too bad . . . good for him! I don't feel sorry for him.

"I'm sorry for you Mom, not him," I answered.

"I hate to say this, but two wrongs don't make a right," Mom added softly.

I remained silent to her, but my mind wasn't silent to myself, or to my dad hovering above. *I wish I was a stronger person right now, Dad, but I'm not, and some wrongs in life can neither be forgotten or forgiven: certainly not compared. I just can't be near him . . . I still need time. Please, Dad, try to understand, help Mom to understand if you have any will over her.*

"Trish, I'm sorry it happened, and I can't erase the fact that it did. But I want to go to my grave knowing you all will be together again, like our family should be," Mom begged. But I think she knew she was asking too much, expecting any child of such abuse to forget.

I understood her love for Bill, her only son, even if he had caused her more worry over the last forty years than any of her offspring. She still continued to love and worry about him; worry because everything he attempted to do failed, from his slowness in school, to the many times he borrowed money for his last try at some crazy fast money making scheme that always failed. Never once did he keep his promises to double their share after he made his fortune, usually landing in jail for misuse of funds. Hardest of all on her, she had spent forty years worrying about Dad's justified lack of pride in his son. Now here she was worrying again, this time about his total aloofness to life in general. Most of Mom's gray hair was the price she paid for loving him so, but I doubted she knew that was the reason.

For a while, we all thought after Bill got married to such an educated girl like Mary, that just maybe a good wife would keep him on the right track; no such luck.

Mom looked at me with tears—years of regret reflecting in her eyes. Her hands gripped the arms of her world tightly as she softly spoke, "We all have wronged you—not just Bill. You should have been able to come to me . . . I failed you."

Her words needed no rebuttal from me. I was learning that silence can be golden.

"Fine, Trish, you do as you need to. But please tell me you'll try to amend your feelings toward Bill, even after I'm long gone . . . keep trying." Mom started to quiver. "I don't say that just for his sake, but for yours as well." She took the last sip of her drink, handing the empty glass to me, touching my hand softly as she released the glass. "You have made your dad and I very proud tonight."

"Thanks, Mom. Angel and I had many hard days, but tonight made it all worth it." I bent over Mom and lightly kissed her cheek. It had been years since I had done that; kissed her in a loving and understanding way, and it had been years since Mom had touched me.

"Think it's time to put you to bed." *Put everything to bed*, is what I was really thinking.

"Yes, as usual, you're right." Then, she turned her head in an attempt to see my face before she spoke. The blasted wheel chair constricted her so . . . I moved around to the side of the chair. Her tears were beautiful to me. I knew right then that I had done the right thing in telling them all about the ugly past.

"Patricia, one last thing before you say good night to me . . . or maybe two things. Thanks for caring enough to put an elevator in, and, do you know what I was thinking the other day?"

"No, Mom, what?" My hands gripped the chair's posts, ready to give her some assistance in getting the chair moving . . . *Please don't ruin the most beautiful moment we've ever shared as mother and daughter. . . .*

"I think if I had married Daniel instead of your father, none of those terrible things would have happened to all of us. Know why?" the wise old lady asked. She now had my curiosity piqued.

"Can't even guess," I replied, exerting a little pressure on her elbow that rested on the chair's forward button.

"Because if Daniel had been your dad, you would have been homely, and for some reason I think your beauty has been the underlying reason for all of this trouble." I never answered, but I did get her chair to start moving in the right direction; the elevator.

After retiring myself, I kept tossing around all the things she had said, looking for any double meanings hidden in her words. I wondered why Mom had used Daniel as an example for another father, letting my imagination wander even farther. Maybe she and Daniel had something going when they were young, I teased with the thought. They have known each other for years and are still very close. . . .

Before I finally dozed off, I admitted Mom was probably half-right. My outside beauty had caused me some pain, but it was my inside beauty that still remained unknown to the people I loved most in life.

• • •

Sunny and clear quoted the newscaster over the car radio. Angel had promised Pete she wouldn't be late, and even though she rarely kept little promises that meant nothing, (a tiny flaw in her angelic being), she was determined to be there on time. It was going to be a great day, and the family would be really amazed when she called them and announced their intentions after they secured the license.

"Wish we didn't have to wait for the results of the tests," commented Pete, who wanted to go straight to the judge's chamber and make it official before she changed her mind.

"It's really a good thing they're forcing such tests. Think of all the consequences a couple could have if either one of them tests positive." Angel was being realistic and very adultish about the aids test.

"Yeah, I know all that stuff, but what difference would it make if the two people really loved each other?" Pete asked.

"A lot of difference, Pete. I know for a fact that if I'm a carrier, I wouldn't want to infect you with it . . . it kills people. I'd be signing your death warrant," Angel stated factually.

Pete gave Angel a small nervous smile. "You'd be doing that anyhow, if you didn't marry me. I'd rather take my chances with AIDS than lose you," Pete spoke honestly and selfishly, as only one so in love might do, as he wrapped his muscular arm around his woman.

"You're talking out of emotion, not smarts!" Angel retorted. She watched his reaction very closely, wondering why he acted so worried.

Mrs. Smithy from the corner furniture store waved as she passed the knitted couple. What a perfect couple they make, she thought. Both had blond hair and blue eyes, although Pete's hair curled naturally. Angel Tillman is nearly perfect, long legged with rounded hips curving up to her tiny waist. Her midriff is so lean, helping to boast her more than ample young breasts, gracefully sloping upward to her stately neck. A work of art, Mrs. Smithy's head nodding in agreement with her own thoughts. What a beautiful pair—the two could pass for twins.

Pete sat thinking about the little house on First Street that he frequented every Monday night, (discount night), worrying about something that only wasted good brain cells. If any of the girls had AIDS, or any other disease for that matter, they certainly didn't act worried about passing anything on, he consoled himself. He thought about all the men who used the place, and concluded or persuaded himself into believing the girls must be clean, because, if not, there wouldn't be a need in the future for any justice of the peace in Pulaski; taking under advisement that every young boy he knew got his sexual start on First Street!

Angel confronted him, "Are you worried about something, Pete? You're miles away from me. Why don't we go to the drug store and have a cup of coffee while we wait until four. Didn't they say to call in by four?" She questioned his large blue-green eyes that she had fallen in love with at first sight.

"Sounds like the right thing to do. I need to see Ned

anyway, find out when the bowling teams meet for spring leagues." Pete took Angel's hand and led her across the street, still deep in thought about the tests and his past escapades with youthful lust.

The drug store on the square was a typical old country store, dimly lit and dimly stocked. The busiest section, the only money producing gimmick in the store, was the soda fountain area.

The new generation owner had mistakenly crowded the the fountain area by adding tables to it, hoping to draw more customers. It was a tactical error that would prove itself in time, once the nightly tallies were read. The owner would soon be seen moving all the tables out, restoring the soda fountain to its reign in history once again. Most locals on their weekly trip to town somehow felt themselves drawn back to their youth, to the soda fountain to sip sodas like they did every night after school, engaged in swapping high school war stories and taking liberties by touching elbows of their high school crushes.

"Lighten up, Pete. I've never seen you so preoccupied with anything. You're scaring me worse than the girl did who took our blood." Angel thought about the middle-aged woman who drew their blood, the way she almost snickered at the fact that three people she had tested in the last month had tested positive. She acted happy with their positive results. If she had divulged one name connected with those previous tests, Angel had decided to turn her in to her supervisor. Such facts were supposed to be kept private, she reflected.

"Oh, I'm not worried, just thinking about the day I visited one of those houses in Nashville about five years ago, on my eighteenth birthday to be exact," boasted Pete, stretching the real truth some to cover his local tracks on the well-worn path on First Street.

Angel chuckled and teased, "I'm not getting a virgin for a husband?"

"Just you hush, young lady, and be thankful one of us has some experience. Two virgins is like the blind leading the blind, so I'm told." Pete gave her a big smile, a proud smile of a male that was not ashamed of his past triumphs. He never did believe in treating every girl like a sister.

"Well, let's call the Milky Way and tell Trish what we're about to do," Angel said. "Got a loose quarter?" she opened her empty palm, waiting for the coin that had absorbed Pete's radiant warmth.

Pete took her hand and squeezed it shut, saying, "Let's wait for the results first, alright?"

"You really are worried, aren't you?" prodded Angel.

"I've been thinking about what you said earlier, and it would be very embarrassing if we told them our plans and then suddenly had to change them. They'd all want to know what went wrong."

Embarrassing, thought Angel. Embarrassment wasn't the problem, the problem would present far more ramifications than embarrassment! Why do small town people worry so much about what their neighbors think, or, is it a town with small people, she wondered.

Pete was worried, more than he wanted to admit to Angel. Angel was worried because Pete was worried. What will I do if he tests positive? Dear God, my world would end without Pete. She closed her mind to such thoughts, moving her chair closer to Pete, seeking added security through his warm touch.

"Here's that quarter, you make the call, okay?" Pete handed her the warmed coin that he'd nervously been-playing with for the last hour.

"Okay, shall do." Angel made the call, and the two lovers headed for the inn.

"Hi Angel, how's everything treating you today?" asked the yard man as she walked up the front path to Galaxy. Louis waited for a return greeting, and stopped trimming the small branches on the lilac bushes long enough to ogle at Angel.

"Just fine, Louis," grunted Angel. She disliked few people; he was one of them. His eyes were wicked, and she had a feeling he was a born thief or possibly even an ex-con. He made her skin tingle in fear, not desire.

A small grin flashed on Angel's face as she and Pete reached for the door knob simultaneously, hands mingling together, as she recalled how I had justified hiring

Louis; Sis thought he would make a natural match for sister Tilly.

They had made plans to be retested the next morning, as soon as the lab opened—something about the results being tainted in the lab. Just one more day to wait, and they'd be headed north on their awaited honeymoon, Angel bubbled secretly to herself.

• • •

Tilly and Mom didn't rush back to the homestead in Nashville after the open house. They wanted to be around the excitement, watching the first paying guests arrive, joining in the opening day with anxiety.

The weather was perfect, better than I had prayed for. Everything was in bloom, beautiful springtime had arrived in Pulaski. Hills weaved up and down, either covered with trees or green pastures, and the flat lands foregrounded the rises with every imaginable color. Farm houses dotted the landscapes, divided by fences of many shades and wood types, and streams of clear water trickled through the properties. Even the so hated dirt roads were appealing, adding hues of brown as if they had been painted into the scene on purpose.

The inn's register was signed in full, and reservations kept piling up. Angel had persuaded me to open the dining room to anyone, (drop-ins), stretching breakfast to dinner for non-guests as well. Her idea was meant to fill the gap of restaurantless Pulaski. I remember worrying about how the restaurant would fare, speculating that possibly the fast food, plastic way of life was too ingrained in the locals.

Our hired crew now totaled fourteen, all full time employees. And believe it or not, I actually found Tilly's presence *was* needed. It felt good to me, ordering Tilly to do the things I preferred not to do. I now began to understand why Tilly had been so reluctant to change her ways when we were young. *Power* can be addictive!

"If this keeps up, Trish, we'll have recouped our

investment by the end of the year. Not bad considering what this place costs you in repairs and redecorating," Tilly acknowledged.

"Daddy knew it was a good idea." I was wearing one of the new outfits that Nathan and I had picked out last week in Birmingham, celebrating with the money we had won at the races. I felt lovely, dressed in shades of blue that snuggled my waist tightly—a little too tightly. I justified a few added pounds here and there by all the partying and my lack of visits to the gym. Pulaski's gym looked like a converted garage housed with equipment purchased from a flea market.

"Phone for you Ms. Tillman," called Susan from the front desk. We both responded, until Susan clarified I was wanted, not Tilly. Mannerly, Tilly disappeared outside, leaving me in privacy.

"Hi, Sis." It was Angel, and she sounded miles away.

"Hi kiddo, what's up?" I asked.

"I'm at church. Do you think you could come down here anytime soon?" Angel asked. I thought I heeded a slightly broken sound in her voice.

"Well, I guess I could. I've got some time around two. Is that soon enough?"

"Please come sooner . . . I need to talk to you . . . away from the inn."

"Sure, let me change and I'll be right down . . . are you alright?" I was worried as I listened to the sound of her nose blowing on the other end of the phone. "Why are you crying, Angel? Tell me what's wrong."

"No, just come."

"Will you be alright until I get there . . . is Father Daniel there with you?" I checked.

"Yes, he's here. Please hurry, but drive safe." Angel always added, "drive safe" to every farewell, even if you were only leaving to go to the ladies room.

I rushed to my room, changing into a pair of blue slacks and contrasting lightweight sweater. I had been overdressed for Pulaski, and hated to flaunt a better-than-thou appearance over the dowdy locals. When the judge wore coveralls, you can imagine what the local farm boys and girls dressed like.

Daniel smiled a greeting at me. He always had a friendly look about him, but I couldn't help thinking about what Mom had said about him being homely. I never really noticed his looks, probably because I thought it was unsaintly to size up a priest. I tried to imagine what I would have looked like if Mom and he had mingled enough to produce me. Instantly I stood still . . . in complete shock with my thoughts. My throat tightened like someone was pulling the noose tight; My God, I'd look like Tilly!

"What's up, Father Daniel? Where's Angel?" I was thankful I could speak. I was anxious about Angel, but shocked at my thoughts about Father Daniel and Tilly looking so much alike. Can it be true? Episcopal priests can marry. . . .

"Go to my study in the back, my dear. She's waiting for you in there," coached our priest as he closed the door behind me and followed me to his den.

Angel looked like she had been to hell and back, I could tell by her swollen eyes that she had been crying hard for some time, and immediately I scoured the room for Pete. No Pete. *My God, I hope she's not pregnant*, I thought as my heart ached for my younger sister. The Tillman baby was in some type of fix.

Father Daniel took his seat behind the desk and told me, in a priestly way, what Angel's predicament was.

"Oh no, not Pete," were the only words ushered from my mouth. I couldn't believe that healthy young man had AIDS, or was a carrier at least. This couldn't be true, be happening to Angel, someone who never hurt anyone . . . never did a wrong in her life.

"What are you two going to do?" I asked as I held her in my arms. I kept brushing my hand down the back of her soft long hair, trying to soothe her into some form of peace. The word *peace* suited Angel; all angels were supposed to be at peace, I thought.

Not waiting for an answer, I asked to be alone with Angel. Father Daniel left us in our misery. He had done all he could do for us.

"I don't want Tilly and Mom knowing about this . . . if I caught Tilly smirking, I'd kill her," threatened Angel, "and

Mom doesn't need this grief."

Still worried about other people, I thought as I groped for something to say to my wounded sibling. "Let's get out of here, Sis. Let's go for a ride, and talk this through." I doubt I could help her through this thing, but I promised myself I'd try.

"Sounds good, I'm tired of crying and my eyes hurt," Angel agreed.

We rode around in silence at first, until I finally asked the one question I feared the answer most to, "Have you slept with him, Angel?" *Please answer no!*

"Thank the good Lord, no!" Sadly, Angel started to ramble on, letting all the rage and anger she held inside come to the surface. "It's not fair! I wish I had slept with him. I keep thinking if I had, then at least I wouldn't be facing the choice I have to make now." Reality was overtaking her. She blew her nose, and I could tell she was feeling the soreness the tissue caused as she wiped it dry. "He's hurting so much already, facing the facts of it all . . . looking his sure death in the face . . . I just can't add to that hurt by telling him we're through." She caught her breath and continued, "Yet, I can't sign my own death warrant that way either. The doctor told us what to expect, all about our children possibly being born with it, and what precautions we could take if we never wanted any kids. But . . . ," she couldn't relate any more feelings, never finishing her words.

"Why don't you plan on going to the homestead for a few days. Get away from here and be alone with your thoughts. There's nothing anyone can say to you that will help you over your grief right now . . . it's too soon," I counseled as an older sister would.

I, too, was angry; bitter at myself as if it was my fault that I couldn't help Angelica for the first time in her life. When she fell out of the tree, I washed away the hurt; when she had a fight with Tilly, I rushed to her aid in winning; when she dirtied her dolly by the river bank, I washed her clean, and when I saw Bill anywhere close to her, I rushed between them; but this I could do nothing about.

"Bill is still there, isn't he?" Angel checked.

"Who knows where he's at? I don't think Mom or Tilly has called him in weeks."

"When we get home, will you drop me off at the stables? I don't want anyone seeing me like this."

"Sure, but what are you going to do? Do you want me to pack some of your things, help you get away without their seeing you?" I aided. "I can shoo Bill home to his family if he's still in hiding in Nashville."

"If I haven't come to the house by seven, come to the barn, okay?" Angel was slowly absorbing the facts and making her plans.

"Sure, honey, sure," I promised as I dropped my sister off at the stables.

Dusk arrived and no Angel appeared on the dinner scene. Before any of the household snoops checked on her whereabouts, I sneaked out the back door and went to meet her, finding her in the hay, fast asleep in the prenatal position. I retrieved two horse blankets, covering her gently so as not to disturb her. She'd be safe there until morning, when she would feel more like seeing people. I brushed some bunched strands of hair from her face, pulling some mouth-trapped, damp hair free, and kissed her lightly on her forehead. I left her there, closing the stable door tightly, deciding I'd tell anyone who was inquisitive that Angel had stayed in town with a friend.

CHAPTER FOUR

The birds chirped too loudly and the sun shown too brightly as I woke up, remembering with pain the situation I had left my younger sister in yesterday. "Stop sounding so happy, you blasted birds. We've got problems to face today," I threatened the colorful little blobs of nature as they flew around outside my window. Problems to face . . . hell, everything seemed doomed lately, I thought as I struggled to get into my jeans; even my waistline is giving me problems this morning!

I hurried to the stable, telling Tom and Gladys that if sister Tilly or Mom came down to breakfast before I got back, tell them I had gone to meet the vet in the main stable. "Sunny is about to foal and I need to check on her."

"Sure thing, Ma'am," replied the better half of the cooking duo.

As I opened the doors to the stable, I wondered how I came up with stories like the one I had just spontaneously contrived. The symbolism was remarkable, except it was Angel who was about to fold-up-her-life instead of foal-a-colt. Maybe my ability to ad-lib so quickly in a pinch was part of the reason everyone always believed Tilly's side of the story instead of mine, I theorized with myself.

Angel was nowhere to be found. I panicked, letting my imagination run from one terrible thought to another. After I checked the stable again, I summoned the help of Nathan, calling him on one of the thirty-six phones I so conveniently had installed. Nathan agreed to meet me at the inn within the hour.

"Let's talk in here," I said as I led him through the kitchen into the large, well-stocked pantry. Privacy around the inn was a luxury.

"Tell me again what Angel said before you left her out there last night," Nathan prodded me for details.

I methodically plowed through the scenario. "She wanted to stay in the stable, until her eyes looked better, and if she didn't return by dinner time, then I was supposed to go back down there to see her." I could feel myself beginning to tremble, and tears started to flow unwillingly down my cheeks. "She was asleep when I went back down last night, so I covered her up and left her there, in peace . . . I thought." At least I could cry, something I could never do with any other man I knew, including my father.

Nathan took me into his arms, tightening his hold on me and gently rocked me back and forth, trying to soothe away my worries. "Come on honey, please stop crying. Angel probably woke up and might even be upstairs. Did you check her room this morning?" Nate quizzed.

I raised my head with a smile of relief, and thinking of Nate's idea, answered him, "You're probably right. Let's go check out her room." I was never very good in handling an emotional crisis, especially if it concerned Angel.

No Angel anywhere. We searched every place, even saddling up and riding to the ridge where she and Pete always rode together. In our state of worry, we forgot to first check to see if any of the horses were missing, and only thought of it after we arrived on the ridge. "Stupid of us Nate, not to look for her horse first, but what difference does it make now. At least it gave us a nice break before we return to the house and tell Tilly and Mom that Angel's disappeared." I dreaded telling them, because I knew they would find me at fault for leaving her alone last night.

No Angel, no messages, just fright! We had exhausted every feasible idea between the four of us, with Tilly and Mom now knowing the whole truth about the situation. She wasn't in Nashville at the homestead, according to Bill, and Pete was at home but unable to come to the phone. His mother did say she would have him call as soon as he woke up. So, the four of us sat around worrying to death, envisioning all types of terrible things, getting more on each others' nerves as the hours ticked away.

"Trish, let's go out back into the garden and get out of

here for awhile," Nathan suggested. Tilly and I had to be separated before the next war broke out, because if Tilly had said one more word about not telling her and Mom when it happened, I was loaded, ready to drop the first bomb on "Tilly the Hun."

"At least the weather is warm, if she's outside somewhere, Trish," Nathan said, trying to find some good in the situation. I appreciated his caring and his help, no matter what he said as long as he said something to keep me from reliving what had happened. He could calm me down faster than any man had ever been able to; I loved him. He loved me. We belonged together in times of trouble, helping each other remain levelheaded and cautious in our secret, suspicious fears. It's a great feeling to have someone who loves you by your side in troubled times. It was great having a protector again.

I remembered how Angel feared Lousy Louis, the yard man, and checked that angle of her disappearance myself. The poor man must have thought I was crazy, challenging his every word as he tried to tell me where he had spent the last ten hours. I got the feeling that if he had known Angel was asleep in the barn all night alone, he would have called on her. I made a mental note to watch the character, and possibly let him go at a later date.

Twenty-four hours passed and no clues to Angel's whereabouts. Nathan rode into town and recruited the help of Bob (Buggy) Bundle, the local police chief.

I had met Buggy at our open house. He was a large glob of a man, with a smile of a Cheshire cat. His stomach hid his belt, and the gun that he so proudly carried on his hip was his false array of power. Men like him needed a gun; one to polish and fondle . . . keeping it erect and ready. I imagined his penis as a small revolver, never loaded and only capable of shooting blanks. His hair was curly, what he had of it, and his eyes reflected an unawareness to everything around him, except his gun. I did wonder at the time if I was being too cruel in my first analysis of him, after all he did get elected. But it became obvious that he was a carry-along by his cronies in power; the small town clique at work. Now I knew how Judge Beacher still held his seat.

After hours of questions that seemed irrelevant to me, the local, inept cop left to organize a search for Angel. The neighbors started to show up offering their help, the Tennessee Bureau of Investigation was called in, and finally Pete came dragging in, looking like he was at death's door. And adding to the confusion, those blasted thirty-six phones kept ringing!

Tilly grabbed the young man, and started to accuse him of infecting her sister, and even went as far as suggesting he had planned the whole thing. She ordered Susan, the desk clerk, to wash all thirty-six phones . . . "Wash them clean of his germs," Tilly retorted angrily. I was ready for her to spray the room with Lysol at any moment. "We're all contaminated," she declared.

"Well, if that's true, Tilly, I wouldn't worry about you giving it to anyone!" I snapped right back at her, thinking she'd be the last person left on earth if AIDS wipes out mankind; no chance in hell she'll get it.

God she was an ugly woman. I often theorized that her ugliness inside came from her homeliness outside. She was tall, with a pimple-pocketed face and titless. I wondered why her weight didn't settle in her chest, giving her at least something someone might want to look at. Her eyes could cut through anyone, always squinting like she had tried an eye-lift and the doctor blew the job, leaving her skin too tight to allow her eyes to open. She never spent any time with her appearance, her clothes hanging instead of clinging to her shapeless gangly look. Lipstick was the only color she had, and that was white/pink, like the type girls wore in the early fifties.

Nature hadn't been kind to Tilly, and to make matters worse, she had fallen when she was young and chipped her front tooth, which added to her wicked, crooked smile. The one corner of her lip rippled upward, which she must have wanted it to do because she practiced daily quirking it like that until it stayed permanently deformed.

I remember when I was a teenager, I thought she'd make a perfect nun. Her habit would cover her ugliness to the world, and she'd only have God to try to maneuver in life. I'd like to see her order him around; fair justice!

Nathan finally shut her up, telling her to gain her senses, and reached into his coat pocket for a pamphlet that held all known facts of the disease. "Here, educate yourself and leave the boy alone. Christ, you know, you can be a real bitch!" Nathan wasn't smiling when he handed her the facts, and when she opened the literature, out fell a pair of white, rubber surgical gloves. "Thought you'd probably need those, Tilly." Now, he was smiling broadly!

Tilly was quite taken back with Nathan's behavior, but I wasn't; he could be so clever when he needed to be.

"Well, who the hell are you to talk to me that way . . . you don't even belong here!" Tilly's nasty side was glowing in our time of trouble. "I think it's only fair to ask him where he got it from . . . we need a list of everyone that he's been with, both men and women!"

I couldn't believe she said that. "Tilly, shut up!" I knew I screamed too loud, and suddenly everyone was looking at me. Then, Nathan saved me from their glares, and started in again.

"At least I don't go around with my head stuck in the sand, dear spinster," countered Nathan.

"Stop it you two," Mom demanded, wheeling her chair forward so the loudest, most interrupting squeak could be heard. Mom had heard enough. "Why do we all have to start attacking each other whenever something rocks the boat in this family?"

I blurted back at her, "That's funny, Mom, coming from you! Isn't that the only time you attack!" I couldn't help saying what I had. Thank God Pete put a stop to our fighting.

"I'm sorry folks," piped in Pete, "the last thing in the world I want to cause is trouble in the family." Pete turned to Mother with pain written all over his face, and continued to explain his stand. "I love Angel, Mrs. Tillman. I would never do anything to hurt her." Embarrassment forced his head to lower. "I never did anything with her. I promise. She hasn't got AIDS." The young boy told all the facts; the fact that he hadn't slept with Angel and the reason they had the tests.

"Come over here Pete," Amanda warmly requested. Taking her hand and looking him straight in the eyes, she pulled him down to her level the best she could, hugging him as close as her precarious position allowed. "No one would hurt our Angel . . ."

I couldn't help but admire my mother's act. She was treating Pete better than one of her own, actually showing him more touching love than she ever had me.

Some families have the tendency to pull together in a time of trouble; others, like ours, drive wedges deeper into their core. I used to wish our family stuck together, protecting each member from the outside world if it was needed. But after my last divorce, I accepted the fact that my family would side with anyone if they thought they could gain something from it. To hell with family loyalty! A complete stranger could dangle a benefit in front of Mom, Dad, sister Tilly or brother Bill, and they'd take the prosecution's side over mine every time.

This abnormality only held true regarding the outside world versus the inner-family world. When it came to family-members-only feuding, the order of fault had fallen in place years ago; first me, Angel second, Tilly third, and then finally Bill, and only Bill if you had conclusive evidence.

Like the time someone drank Dad's last bottle of Coke. "Okay, who drank my last bottle of Coke?" Dad's Coke was his life line, and he kept a mental count of every six-pack he brought home. He knew how many he had slurped down, and how many remained cooling in the refrigerator. God forbid if one was missing!

"You kids better get down here fast!" Dad summoned his line-up! The procession would amble in, one at a time, each one of us ready with our testimony and alibis. Four "Not me's" sounded off, from oldest child to youngest. "I suppose the rat drank them!" Dad would search the line-up's eyes, looking and watching for the least little flinch of guilt.

"Honest, Dad, I didn't drink it," Bill would say.

"Me neither!" Tilly testified.

"Me neither!" I said, beefing up my testimony with a no-shake of my head.

"Me neither!" Angel meekly repeated and followed the lead. No one ever believed Angel capable of lying or stealing one of Dad's Cokes. She didn't know it, but she didn't even have to show up for the line up.

"Well, who's going to say me neither for the rat who seems guilty around here for everything?" Whenever no one owned up to being guilty, Dad always said that the family rat was the culprit.

Then, when it looked like no one was going to own up, and for sure we all were going to be punished severely, Tilly added a fictitious clue to the mystery. "I saw you drink it, Trish," pointing her dagger finger at me. "Yesterday, I heard you *burp* afterwards! Honest Dad, she did it! I heard the *burp*!"

Burping! The conclusive evidence Dad needed. Bang went his gavel, finding me guilty as usual. It didn't matter if the witness was unreliable, or that the judge was drunk from Coke and rum!

My punishment was always the worst form of cruelty a thirsty young girl could bear; everyone else got a nice cold bottle of Coke, a whole bottle to themselves, and I was forced to watch as they swallowed every last drop! But, unknown to the paid witness and the judge, Angel always showed mercy and saved her last swallow for the convicted.

I decided it was time to take some action of our own in locating our Angel. "Mom, you have to be here anyway, so can you handle the phones? I was thinking it might do us all good to go looking for her ourselves. This waiting around is getting to me, and I don't have much faith in Buggy Bundle," I suggested an out for everyone.

"Good idea, Trish, I'll man the phones with Susan, and keep the inn running. You all go and find our Angel," and turning to Tilly, she added, "Take the pamphlet with you, Tilly." Mother was definitely changing.

"I'm not going, Mother. I'd be of no help out riding around." Tilly was right about that.

Pete, Nathan and I left the inn in search of our lost Angel.

• • •

Things didn't change, the thirty-six phones kept ringing, and I was always waiting in anticipation that just maybe one of the calls would produce news of Angel. It had been a month now, and no clues of any kind. It was almost like she had spread her wings and flew off. The town folks had come to our sides, offering help and all kinds of suspicious theories. I sometimes felt like they were just plain nosy and wanted to further their position on the square, and in the community, by using what knowledge they had learned from their visits as the in-things-to-know! Coffee gossip!

Meanwhile, I was feeling sick every morning, and my weight kept creeping up around my middle. My thoughts were divided over Angel's disappearance and my disappearing period; everything seemed to be disappearing! Although I knew it was common for ladies of my age to skip a period once in awhile, as I *was approaching* middle-age and menopause, I wasn't quite ready yet to let nature nudge me into mellowness.

"Well, Ms. Tillman, I don't know if this is good news or not, but we can't trick Mother Nature; *you're pregnant!*" The good doctor even had a funny personality, I thought.

"At your age, thirty-eight, we'll need to have some tests." She handed me some pink and blue folders, and I remember thinking how very fitting and cute the colors were, while she continued to relate the risks of having a child this late in life. As she talked on and on, all I could feel was fright! Is this the price I have to pay for departing from the homestead again? I wondered.

I drove slowly to Nathan's office on First Street, bypassed his receptionist and barged into his treatment room, unannounced. I invaded the poor patient's privacy on the table, but then I wasn't really concerned with it anyhow. "Trish, what's wrong?" Nathan asked as he halted his magic rub and opened the door, ushering me into the hallway. My hand reached subconsciously to my stomach, and then I started to laugh hysterically. One look at the graying old boy and my condition struck me as funny! "Tell me what's wrong, Trish," demanded Nathan as he searched my eyes for a clue.

"You're going to be a papa!" I blurted out the fact between gasps as I reached deep within me for more air to laugh again. "And to think at your age, Nathan." I shook my finger and gestured toward him; naughty, naughty!

Nathan let go of me, he was in shock; maybe after shock! My words ran off of him. He thought I was crazy. He told me later that his first thought was he hadn't been messing around with any of the local girls since he had met me. "Trish, who ever told you such a stupid lie is crazy and full of shit!" He paused, then rambled on. "You don't believe I've been with anyone else, do you?" He waited for an answer, and when I didn't reply, he started up again. His face was ghostly white.

"What's her name? When did she tell you this?" Nathan wanted some facts, and fast. For some reason, I guess he didn't think it could possibly be me that was pregnant.

The receptionist and patient sat listening to every word, with Nathan and I oblivious to the fact that anyone else was around. The office phone kept ringing, and finally he turned to the girl behind his desk, hollering loud enough to shake his trailer which housed his medical practice, "God damn it, Brenda, answer the phone and mind your own business."

"Please Trish, tell me who is starting the rumor."

Coming to my senses after both feet were back on the shaking trailer floor, I realized not only his receptionist was getting an earful, but also his patient whom I had rudely interrupted. "I'll wait in your office, honey . . . Papa. Better clear the trailer out, we need to talk."

Nathan followed my orders to a tee, putting the closed sign in the front window. I guess he concluded that certain things are more important than someone's ass-ache.

"Okay, honey, tell me who's causing us all this trouble, so I can put a stop to it before it's all over town." Nate looked flushed. "Probably some young girl who needs a name for her child."

He acted like he had been here before . . .

"We aren't going to put a stop to it, Nathan, not unless there's some problem at my age . . ." My eyes were twinkling with tears of delight!

"Oh, my God, it's you! You're pregnant?" Now Nathan was lost in his first reaction to the news, although I think he was having trouble believing it.

I was thinking about our lovemaking; the way we went at it. Pure heaven, pure bliss, nothing ever felt so good. We fit together like we had been molded or sized before birth, guaranteeing us a perfect, heavenly fit later in life. If someone had just seen fit to spread some bread crumbs along our paths in life so we could have met a little sooner.

It was obvious to me that a child wasn't one of the things Nathan had expected in return for our passion. The price was high. He was a confirmed bachelor, nearing fifty years. He knew better than to let something like this happen, he usually took precautions, but not with me. He knew it had to be love with me, or no nookie!

Again, my past must have caused my feelings toward those slimy things men use. Even though I knew my parents used them, I still felt they stood for *sex*, not lovemaking. I had to know the man wanted me, desired me out of love, not dirty sex, and if he loved me enough, he'd be willing to pay the price of no protection. I know my reasoning isn't safe, and was stupid, but it's the way I thought and the way I felt. Rubbers stood for *sex*. Rubbers stood for *incest*. Condoms are just a *cover up*! The consequences of not using protection were second in priority to my convictions, and now I found myself challenging those old convictions!

"Well, say something, anything, Nathan. Just don't sit there staring at my belly."

"What can I say, or do . . . it looks like I've already done it!" A sense of humor Nathan had, but his timing was definitely off this time!

"Why don't you try to smile if you're lost for words," I replied, biting my lower lip. I didn't know how I expected Nathan to act when he heard the news, but I knew I was beginning to dislike his reaction. Dear Lord . . . help me save my pride . . . don't let me cry. Don't let this man hurt me like the others.

"I love you, Trish. You know that, and I shouldn't have to tell you. We'll get married as soon as we can, if you plan on seeing this thing through," he forced a smile, then stared at his damn diploma on the wall.

Another conviction! Back then I wasn't in favor of abortion, unless medically it was proven that something was wrong with the child. I believed that if one was lucky enough to conceive, then the Lord had helped the little fishy swim up the channel to spawn. It would be blasphemy to mess with God's creation. God and nature are one in the same, and I knew better than to trick Father Nature!

"I don't know what I expected you to do or say . . . I was shocked at first, too. But after the ride from the doctor's in Columbia, after I found out I was pregnant, I had some time to think what all this means. God knows I've already done my fair share of worrying, with my period missing for the last two months. I wrote it off to menopause . . . but obviously my *man-didn't-pause* when it counted!" I flashed a big wink at him.

"I'm sorry, Trish, I never imagined you'd get pregnant. I used to worry about such things when I was younger, but since I've been with you, I've just enjoyed myself, worry free!"

"*Free*! Daddy always told me to expect nothing for *free*!"

"Come here, honey," motioned Nate, opening his arms and lap to his wife-to-be.

I put my arms around his neck, placing a small kiss on his forehead. "Do you think we're too old to raise a child together, Nathan?" I did fear our ages under the circumstances.

"Hell, we're as young as folks who are twenty . . . and this just goes to proved it." His hand reached out and patted my belly, softly. "When are we due?"

"Sometime in December." Now I was proud and surprisingly happy. "But we won't get married until I know my test results," I announced with some concern in my voice.

"Why not? Why wait?"

"What if it has to be aborted?" I asked. I was testing him to see if he really wanted me as his wife.

"So, no one will know we had to get married. I want to marry you, have been going to ask you anyway."

"Oh, and why didn't you?" A likely story I figured.

"Well, with Angel missing and my trying to help Pete through his problems, I thought it was best to wait. But, I was tired of sneaking out of the inn every night like a paid guest . . . and besides, you're like a heating blanket to sleep with." Nathan's arms were wrapped around my belly, holding us all tightly. "I should know that heat applied to the right places produces overwhelming results!" We both broke out in laughter, thinking we must have applied too much heat!

"I want a big, white wedding, one that will set this town to talking for years. I'd like to shock this place, playing right along their lines of expectation." I winked at Nathan, then told him, "I'd love to give them something to talk about—it's good for business!" I removed my butt from his heated lap.

"You're wicked, you know, and a hell of a lot of woman. I love you." He picked me up and carried me out of his office and to the closest treatment room. "Let's celebrate our seedling, Mama. Maybe our son can feel me probing . . . the sooner I get to know him the better, right?" How I loved that devilish grin.

"Son? What makes you think it's a son?"

"Just a hunch. Maybe my probing will give us a clue." Nathan adjusted his treatment table, and I stood watching and thinking about all the fantasies I had about that table.

The chiropractor's table lends itself to the easiest positions in life's lustful ways. First, the way it delivers me into position is unique. With the table in an upright position, perpendicular to me, I place my arms around the front of the table, holding on as the table is lowered, taking me from a standing position to a reclining one automatically; no bending or flopping required. Once the table and I are flat, me on my stomach, my mate lowers the shelf of the table directly under my breasts, removing any pressure from my previously squashed boobs. (An added advantage to the shelf is no matter what size cup your lover's breasts are, the table can be adjusted up or down for a perfect hang.) Next, the lower half of the table can automatically force my knees to rise and bend, raising my firm, small ass high, as well as assisting me in supporting my mate's weight once he's in the grove. With another push of the button, the table can be made to rock, slowly at first, and then with just a little turn of the knob, the speed picks up to quicken the thrusts. As for release, the table so effortlessly returns both tired mates to a standing position. Dogs should have it so easy. I think the treatment tables should be covered under medicare!

Naturally, my tests came back confirming the only thing that they could have possibly projected; anything dealing with Nathan and I had to be good, even the bundle that was growing so patiently inside me.

• • •

The night before we announced our wedding plans, I made a special visit to Becky's room before I retired for the evening. I wanted a chance in private to tell my daughter before I shocked the rest of the family. I was actually afraid of Becky's reaction, afraid she'd hurt Nathan and I by not accepting the news joyfully.

"Did I shock you, Becky? Are you ashamed of your mother?" I asked, imagining the answer would be a cruel one.

Becky came leaping off her bed and threw her arms around me, which literally shocked the hell out of me. She was happy for us; one should never prejudge their children. "Mom, that's wonderful for you both." Her eyes spoke her happiness. "It's quite a shocker, at your age and all . . . but, who cares nowadays when you got pregnant. I really think it's great! I wish I had seen Nate when you told him," and by the look on her face, she was telling me she knew how shocked he had been.

"You know, Mother, you make it easy being your daughter. I never know what you'll be doing next that will shock us all! I can't think of anything you haven't done in life." The words sounded cruel to me, but my daughter always let her feelings out boldly, and sometimes I appreciated it, and other times I didn't. One never doubted where she stood on any issue; definitely an inherited trait passed from Dad to me, and from me to her.

"What do you think your brother's will say?" I was worried about both sons' reactions, because I never really knew how to read each of them as well as Becky.

My oldest son, Tim, was wrapped up in his college life, which was fine with me now that I had Nathan. It was hard when he first flew the coop. Tim was a loving son, and if I hadn't freed him to live his own life, he'd have stayed next to my side out of obligation forever. I looked forward to Tim finding his love and settling down, producing grandchildren by the bundles.

John, my last child, who no longer would be able to claim that title once my bundle was born, was raised under different circumstances than his half-brother and -sister, having spent most of his teenage years as an only child. With the older two away in college, he had become very close to Nathan and I. I felt sure he would be happy for us both, after the initial shock of it wore off.

Becky jumped all over me. I had asked the wrong question. "I don't know how the boys will react! Why do you always ask me about them? I keep telling you, Mom, that how they feel and what they do is their own business. I hate you using me where they are concerned."

"Yes, I forgot. I just thought I'd ask. Sorry, I forget how touchy you are on that subject. Well, I'll let you go back to your sleep, and thanks for your kind reaction." I was a little tiffed at her for her bluntness . . .

I rested well that night, figuring one out of three children had accepted the news quite well. I always contended that if I could keep a third of my children happy with me, then I was doing a good job.

The timing of our announcement couldn't have been better. It was Mother's Day, and the dining room was decorated for the occasion with lovely floral arrangements on each table. When the guests finished their meals, and before they left the inn, the waitresses had been instructed to give each mother the flowers on their table in celebration of their big day.

After the room was closed off to the dinner guests, the family was asked to join us in our own celebration, with everyone assuming we were going to pay homage to our dear mother. All the children had returned home from college, and Johnny even managed to be present on this day. His being a local usually preempted his presence from the inn, always cruising around town with his buddies, peeking up young girls' skirts.

Nathan was dressed to please, when he rapped his fork

against the crystal goblet, clinking the family to attention. I rose from my chair and stood next to him, thinking how it always seemed to be me that was announcing something, or shocking them by relating something that they didn't either believe or want to hear; more often the latter.

Nathan held his glass high and looked at Mom, gesturing forward with his rehearsed announcement, "A toast to the mother who brought the most beautiful creature into this world, the woman next to me who has agreed to marry me as soon as I can carry her to the altar." Nathan secretly hoped the wedding would be soon, because he'd never be able to carry me if another month went by. I could read his mind. We exchanged little pecks.

Glasses clicked, and Tilly bent over and kissed Mom, handing her a small gift. Then, almost as if her mind had to take time to replay what Nathan had said, she abruptly turned to us with her mouth falling open, and asking, "Did I hear you right? You two are getting married?" Tilly was surprised, in shock, or maybe it was fear of her own loneliness.

"Sure did, Sis!" answered Nathan before I could even begin to formulate a clever comeback. I smiled at Nate, and then at Tilly, but my eyes were searching my children's faces. What did my sons think?

Timothy had learned poise at college. He jumped up and gingerly walked over to Nathan, extending his hand in congratulations. "Finally, she'll have a good man to care for her. Too bad you didn't come around twenty years ago." His words were music to me. He was elated for us both. He made me proud.

I waited for Johnny's reaction. He just sat next to his grandmother, and I could tell he was embarrassed by the announcement, because he wouldn't look at me. He finally rose and joined his brother by our sides, speaking directly to Nathan, not me. "I thought we talked about everything, Nate. Why didn't you tell me you planned on asking Mom to marry you?" His words were feelings of hurt, of not being the first child to hear the news. I never surmised his reaction would be like that. He finally wished us well, and at least remained polite. Well, two out of three wasn't so bad, I thought.

After seeing everyone's reaction to the first part of our news, we coyly decided to wait and spring the ever-growing news on them all at a later date. I thought of what the blow would do to Tilly, and figured we'd better give her some time to get used to the first half. Tilly would never admit it, but she worried about ending up childless in life.

We opened champagne, showered all moms with gifts, and tried to celebrate without Angel's presence. I missed her terribly.

CHAPTER FIVE

As far as I was concerned, dear little Angel had spread her wings and lost her halo. Three months ago she had completely disappeared from my life, frightening me beyond words, and never as much as one phone call came assuring me she was safe. I was disturbed by her, but, how much, I would never let on to the rest of the family.

"Mother, please don't worry. At least we haven't heard the worst. She's still alive somewhere, but God only knows where. We would have heard something by now if she is dead!"

"I don't know, Trish, it all seems so odd. Not a trace of her, after three months and no word. It's so unlike her," worried Mom. "I know she would have contacted you, or Pete."

"I still think she's okay, Mom. I just feel it inside . . . she'll call soon. Maybe when Pete passes away, she'll show up for his funeral," I boldly stated what I was thinking.

Mom sat squirming in her chair, with her eyes rolling up toward the ceiling, and then back down to meet mine. "Trish, for once in your life, please try to spare me your thoughts. The way you say things, you sound so cold and calculating."

"Guess I could try to change, just for you, but to be perfectly honest with you, I don't care to! By now you'd think you could accept what you developed in this life—or what you let develop, I should say." I felt terrible after I spoke to her like that.

Before father died, and after my last divorce, I did try to change. All it did was make me miserable. For so many years, I had kept everything inside, managing to somehow forget everything that had happened to me. It was like I took all the hurt and pushed it into the right side of my brain; the emotional reacting side. I seldom found any use for that side of my head back then, treating everything emotional with the logical thoughts of my left side brain. Insanity lodged itself in the right side—I didn't like my right side thoughts until now. I was finding out that the smartest people had learned to use both sides of their minds, and after trying it, I was pleased with the results.

The closer I got to true love, the more I trusted Nathan, the more I let him guide me along a clean, harmless path of caring, the more I wanted to tell the world what had happened to me. I was glad I no longer had to keep my secret, I wanted the person who had hurt me to know what I had been living. I wasn't the guilty one, I didn't ask Bill to rape me, and it was right that I told on him. Now, my only regret was not having a father to tell. Would Dad have punished him? I'll never know.

Mother, dear Mother, what are you thinking? Why can't you see what he did to me was not my fault. Yes, I'm who I am because of it, but I no longer have to run and hide. Like me, or leave. Accept me as an abused child who had such a short childhood, one who is now trying to protect what few good memories of that time I still have left. What I don't understand and have answers to, well, I'll find those answers through you and Tilly before I die.

"Mother, why didn't you ever bake me a birthday cake, like you did Tilly every year? Like you did for the rest?" I don't know why I asked that question, and realized how completely out of context my question was with the subject at hand.

"What did you say, Trish?" Mom asked me to repeat it again.

Better close the trap door to the right side, I thought, as a pause of pain came between us. I knew damn well she heard the question but didn't want to answer it, or more likely, she needed time to think up an excuse.

"It doesn't matter, Mom. Forget I ever asked a question." I know the answer, I told myself.

"I would if I could. Are you going to make me sit through what remaining years I have, scared to death that you will come out with questions like that. Do you still have such a need to hurt everyone connected with your past? I thought maybe you were changing. . . . "

"Yes, I am changing, I'm not so sure you'll like what you see, but I am changing. The truth surfacing has uncovered me . . . like frosting put on a cake when it was too hot and it all ran off! The past is dripping away, slowly, but it's not gone."

"I just don't understand you, never will I guess. We seem to get closer, and I begin to trust you, and then you attack my past ways." She didn't look at me when she answered, she played with her rings that Dad had given her. "You've had your say, why can't you forget the past?"

"Come on, Mom, no one ever forgets. Memories are only saved as long as there is a purpose or a need. Then, God erases all the hurt and pain by passing along Alzheimer's disease to the ones he feels have suffered enough, or the ones that he thinks have all they answers they'll ever need, or want."

The older lady nodded, wishing inside God would pass the cure on to her. "Possibly so!" Then, she wheeled her chair around once, and before leaving the room, turned her head high and asked, "Where do you suppose all of the good jewelry your father bought me went, Trish?"

"Well, I didn't pawn it. You'd better look closer at your two darlings for that answer!" I wanted to tell her that I thought my trophies had been melted down for her cause, but didn't. I knew I had said enough that bothered her, and even though it felt good being able to say what I was really feeling and thinking, sometimes guilt would still creep into me and I'd find myself trying to make amends. I still had to keep telling myself she was my mother.

"Mom, how about a nice ride out on Pulaski's famous and potty dirt roads? You haven't been out in so long," I asked, hoping to change the subject and mend the wound like I had been taught to do so many times in the past. The Tillman's never really faced facts, and were masters at changing subjects!

"No, not today. I'd like to go outside and sit in the sun for awhile. Call Tilly and make her take me for a walk. The new paths you had put in for me really are lovely," Mom complimented me, again, for my caring. If only she had known how much I had always cared as a child, before I gave up trying to get some love from her.

I rose from my chair and started to call Tilly, but before I did, I let Mom know how Tilly had impressed me with her work efforts. "Sure Mom, Tilly could use the fresh air. She's been working hard around here. I didn't know she knew how." I was amazed at her efforts, because she never lifted one hand to help when we were young. She always acted like it was beneath her to work.

With Mom gone, leaving me to my own thoughts again, I found my mind wondering back to Angel's disappearance. I was overwhelmed by it, and as the days began to add up, my own fears started to consume more and more of my thoughts. A piece of me was missing, and although I was overjoyed because I was growing another human being inside me, I still felt consumed lately by the lack of news and the scare of eventually finding out that Angel was gone from me forever. Not even Nathan or a future child could replace my best friend and partner in life. Even the children seemed to be visiting more lately, trying to fill the gap for me, but no one could.

Where are you, Angel? Please come home!

• • •

Angel was in the middle of a voyage! As she sat on the old, board-broken dock, remembering all the times the family had spent there, she recalled how summer after summer we packed our most treasured belongings and traveled to the north; far north, the trip taking two days. She was well aware of being very alone in life for the first time, and her thoughts ran deep, searching to recall distant memories. . . .

Summer in the Adirondacks was always so cold, I reminisced, as I wrapped my only sweater around me tightly. The water of First Lake rippled at my feet, as I continued watching the sand come and go with the waves. So many memories . . . and so much to handle.

I remembered swimming together, driving Grandmother Timmons crazy by diving under and holding our breaths as long as we could. Grandma couldn't swim, and she counted heads the entire time we swam. Even worse, we played into her nervousness by taunting her and yelling, "We're drowning Gram, call Dad to save us," and as our heads bobbed under the cold water, we'd hold our breaths for what seemed like eternity, letting some bubbles surface for added proof that we were really drowning, and poor Gram would scream for help to her second husband, Tom.

We weren't' allowed to call him Grandpa because Mom didn't like her stepfather, although he was by far the greatest grandfather any child could ask for. I think Mother always felt like she was getting even by not allowing us to call him Grandpa. It was her way to hurt Gram. Mom mastered the use of her children to hurt others, being coy enough to let someone else do it for her. Cowardly, I thought, after all, Gram was a widow when she married Tom.

I found myself rising from the the old bench and walking along the waterfront. The water was low; the time of year when everyone came to the lake to repair their docks and get ready for another warm season of fun. It was the time of year when the birds flock north to escape the southern heat, mating and sheltering their young until they could fly south by their sides in the fall. Bird's parents didn't leave their flock alone all of the time. Mother birds even fed their little, taught them to fly before they kicked them out of their lives.

We did have some good times here, or at least I thought they were good times. My mind wandered back, thinking about all the times we walked to town with Mom; walking to meet Dad, who at six-thirty on Friday nights would be headed up to our cabin on the lake for his weekend retreat before returning to the city early Monday morning. Funny how I always felt Mom was half a person without him, filling in her day hours by appeasing her kids with anything we wanted to do—anything just to get her through the hours of his absence. After thinking about it for awhile, I finally realized that we raised ourselves while Mother paced our early years away.

I tried hard to remember what Mom did all day; five days without Dad. Did she read? Sew? I couldn't remember any details. I remembered her talking for hours with some old German lady, sitting on the front porch while us kids did something we shouldn't have been doing. Then, I remembered something odd. . . .

Tilly getting a razor and shaving Trish and I down there, where the hair was just starting to come in. What were we playing, out back in the woods, in one of our many forts that we built? I could hear Trish crying and then that night, she took a pen and drew dark blue ball-point circles all over her pubic area. Trish told me she was afraid it would never grow back . . . that she'd be bald like a plucked chicken the rest of her life. Worst of all, poor Trish thought she'd never have a period because she had heard Tilly tell Mom that she didn't have any hair there yet, so she couldn't have started her period. I think we must have all been a little sick then, or was that normal behavior for three young, curious little girls?

Mom and Dad were so tied up in each other, their friends and social clubs, that they forgot to watch us . . . or maybe they didn't forget! Maybe it was easier that way. No wonder Bill got away with abusing Trish! It makes sense why they let Tilly boss us around so much: she was dong their job for them. But why would they have us if they didn't want to raise us?

I felt drawn to the sky and the passing clouds, and my insides became twisted and squeezed like a lemon . . . sour tears flowed involuntarily down my cold cheeks. I wasn't one to delve into the past and analyze things that had happened to us back then, so feeling and thinking like I was came hard for me. I actually could feel the pressurized weight pushing against my chest.

I vowed right there and then that my marriage would be as good as my parents in respect to each other, but better at raising a family.

Trish is right . . . I thought about our early family years at the lake when Mom counted on Bill in Dad's absence. Boy, if I had known back then what I know now about him, I would have been scared to stay here without Dad all day.

We only had a boat to get to town with, in case of an emergency, no phone back then, not this far out in the woods. The phone came many years later when it wasn't really needed, but, we had an older brother who could drive the only boat to town! Glad it wasn't ever necessary, because he would have screwed that up, too. I mocked at the memory. I never worried about him being our only savior back then, but I sure bet Trish did!

Trish. I'm being so unfair to her. She's probably worried sick over me. I wish I could call her, but she'd come running to help. I need to think for myself. It's about time I handled my own problems! And it's about time someone helped Trish cope with her horrid past. My God, I'm growing up! People need me . . . Trish and Pete need me. . . .

"Hello, Pete. It's me," I spoke shakily into the telephone receiver.

"Angel! God Angel, are you alright? Where are you?" Pete felt sick, and he knew it wasn't AIDS, or missing Angel, that caused his anguish.

"Sorry, but I needed to get away. For the first time in my life, I needed no one . . . no one to help me." I was proud of my new independence.

"Where are you? I'll come to you. I love you."

I wiped my tear-stained cheek, and felt the instant happiness that Pete's voice and words of love brought to me. "I love you, too, Pete. I'm twenty years in the past . . . somewhere you've never been, and I needed to make the voyage alone." I prayed Pete would understand.

"Are you coming home, or will you at least tell me

where you are?" Pete asked with warm concern.

"Tell everyone I'm fine, and that I'll be home when the voyage ends. Are you doing better, or has it gotten worse?" I felt like a nurse that had entered the battle to heal, but had gotten so sick at the sight of death that I had to run away; traitor to my wounded soldier! I began to feel what guilt felt like for the first time in my life.

"I'm holding in there. I actually seemed to do better before I found out about the damned thing, except . . . I miss you so very much and have been half-crazy with worry."

"Mind over matter they call it, Pete. You're voice sounds so good to me. I've missed you, too. You'll never know how much I've wanted you here with me, but this was the only way I could think out our problem; alone."

A loud click interrupted my explanation and I listened as a recording replaced Pete's rasping breath. "Please deposit another three dollars and sixty cents, or discontinue the call," informed the operator.

Just as well, I thought, we've talked long enough . . . "Got to run, Pete, no more money. I love you, and I'll be home soon," is all Pete heard as the line to our love disappeared once again.

I began to feel sleepy with the thought of the long walk back to the cabin. Mom and Dad had sold the place many years ago, after Dad's business expanded and he no longer had the time for vacations with the family. I was glad that I found the place still standing, and very easy to break into.

I remember Trish telling me how easy it was to break into . . . that was the year of her graduation when she and Mom had a terrible fight and Mom hit her with the broom. All Trish wanted to do was stay out all night with her class on Lookout Point. I laughed at the memory, seeing Mom chasing her around the downstairs, swinging the broom and screaming, "Get out of my sight!" Trish ran away that same day. She stayed here all summer, surviving her ordeal just fine. Trish is a born survivalist . . . always will be, I convicted.

I mentally counted backwards and figured out I had to have been around seventeen. Then a smile broke out on my face, thinking what a boring summer everyone had without controversial Trish around. Maybe Mom and Dad thought of her as trouble, but to me she stood for *life!*

As I cuddled up on the sofa in the living room, feeling very tired from the walk back, I laughed inside about another memory; my parents always making love on Sunday night . . . no other night seemed to suit them. Maybe Mother was performing some kind of duty to Dad, wanting him to go back to the city "taken care of," I surmised. Surely Mom never enjoyed sex, not stately, cold Mom. I could hear her voice as she told me how she hated the mess it made!

The sounds of my parents grinding it away would come through the thin walls, when they thought all their children were asleep, and the next morning, Mom would declare she needed to get in the lake to bathe, which was the only time she ever crept in the water above her wobbly knees. Mom couldn't swim because Grandma never let her learn.

Now where would the Tillman children be today if we never did anything we weren't supposed to do? I thought. Trish wouldn't be Trish, and maybe Bill would be different; clean. Tilly, well, she was just somebody who was never around unless she needed something done. I think she was too in love with Elvis to pay much attention to me.

Nothing but a flimsy excuse; Grandma was to blame for her *lack-of-everything* in life, or so she led us to believe!

Well, I want sex, messy or not, and I want it with Pete; AIDS and all. Guess I just won't have any children to raise, but I'll have him and lots of love! I won't be alone. I have my family, I have Trish to help me. I just can't walk away from him, he's part of my past now, too. You just can't shut the past out. . . .

• • •

Pete ran breathlessly through the inn calling, "Trish, Tilly, anyone? I've got great news . . . Angel is okay!"

"Yes, Pete, what's up?" I felt my stomach muscles tightening as I approached the young man.

We all descended on him like vultures, ready to pick his brain. We were half-crazy with delight, not quite willing to believe what we heard.

"Trish, she called me about an hour ago. Maybe you can make sense out of this . . . I don't know where she is, somewhere twenty years in her past, on some crazy voyage. It was a long-distance telephone call." Pete's appearance looked terrific, like he had been given an injection of the *cure!*

"Thank God, Pete. Is she coming home, or did she tell you her plans?" I couldn't pick the kid's brain fast enough.

"Yes, she's coming home soon." I could detect a large sigh of relief in his voice.

I instinctively touched my stomach, feeling a sudden strong pull from within. It was like I had been feeding and carrying Angel around covertly, keeping her under wraps during her vigil. Suddenly, I felt my next child move for the first time—signaling my *instincts* had paid off; both beings that meant so much to me were doing fine. Today was a memorial day, and I thanked Dad for telling me to trust my *instincts!*

Angel literally flew back into our lives as quickly as she had flown out. The day after her arrival, after the initial Angel dust had settled back into the corners of the inn, I had to make certain that Tilly didn't follow through with her plans regarding Angel.

I had overheard the witch prodding Mom into shaming Angel for all the worry she had caused us. Tilly's voice could be heard plotting again, "Mother, you need to come down very hard on Angel. After all, she didn't show any concern for you . . . you could have died of worry. I told you Trish knew all along where she was. That's why she never acted so alarmed like the rest of us. Those two were obviously just trying to worry you to death."

I stood very still outside Mom's lovely room, not letting on that I was there. I didn't burst forward with anger, because I wanted to hear Mom's reply first.

"Tilly, I'm just glad she's safe and home. Angel isn't my small child any more . . . I can't just spank her like I used to."

When did she ever spank Angel? I questioned my memory bank.

"Well, if you ask me, you have every right. If you don't confront her, then I will," Tilly declared with glee in her anticipation off doing just that. "And someone has to tell her to keep her AIDS spreader away from here."

I had heard enough, and was furious. I interrupted cruel Tilly, after I purposely moved Mom's chair away from Tilly's side. If I had a need to slug her, I didn't want to hurt Mom, or let her get in the way of my blow. "You'll never change, will you? Always scheming to hurt someone, but what I can't figure out is *why*. You've got Mom right where you've always wanted her, so why try to persuade her into hurting Angel? What purpose does it serve?"

Tilly offered no defense or reasoning, too shocked to quickly think up an alibi, I assumed. After a pause, I kindly let her know that if she said one word or questioned Angel about her reason for disappearing, I'd beat the tar out of her. Tilly knew I meant every word of my threat, and knew physically I was well capable of doing just that, pregnant or not!

"If, when and to whom Angel wants to talk about her little voyage, it's her decision and hers alone. I'm sure by now that you both realize that she is very capable of making her own decisions in life. Leave her alone. Understand?"

Tilly and Mom were embarrassed by my confrontation. Maybe that's what I needed to do when we were kids, threaten to beat the hell out of Tilly when she pulled one of her stunts and tried to stir up trouble. I thought about our paddlings, and for the first time realized I could never remember Tilly ever getting a spanking.

"If you ever mention anything to her about keeping Pete away from the inn, I'll do more than beat you." As I started for the door, I turned and stared at Tilly and added my credentials, "Remember, I had a good teacher when it came to beatings, and experience counts!"

My threat worked, neither one of them pestered Angel about her voyage into her past.

• • •

Summer days in Pulaski justified its founding. The trees were a natural asset, adorned with every shade of green leaves, made visible by their fluttering in the warm breezes. The heat of July helped the farmers' harvest grow, as well as Nathan's and my little seedling. I was definitely eating for two, and my feet began to disappear, becoming well-tucked under my protruding belly. I was beginning to resemble Buggy Bundle.

The formal white wedding I wanted in town was long overdue by standards imposed by others. Actually, when Angel and Pete asked us about a double wedding, we were delighted in delaying ours to coincide with theirs. Now, instead of two sisters sticking life out together, it became two couples—joined as partners on July 4, 1981.

It was a grand, large wedding that set off many charges in Pulaski on that hot July Fourth day, and our explosion in uniting caused quite a celebration for the local gossips.

The Church of the Angels never looked so beautiful, only being outdone by the lavish and very expensive attire of the guests. I knew for certain that they didn't purchase their outfits on the square; the cash registers, or the cigar boxes, couldn't have held the amount spent. And I have no doubt that banker Lilly would have panicked if the merchants tried to cash all those checks on the same day.

It was a pleasant sight, although all of those big hats and furs seemed to walk themselves into God's house in search of air conditioning.

Angel wore a creation by Queen Anne of Palm Beach. The gown was white sheer organza and Chantilly lace that featured a lace-covered fitted bodice. Her halo was trimmed in little pearls, allowing only a slight glimpse of her beautiful facial features as she walked down the aisle to Pete. She never looked more like a cherub, as her wings made of Chantilly lace fluttered behind her. Johnny stood almost a foot taller than Angel, as he guided her to her future.

Of course, my halo had long ago vanished, but I still had wings, and had to rely on them heavily to flutter like hell, in order to make my arrival at the altar possible. My dress was lovely, and I was as proud of mine as Angel was of hers. The bodice was similar, assuring every envious guest that both sisters were amply endowed. I snickered as I imagined the guests had figured my assets in my bodice area were one of the reasons the lower half of my gown pugged. I knew the way the designer had flouted the waistline was enough to make their tongues begin to chatter.

Sir William of Nashville, my dressmaker, was quite proud of his work. It was his first and only maternity creation, and neither one of us saw any sense in hiding my belly; it didn't like being pinched any more.

After my tight bodice came the sack of white organza, which was pleated around my bulging waistline. I hadn't begun to waddle yet, so at least I carried my load to the altar with some poise. As I walked down the aisle, I was thinking about the press release and wondering how the newspaper's description of my gown would read. . . .

Tradition is hard to overcome, and I never understood why white was saved for virgins only. I grinned, thinking how I justified white to my family, this time around.

I had taken Mom with me to Nashville, telling her the outing would be good for her. I wanted to get her away from Tilly when I told her I was pregnant, and just in case I needed it, her hospital and doctor would be close by. "Mom, Nathan and I are going to wait to get married in the church, because Angel and Pete want a double wedding. But, you might find the wedding a little embarrassing . . . because by July I won't be able to hide my condition, and furthermore, I'm wearing white!" Mom's face was expressionless. For some reason, she hadn't interrupted my story.

"Does it bother Angel that you'll steal the show?" I looked at her smile, and I started to laugh. She laughed.

"You mean the baby will steal the show!" Mom wasn't furious, or embarrassed, maybe she was finally learning to accept me.

"Nathan told me after your Mother's Day announcement." I was shocked. He never told me that he had told her. My, aren't they getting chummy, I thought. My insecurities were cropping up! Not again, not like Jimmy. . . .

When Tilly found out and challenged my choice of white for my gown, I told her that my baby was pure, and would display the color proudly. She pissed me off and I felt bad after I told her, "You should be so lucky . . . that gown of yours has been hanging in your closet for ten years and is already off-white!" I apologized for saying that, and told her she needn't attend the wedding if it bothered her.

As I joined Nathan at the altar, releasing Tim's arm, I watched Tilly lift Angel's veil. I wore no veil because I didn't want to hide from all the accusing eyes. Dad always taught me to meet my *foes* head-on, eye-to-eye, especially if I had something to hide. He used to say it took the sting out of their stinger.

Tilly actually looked attractive in her street-length gown of blue, but I couldn't help wishing she were wearing white also.

Becky was my maid of honor. She was wearing blue, and I wished her gown's color symbolized her lack of virginity, because her lack of a "first time" bothered me. Most mothers would be proud if their daughter at twenty-two was still a virgin, but then again I was different. I worried she'd never be able to love and share herself with any man. I held a lot of guilt inside, always wondering if my two previous marriages had turned her sour on men. I prayed constantly that someday she would have something in common with me; the ability to give love. (Maybe not quite as easily as I had, but at least to some lesser degree be able to give a little potion of the magic!) God forbid her to end up like Tilly; a very bad, recurring nightmare of mine.

I stood tall and tried to hold my pride in. Tim and John had taken their places next to Nathan, who had asked both sons to be best men. Pete had his brother, Bob, as his. What a lovely family wedding picture this would make.

My thoughts should have been on the sacred vows, but after two previous marriages, I knew them by heart. I didn't hold much faith in the words anymore. I knew no words could bind Nathan and I for the rest of our lives; only actions could. After all, the two previous princes I married swore their vows to our unions also, and it was their *actions* that destroyed those unions, not their *words*.

As Angel and Pete attentively listened to Father Daniel, my mind kept drifting to thoughts on the right side of my brain.

I often wished the men in my past had just sired my children; that I had never married either one of them. I wish we humans did it like horses, which I used to believe had a better way; let the studs do their trick and then leave their calling cards to be nursed and raised by their mothers. But now that Nathan was my stud, I felt differently. I looked forward to my next child having a father, and knew this time that I wouldn't be so protective of my child. I'd let Nathan be a part of this one's life.

With Angel and Pete's vows completed, Father Daniel turned his focus to Nathan and I. He had a sly grin on his face as he turned to the guests, and said very proudly, "Patricia Tillman Brawn and Nathan Howard Brawn are here today to bless their marriage in God's eyes, according to the laws of the church!"

He had just popped the gossips' bubble with that declaration. I loved it! For you see, we had been married by Father Daniel two days after I found out I was pregnant, some four months ago, and now our marriage was blessed in the church.

CHAPTER SIX

With Angel and Pete in Alaska on their honeymoon, and Nathan and I in Miami on ours, I imagined the inn's business was getting to Tilly and Mom. I had left comprehensive instructions, but I was secretly worried that the place would be too much for the duo to handle. I also had seen to Bill's monthly check, so there wouldn't be any need for him to contact Mom and Tilly, or view my home for the first time. I never wanted him to feel free to enter my home again, or my life. I hadn't had to look at his face since I departed the homestead, and I wanted it to stay that way.

Although I wanted to get away with Nathan to spend some time alone together, I also worried too much to really enjoy it. I never did think anyone could handle business as well as I could. If I made a mistake, it was just that, a mistake. If someone else made a mistake, I constantly searched for a hidden evil purpose behind their error. I had come a long way in trusting people, but trusting Tilly was not a way of life, at least not yet.

"I'd better get you out of the sun, honey, or you'll roast that child of ours," doted Nathan. I found his constant attention something new in my life; it was like I had been starving for years for the type of affection he bestowed on me, and now that it had come my way, I was milking it for all I could get. He knew about my past, my future dreams, and still loved me. Nathan found little fault with my personal traits, and acted like he enjoyed my wild schemes and active imagination. He loved all of me, the good and bad, the strange and normal, the sadness and the happiness, the crazy things I said and did . . . he loved me.

Although his love was sharing and straightforward,

never once giving me a valid reason to second guess his intentions, my old distrusting habits would never quite leave me, not completely. Distrust is a hard feeling to explain to anyone, it's just a feeling that keeps edging its way to the surface from time to time, without any apparent reason. As hard as I tried to change, to trust, I lapsed from time to time. My past legacy was deeply ingrained in me.

"I love you, Nate. I always will. I can't imagine having to say good-bye to you . . . will you wait in heaven for me, after you finally get out of hell and make it there? No hanky-panky while you wait, promise?"

"I'm yours forever and three days! No one else could ever replace you. I promise." Nathan was always looking at me with those honest blue eyes, the ones that captured my heart so quickly. Forever and three days means his entire time on earth and the three days it'll take him to rise to heaven. It was our personal promise to each other, a promise that no one but ourselves could understand the meaning of. It meant loyalty, forever and beyond.

After two unsuccessful marriages, I always felt like everyone took for granted that I couldn't love anyone, not the true love that so few people find and keep forever. I could tell by the way Mom and Tilly looked at Nathan, like he was the next victim in my love nest and soon, any day now, I'd cast him aside like the other two. It was hard for them to believe I was as happy as I was, and saying they were happy for me was most difficult for them. I imagined I felt a lot like a liar does, crying wolf, wolf one too many times, and consequently, no one believed that Nathan was the right man for me. No one believed there would ever be the Mr. Right for me.

We would talk about what we had done in our pasts, and with him I could share anything and everything. He was the first man I'd ever let watch me when I dressed and undressed, the only man I ever let share my shower, and the first man I ever took a good damn hard look at physically. It felt right, and without any drums rolling or overture thundering its presence, trust had crept into my inner soul and magically let me enjoy the art of loving. If I had known that unleashing all the hurt done to me as a child would have freed me, made me capable of loving someone wholly, then I would have told the world about my brother's incestuous acts years ago.

The soft warm climate breeze swirled the loose beach sand around my swollen ankles. I dug my toes deeper into the hot, gritty sand, absorbing the heat. I was relaxing and enjoying the scenery dotted with palm trees. For the hundredth time Nathan had put my distrusting feelings at ease. I found those testing times, the times I asked him for the trusting words I needed to hear, the ones he so willingly came forward with, happening less frequently as our love grew with new trusting memories.

The ocean was bluer today, and much rougher than yesterday. A large shell washed up on the beach, and I watched Nathan as he strolled over to the bubble of coral to examine one of nature's polished inhabitants. I reflected back to a childhood vacation we Tillmans had spent here one cold winter as a happy family, remembering how a man-of-war wrapped itself around my foot, causing me to lose my voice for three days. My kidneys malfunctioned and I swelled up like a puff ball . . . very similar to the way I looked and felt as I sat sunning on the beach. I was only in my fifth month, and I was gaining at at rate of ten pounds a month. Consequently, we both found it hard to tell inquisitive people that we were honeymooners.

Nathan knelt down beside me, and placed his hand on my belly. "I can't wait to see what we've created." He made it sound like we were chefs, and had created some new lavish, tantalizing desert that needed a little longer in the oven.

"It's amazing, Nathan, because I often try visualizing what our child will look like, too. Not having known your parents, or your brother, I can only draw on your features when I form our child's face in my mind." I rolled over closer to him, putting his hand next to my cheek. "It'll be beautiful, both inside and out."

Nathan whistled for the beach bar hop and ordered two more drinks . . . mine a Shirley Temple. There are some things I hated about being pregnant, and a Shirley Temple was definitely one of them.

"Nathan, I think I'd like to go home before next week. I'm bored with the sun already."

"Are you bored with the sun, or are you worried about the inn?" He knew me. I no longer had any private thoughts.

I picked up some sand and tossed it on his belly, wishing I were more agile, so that I could roll in the grit with him, play with him, laugh with him. "Do you need the answer to that?"

"No, guess I don't. What do you say we go to our room and call the airlines? I'm ready to go home, too." He was obviously ready for something other than going home, his manhood showing its life with a pulsating throb once, then twice. He wanted some loving, and I was ready to give him some. I thought about my mouth licking his throb as one hundred and sixty pounds of me actually jumped up!

• • •

We arrived home without any preannouncement of our change of plans. The inn was still standing, and cars filled the parking lot, so I assumed all was normal. I felt relief, seeing the inn and just being home, until I saw Bill sitting in the main room, relaxed and sharing a drink with Mom and Tilly. I remember the sick feeling I felt inside when I saw him.

"What the hell are you doing here?" I stood glued to the floor, clenching Nathan's hand tighter by the minute. Bill was sitting next to Tilly, flanked on the right by Mom. Mom was nervous. Her squeak started to move. "Why, Nathan and Trish, you're home so early. We didn't expect you, not until next week. Are you feeling alright, Trish?"

"I *was* doing just fine, until I laid eyes on him in my house. Have your *guest* leave as soon as he can find his way out." I coldly stared at Bill as I ordered him to leave.

I continued to hold Nathan's hand, letting him guide me up the stairs to our room. I knew I was shaking, and perspiration started to bead on my forehead. The sight of him made me sick, and the gall of those two inviting him here behind my back made me even more sick. They both knew how I felt about him, and I had been betrayed.

After taking my pulse, the good chiropractor put me to bed, forcing two aspirins down me before he closed the door and fled back downstairs. I crept, or more like heavily bounded, to the door as soon as Nathan left our room, and listened to what his protective voice was thundering at Tilly and Bill.

"Leave now, Bill. You've upset her and I want you off the property. Don't come back unless she calls for you, understand?" He was demanding. Nathan was as angry as I, and he wasn't any man Bill would want to tangle with. I stood listening, wishing that Bill would say something to my protector, irritating himself into a fist full of trouble. Baby or no baby, for that I would have rushed downstairs just to see Bill fall to the floor.

Tilly butted in, as usual, and reminded Nathan that Bill was her brother and Mom's son, giving him no right to talk to him like that. "This house is as much mine as it is Trish's, Nathan, and whereas you have absolutely no claim to it, I suggest you keep your demands to yourself. After all, Bill has more right here than you do. . . ."

I swallowed hard, waiting for Nathan's reply, but to my surprise, Mom piped in first. "Tilly, Nathan has as much right here as you . . . actually more. He's my son-in-law and Trish's husband. What's hers is his! I told you both that it was wrong." Then Mom demanded he leave, "Bill, please leave. Maybe I'll be up to see you later on in the month." I was afraid that Mom knew the truth, that Dad had really left the deed only in my name, something I had never disclosed to any family member. Did she know that Nathan legally had more right to the place than they did?

Bill faded from the scene, and Tilly was disgusted with Mom, and fled to her room. As she passed my door, she was mumbling something obscene. I wanted to do what she would have done as a child, open the door and flash a satisfying ha, ha look at her; how I remember that look.

With that minor family fight over, I fell asleep from the combined effects of the aspirin and my nightly back rub by the "magic-hand-man"—my man, my protector, my Nathan.

The next morning I woke with the thoughts of how Nathan had protected my feelings yesterday. He was the first person since Jimmy ever to protect me. Although my first husband didn't know he had any reason to protect me, my second husband surely did, and he chose not to protect any of us.

When I was married to John Senior, number two husband, I had disclosed a few details about the abuse Bill had so roughly subjected me to. I never went into much detail, but did tell him Bill had raped me, which I thought was enough to justify why I wouldn't let my daughter stay over at Bill's farm with her cousins. He was the first person I ever told.

You can be sure that I never anticipated John's ploy, when he took Becky over to Bill's place and left her there for a week when I was out of town on business during my illustrious career with IBM. Becky was ten years old at the time. I returned to find Becky gone, and heard him so proudly flaunt, "I took Becky over to Bill's place for the week. They keep asking her and I saw no harm." The gleam in his eye told me he was finding pleasure in my scared reaction. I could have killed him with my lady hands. It hurt me deeply that he saw no harm in it. I concluded from that incident that either he didn't believe Bill had ever raped me, or he didn't care about his daughter's safety, or my concerns. He might not have been Becky's biological father, but he was her legal one, having adopted her when she was two years old. Possibly, he was attempting to hurt me, but for what, I didn't know. The thought of him using my daughter to hurt me brought me to the alertness of what he was really capable of! I began to wonder if he was like my brother. Any trust I held for him was gone.

I don't know if Becky remembers me asking her all the detailed questions I asked after I dragged her off of Bill's farm on the very night I had learned where she was. Thank God nothing happened to her, because I would be sitting in some jail, convicted of murdering two males!

Now, years later, as I relate this to you, I know that my feelings for Bill caused my family a lot of confusion. That night at his farm, his wife must have thought I was crazy, dragging Becky off in the middle of the night for no apparent reason. I know my mom couldn't understand why I wasn't close to Bill, especially since our homes were only twenty minutes apart and our children's ages were so close in years.

Unlike the others, whenever he came weeping for help (money) I never had any sympathy. It actually galled me to think he'd have the guts to ask me for help of any kind. I was doing good just being able to stomach his presence whenever we accidentally showed up in the same place. I avoided him as much as possible, and because of this I think my parents thought I was a cold, unfeeling person. Bottom line, when it came to Bill, they were right; they just didn't know the reason why.

I rolled over and watched Nathan as he so peacefully slept. Nathan, Nathan, Nathan, as our child grows in me, so does my love for you. I actually found myself shocked at my deep feelings for this man. Everything we shared became one. We are one. I had changed! I had faith in trust. I thanked God for the new day, and for the past protection Nathan had provided me. I asked my God for patience in dealing with Tilly and Mom, because somehow I knew I was going to get my point across to them; no Bill at the inn!

● ● ●

"I know you're probably as excited as me about the baby, Angel."

"Oh, Trish, I envy you so. Yes, I'm excited for you and Papa." Angel had begun calling Nathan Papa as soon as she found out about our pregnancy. "I wish just once the damn dirty condom would break, or leak, impregnating me with triplets!"

"What did you say, Angel . . . not what I think I heard, I hope." I never thought about Angel and Pete having to use condoms, and Angel's use of that word had shocked me. Angels weren't supposed to have to worry about the use of such things.

"You know, Sis, Pete checks the thing to be sure all was safe, and I check them hoping they weren't!"

I arranged Angel's hair in a bun on the back of her head, securing it with a lovely ivory hair comb. "Angel, do you remember sneaking into Dad's dresser and playing with those things when we were kids, making believe they were balloons? Remember filling them up, and the one that broke when you threw the thing at me?"

"We were crazy kids!" We both laughed at the memory.

"You know, when they rode to Sandford on Sundays to the drugstore, and asked us if we wanted to ride . . . they were going out of town to buy rubbers! No wonder Dad never let us go in the store with him. I thought he was just in one of his no-moods, and felt like being mean. You know how he said no, just to say no sometimes?"

"Yeah, I thought about that, too. Can you imagine driving twenty miles just to buy rubbers?" We smirked and shared giggles, while Angel sat looking at our images in the mirror as I continued to fuss with her beautiful hair. "They were so afraid their friends would talk about them using the things if they were caught buying them in town."

"Funny how we both remembered the same thing," I said.

"They always worried what everyone else was thinking, actually lived their lives like they did because of what people thought!" Angel made her face grimace.

"I know! Believe me, I know better than anyone."

"Remember the time they went to Texas to see Bill graduate from boot camp? God, they raised hell with you over that accident you were in with Sally, and what was her name . . . Sue something?" Angel asked.

"Yeah, Sue," and I tried hard to recall her last name also, "hell, I can't even remember her last name. They only raised hell because Mom's local gossip-connection found out about Sue having beer in her car. If old Maud's nose hadn't smelled the opportunity to get at Mom, nothing would have been said to me! God, I hated that nosy old bitch."

My mind reflected a vision of the fat, unkempt biddy who haunted me for years, trying to catch me doing some wrong, just so she could needle Mom about it. Of course she had another motive, too—her ugly daughter's cause. She couldn't take my looks away from me, but she could try to ruin my reputation with her games and malicious gossip.

"I was prepared for the worst punishment, once everyone in town learned of it via Maud's exaggerated mouth. They had to punish me to save face." We both sat remembering the incident. Then, I started to reflect again. "Mom liked her friends feeling sorry for her, for having such a difficult child to raise! You know, I think she was a master at playing both sides; our inside world and their outside world. If I didn't get caught by Maud, it was okay, but if I did get caught by her, then I had to pay . . . so they could tell everyone they punished me. Nothing like flushing your kid down the drain to advance your position in town."

"I thought the accident was funny. Sally sitting in a field of corn, flapping her arms like an angel who was on her way to heaven! It could have happened to anyone . . . I never did understand why they made such a big fuss over it. You know Trish, I was envious of you . . . you always did exciting things and had fun!"

"Envious of me? Shit, I paid a high price for fun, kiddo. I've never told you this, but I was always envious of you. Your mind had such beautiful, kind thoughts of everything and everyone. I used to imagine how great it must have been to feel so good about everything."

"Well, Sis, I think I've changed. I don't have nice thoughts about everything anymore. I changed after I went to the cabin and took my little voyage back in time." Angel was right, she had changed, I felt somewhat responsible, afraid that my core dump of the past was the reason she had changed.

"Angel, I wish you could get pregnant." The joy I felt with child was dampened only by Angel's lack of one. I decided I'd approach a topic that I knew was very touchy under the circumstances. "Did you ever think of artificial insemination?"

Her eyes grew very large. "No . . . but now that you brought it up, I will. It couldn't be Pete's sperm, and God knows I won't do anything to hurt him. Have you noticed how fast he's failing?" She titled her head back to look directly at me.

"Yes. What does the doctor have to say . . . how long?" My mind was turning like a well-greased wheel in a Fortune 500 company. My years spent at IBM had paid off in more ways than I had realized, because I was coldly capitalizing on a victim's misfortune; Pete's. "This may sound cold, Toots, but if he goes pretty soon, you could get pregnant by whomever, and let the world think it's his . . . as long as he never finds out."

After hearing the way my deceitful plan had come out, I was shocked to think I had some of Tilly's traits in me. "I didn't mean that the way it sounded, Angel. You can always wait until he passes and then get it done as soon as possible."

"But my child will never know Pete's love and never have a father. Oh, Trish, I don't know if I could do such a thing."

"It doesn't take a father to raise a child. Look at Tim and Becky, and Johnny. They're turning out just fine, and they share a love with me that few mothers ever share with their kids. Hell, most husbands demand too much of their wife's time: demanding more than their fair share of attention when the kids are small. I think men are jealous of their own kids when it comes to sharing their wife's time with them."

"What about Nathan? If you believe what you just said, you'll have trouble with him when your baby is born, won't you?" Angel was very astute, and forced me to rethink what I had just said.

"I think it will be different with Nathan and I . . . he's so understanding and anyway, we love each other. I didn't really love the other two. Well, at least not the second one. I try to remember the first one, but it's like he never existed either. We were just too young."

"He was a handsome devil. If you two could have made it through the lean years together, I think you would have ended up with him. I sort of felt sorry for him, he was like a little lost boy when you left him."

"That's what I mean . . . he wanted me to be his mother, not his wife. I wanted to be a mother, one who devoted her time to her children, especially when they were so young. You know Angel, I'm as much at fault as my past husbands . . . they never had a chance. I could never trust a man."

A silence came over us both, momentarily. I added, "Everything was alright, until they tried to force me to do anything I didn't want to do. But I could trust my children . . . they never hurt me. They were mine, and I never let their fathers be fathers to them. I guess I was afraid someone would take them away from me, like Jimmy." I wiped a tear of regret from my aged face, and then added, "I hate talking about them, the old ones. The only thing good that came of those years was the kids. That's why I think artificial insemination would be perfect for you. Maybe you'll never find anyone else to love, and you were meant to have kids, Angel." I squeezed her shoulders, and tried to perk myself up by saying, "Just think, you're child will have an angel for a mother!"

"Maybe I should . . . oh, I don't know. I'll sleep on the thought some."

"Well, think it over. It's a big step. I'm sure you'll weigh the pros and cons and make the right decision. Besides, you're young and probably will meet another Mr. Right before it's too late to conceive." I was waddling proof of that!

Angel let me take my place at the dressing table and started to fuss with my recently streaked, perky haircut. When I had shed my halo, I also had shed my long hair. "Trish, do you think Nathan would step in and be a part-time dad to my child . . . if I decide to have one?"

I was astounded with her question and wondered why Angel would even need to ask. Nathan would treat any child like his own: my three children were proof of that. He didn't know the meaning of the word *take*, just *give*. "Why don't you ask him," is all I said.

"You wouldn't mind him sharing your child's time with mine?"

I had never thought of that angle. "No . . . guess not. If you had a baby as soon as possible, their ages would be close and I assume they'd be together all of the time anyhow."

Both of us were as pretty as any brush strokes could make us. We were ready to embark on what we thought was a routine, fast-paced day at the inn.

The date was December 12, 1981. Too soon after our primping, we learned that day would be anything but routine: fast paced, but not routine.

I was sitting with my second cup of warned-against coffee, and Angel was downing flapjacks like she had already visited the insemination bank, and having had positive results, was already eating for two. "Thirty-four people here for breakfast, Angel. Got any more good ideas for the inn?"

As we conversed, Pete joined us at the table, looking very thin and constantly coughing like hell. At times, I have to admit, I worried about catching something from him, but never shared the thought with anyone. It must have been my protective, motherly instincts working overtime.

Pete injected his morbid "food for thought" of the day, which made both Angel and I choke.

"This is my last breakfast I'll share with you two. I'm going to meet your Dad today." Forks dropped, coffee splashed over the cups and onto the saucers, and two hearts stopped. Angel grabbed for her husband's hand, encasing her's over his.

"Pete, I know the reality of death is frightening you, and it must always be foremost in your mind, but please don't say such things. Your illness is hell on all of us." Angel's words flowed with care and concern. "I know they will find the cure, or you'll lick this thing on your own. Do you want to call Father Daniel, so that you have someone to talk to that understands?"

For someone so young, Pete looked like he had survived half a century here on earth. I looked into his bloodshot eyes, and my heart ached for them both.

"So doubt what I've said, you two. But I know the fight is over for me, and all I want is some peaceful time with my wife . . . in her arms, alone. Please leave, Trish. I don't want to share Angel with you any longer."

I knew my place and manners. "Got to go, kids, need to pay the help early so they show their gratitude and work even harder the remainder of the day. Friday is always our busiest. You two have a nice day." What a dumb thing to say, have a nice day to a dying man, I thought, as I poured the coffee in my saucer back into my cup, picked up both, rose from the table and waddled toward the kitchen.

As I approached the swinging doors that led to the kitchen, I suddenly felt a long forgotten feeling; water gush-ing out of me, soaking me thoroughly, and puddling at my feet. My water broke, and Pete was dying today. I wondered if the old wives tale was true, that for every death, a birth occurs.

"Get a mop, Tom. Someone spilled something here and I don't want anyone slipping," I called out to the kitchen detail as calmly as I could.

"Sure thing, Ma'am. Take right care of it for you."

"I'll be back with your paychecks soon." I then proceeded to step across the kitchen to the old servant's stairway in the back of the house, which was the fastest way to my room. I hoped I wasn't leaving a drip path behind me.

Nathan, where are you? Angel, please help! Hell, I remembered her husband is dying today and she can't help. Tilly . . . forget it! Mom and her squeak, please be heard! In spite of a sharp cramp, I made it to my bed and crawled up on it like the elephant I was. The bed squeaked from my weight, but no squeaking Mom. I promised myself I'd never curse her squeak again. Never!

I dialed soon-to-be Papa, counting the minutes between cramps that had now hardened into pains. Papa responded, agreeing to meet me at the front door in ten minutes. Next, I called Dr. Nashe, warning him that his early morning office visits would need reshuffling. I then rose and retrieved my overnight bag that had been ready for a month. After entering the hallway, I saw Mom at the elevator door.

She noticed my suitcase, and smiled, then maneuvered her chair, wedging it in the elevator doorway, holding it open for my slow entrance.

"Don't rush Trish, I've got all the time in the world." I heard her witty words of wisdom, and finally made it to the "automatic-crane" as she called it. "Time for production, huh? You okay?" she checked.

"Yes, but the pains are close, maybe too close to make it to town."

"Have you summoned Nathan? Called your doctor?"

"Yes!" I doubled over in pain, which in my shape was a fete in itself! Mother stopped the crane, then reversed its direction, and said, "Going up, anyone?"

I never remember her being so comical, I thought.

"What are you doing, Mom? For God's sake, I don't want to have this baby in a crane . . . I think I feel its head."

She squeaked and wheeled to my side, ordering me to sit down on her lap, assuring me, "I won't break anymore than I already have." As the elevator stopped where it had originated from minutes ago, she wheeled us both out the door and down the hall to my room, dropping me off at the edge of the bed. "That free ride will cost you a granddaughter, dearie! Climb up there after you strip, and I'll be right back."

"Mom, be sure you take good notes of this delivery. Dad will want all the details, especially the part with me riding on your lap!" We must have been quite a sight. It's a wonder the old chair's wheels didn't crumble.

What seemed like an hour was actually only four minutes, long enough for Mom to summon all the help any pregnant woman would ever need. I was surprised Mr. Hunk hadn't been invited.

The parade of do-gooders was led by Nathan, and thank God for that! Next came Angel and Pete, then Tilly, followed by Tom and his wife, Gladys. Gladys was decked out with blankets, towels and sheets; a perfectly prepared midwife. The rest came empty-handed, and I was afraid empty-headed as well. Everyone's appearance in the room made me very self-conscious and nervous. I was too embarrassed to moan, and wanted to be left alone with Nathan.

I began thinking about my other deliveries, and wondered why I couldn't do anything normal. My first child had been brought into this world by some strange intern from India, my second child by a covering orthopedic doctor, and my third by a qualified, wise nurse. Not again . . . no, I wanted the overly paid doctor of seven months to earn his damn fee!

After being told I was pregnant by the female doctor in Columbia, Nathan suggested I change doctors and go to his best friend, Dr. Tommy Nashe. Conveniently, Dr. Nashe was located only ten minutes away in Pulaski, and Nathan had felt his proximity made it safer and wiser to use him. He was only a family practitioner, but his availability was supposed to count for something. But now, when the time was near, I no longer was sure his proximity counted for anything. "Where is Tommy? Did anyone think to call him at the hospital where he's supposed to be waiting for me?" I panicked at the thought of no doctor, again.

"Yes, I called him. Please, honey, just relax and don't push. He'll be here any minute." Nathan was a rotten liar, and I knew by the look on Nathan's frightened face, that the paid in full doctor would never make it! I wondered if my American Express warranty clause would cover his negligence . . . my fourth child would be brought into this world by a chiropractor—its father!

"Nathan, please . . . this isn't going to be some community thing. Make them all leave, that is everyone but Angel. Oh, let Mom stay if she wants . . . oooooWeeee . . . hell, it's close! Why don't we just video-tape it!" My grip on Nathan's hand and my sarcasm, reflected the pain every two minutes. Finally, the unwanted guests respected my wishes, or Nathan's orders, and left.

"Okay, my man-with-the-slow-hand, deliver our creation . . . she's . . . she's ready to show herself."

Grunt, push, breathe . . .

Grunt, push, breathe . . . easy as pie!

Papa was now holding his daughter: perfect, Patience Brawn!

Grunt, push, breathe . . . why don't the pains stop?

Nathan handed Patience to Angel . . . grunt . . . push . . .

Papa was holding his son: perfect, Patrick Brawn.

Grunt, push, breathe . . . dear God what have we done?

Afterbirth, thank God!

Twins!

I woke the next morning to find I was seeing double; two cribs, two highchairs, two of everything. Nathan was awake and feeding one little surprise, while Angel sat rocking the other. I hadn't even heard the two look-alikes whimper, and felt like I had slept for days. "Good morning you two, I see you've got your hands full." I instinctively reached down to feel my flat stomach. Thank God for small favors.

Angel spoke first, smiling from ear to ear. "Oh, Sis, you've outdone yourself this time. Isn't she just beautiful?" Patience had already captured Angel's heart.

"I don't know, Sis. I didn't see their faces from the angle I was at!"

Nathan rose and brought me our son, Patrick, and his bottle. He had such black hair, and tiny ears. I always checked out my children's ears first thing, then their toes, and finally each little finger. Patrick was beautiful, his ears were well tucked and small like a Tillman's. I was proud. I asked Angel to bring my daughter to me, so I could compare the two. Yes, they were identical twins. I was even prouder. "Honey, you might have gotten a late start on this fathering thing, but you certainly did yourself proud." I pulled on his snowy white trimmed beard and planted a thankful kiss on his cheek. " A new generation of doublemint twins! Thank you, sweetheart!"

Later in the day, Tim and Becky called to wish us well, both sounding delighted in our happiness. They were shocked that their mama had twins, and at my age, no less. Son John even made a pit stop while out cruising, to check on his new brother and sister. Johnny seemed amazed that two babies could look so much alike, and I found him sneaking peeks at them when he thought I was sleeping.

One week later, Father Daniel baptized the twins, with Becky as Godmother and Tim and Johnny as co-Godfathers.

So, as Christmas approached at the inn, we all settled in for a hectic and crowded holiday. Our two unexpected guests had arrived safely, although they did cause some additional confusion around the inn. Angel and I had decided to close the inn for a few days over the holidays, and planned on accepting the public again on January 2, 1982. Tilly and Mom were still delaying their return to Nashville, offering to help until I got back on my feet and adjusted to the twins. (I just knew they hated to leave all the excitement.) And Pete didn't die on the twin's birthday, putting to rest the old wives tale, so it looked like our family would be intact when the new year rolled in.

CHAPTER SEVEN

It had been fourteen years since I had enjoyed a New Year's welcoming as much as I had the one of 1982. The inn rocked with the music of Johnny's band, which surprised us all because they were good. Somehow, Angel's gift of music had crossed into John's genes, and "The New Generation Band" was well-rehearsed and softer to the ear than I thought they would be.

We all danced, drank and amazingly got along like a loving family should. We all faced one thing in common: the hangovers that snuck into our next day. I can speak for my own head, and Becky's, because we both met at the same time the next morning seeking aspirins from the medicine cabinet. It hurt to laugh, but I couldn't help it when I looked at myself twenty years younger, and she looked at herself twenty years older, and we both decided we looked more alike on that morning than we had in years. We certainly felt more alike!

Thank God Nathan had hired a baby nurse, who moved in with zeal and took over the care of the twins. Tina Stella was a jolly, rounded woman, representing motherhood in every facet of her personality and appearance. She wasn't highly intelligent, but she was capable of bestowing love on the twins when I was missing for one reason or another. Like many native Pulaskians, she hadn't finished high school, lacked book knowledge, but was most efficient in raising children. She was the mother of two grown children and was super with kids. Often, her little grandson would stay at the inn with her, and Patrick and Bruce became great playmates. The twins responded to her care, and Tina would remain with our family, molding in like she had been born a member, for the next four years.

"Trish, will you help me get Pete to the doctor today?" Angel was beginning to pay the price of Pete's illness. She looked drawn and tired all of the time. Her duties in aiding Pete had become jump, respond, get this and that every waking hour. Even during the night, in the room next to mine, I could hear that damn bell she had purchased for Pete to summon her when he needed her help.

Her patience was remarkable, because if we had switched roles, I would have rung Pete's head with the damn clanging thing!"

We had moved Pete to his own room in December when he seemed to be failing faster every day. The bell was Angel's answer to security for Pete, and he sure learned how to use it quickly enough. The bell ringing was a sad sound that was heard on the second floor every night since we separated the two of them, for the purpose of Angel getting some much needed sleep. With every clang, clang, we all woke and laid still, waiting for the next clang to come. Usually, it took four clangs until Angel arrived at his side. We all waited for the day when the bell stopped clanging . . . afraid with every first clang that the next three wouldn't come.

Clang, clang . . . I waited, Nathan waited, Mom rolled over listening, Tilly sat up in bed, the twins whimpered, Tina's ears tuned to the whimpers from the nursery, and Angel's feet were heard trotting down the hall. The family was awake, all waiting for the next clang. No third clang! Just a scream!

"*No!*" pierced the night, then a thud, Angel must have fallen to the floor. I listened, the house listened . . . quiet followed. The stillness took over the darkness . . . it was so still that shivers ran up and down my spine. I was going to have the runs—cramps prevailed. My nerves were reacting in a stinking way!

Nathan jumped up and ran to Pete's room while I headed for our bathroom. My nervous colon had reacted to death like this once before in my life . . . the second my dad took his last breath, and I found myself in his hospital bathroom losing control just as I was now. My innards were purged . . . everything old was gone. I knew Pete had passed. Two men I was very close to had died the instant I was sitting on the throne; maybe the real gate to heaven?

Nathan called for my help, and guided Angel to my arms as I stood at Pete's doorway. "Don't look in here Trish, just get her out of here," he demanded as he pushed us both clear of the door and closed it.

Why is it when someone says, "Don't look," you find yourself looking? I'll never forget the glimpse I caught of Pete dangling from the rope, chair turned over beneath his limp body. His neck was crooked, causing his head to flop to one side and his eyes were popping from their sockets like a magnet had pulled them out. The damn bell was tied to the rope around his neck, swinging with his body and emitting a soft, constant ring. The room's ceiling light, his hitching post, was broadcasting a beam over the ugly sight! God forbid! Pete had ended his pain!

Angel's legs were water. I had to pick her up and almost fell from her weight as I struggled to get her down the hall to her room. She started to scream, some haunting sound that I had never heard before. It wasn't a sound an angel would make, more like a devil's wail. The tone was deep, deeper than Angel's voice could range. It sounded like Pete's voice, accompanied by the sound of clangs, coming from within Angel. The clangs kept perfect beat with her cries of fright and horror.

Even though we knew Pete's death was close, we never expected him to take his own life. He never gave us a clue, and the mental health clinic that counseled him never warned us that he was contemplating such a thing.

Nathan took care of the body, calling all the appropriate people in town. He administered a sedative to Angel, and took control of everything. I stayed with Angel, holding her in my arms as she slept the results of the sedative off. She would wake, scream, and then go blank. Her eyes looked like marbles that rolled to a rest and stayed glued in one place. I'm not sure, but I don't think she even knew I was next to her during the following three days. She never spoke, never responded to my care in any way.

Mom and Tilly helped with the inn's daily needs, and someone must have directed them to close the place to the public, because I doubted they did it without someone else suggesting it first.

The police and coroner removed the cold body from the inn. Why in hell did he kill himself? Why? The authorities needed to have some questions answered, but Angel was out; sleeping in peace, I hoped. The police wanted to talk to me, but I refused to leave her side. My big baby needed me, and I needed to be by her side. No one would separate the first Tillman twins.

Four more fuzzy days passed before Angel and I were coherent enough to meet with anyone outside of the family. At least we were up and moving around. We missed Pete's cremation, which is the way he requested his disposal. He wanted no one present at his melting, and wanted his ashes dumped on the lawn of a dingy little house on First Street.

Angel couldn't conceive why his last request was so odd, but later in the week Nathan explained to me the symbolism of that dirty little house and Pete's hot ashes! He also vowed to me to do something about that place, ridding the town of its plague.

Our family size had shrunk by two, not one. Angel was lost in her own thoughts and was oblivious to us all. She sat in Pete's room holding that damn bell for almost a month straight. Tilly and I saw to her feeding needs, but she fought every one of us. She refused to bathe, and if the bathroom wasn't adjoining, I'm not sure of what she would have used for a toilet. It was absolutely pathetic, the way she seemed to snap and lose reality with the world.

Mom would sit with her for hours, reading to her and just warmly touching her, brushing her hair, and fussing over her. I had never seen Mom so emotionally strong, stronger than I was when it came to helping Angel. I found it more difficult every day to visit her prison, and when I'd look at my Angel suffering so, I would break down and suffer more. I couldn't help her. No one could.

"Pete," clang, "Pete," clang, "did the rubber break? It's God's way—we should have a child. Oh, Pete, isn't it wonderful?" Clang! Clang!

Nathan was right, we had to do something. "Either she comes out of it by next week, or I'm having her committed, Trish. Look at what it's doing to you . . . I can't just sit by and watch you both suffer like this. I have to get her help. Do you understand?" His tender arms encircled me, squeezed me. I wouldn't listen to his sensible words.

I looked into his eyes, demanding my way. "I won't let you commit her anywhere. You can't separate us. Never! I'll leave and go with her!" My threat was real. Someone had hurt my Angel. I had let Dad down, she no longer could fly around and make the world happy.

"Please Trish, get hold of yourself. Don't you want her to get over this? It's obvious that her mind snapped and she needs professional help. Christ, she thinks she's pregnant."

"You heard my decision. No nut house for my Angel, ever!" Nathan was holding me tighter, trying to make me see reality.

"You can't go with her, Honey. What about the twins, and John? They need you here." His words meant nothing to me.

"Then hire a private doctor, move him or her in here with Angel. I want to be near her . . . I need to know what they're doing to her. I don't trust those hospitals." My heart held fear as I told Nathan how I felt . . . "She's an angel, angels don't go to hell."

I thought about my cousin on my mother's side, the one who had all of those shock treatments, the one who never got better . . . our crazy family skeleton.

Elizabeth Timmons, beautiful by any standards, but crazy as a loon. She mystified me as a child, and when she came to the house to visit with my mother, I would join them and stare at her, looking for something different about her, something that would jump out at me. Everyone whispered about her, and my mom acted like she felt sorry for her and was especially kind to her. Once, after I asked Mom why her mind was sick, I remember she told me, "Her parents broke her and her farmer boyfriend up when they were going to be married. He wasn't good enough for her, according to Aunt Sophie and Uncle Clarence. She never got over losing him."

I would look at Elizabeth, trying to find the scars that must be somewhere on her. I was too young to comprehend mental illness, and was sure her battle wounds would show themselves on her body somewhere.

I went once, to Marcy Hospital with my mom when she was going to have an experimental shock treatment. Mom said they put her on a table and wired her up, then turned the switch and sent shock waves through her body and brain. "Why does Aunt Sophie want her to forget her farmer, Mom?" It seemed to me that it was too cruel of a way to make someone forget happiness in their life . . . why try to forget someone you love?

Elizabeth had style and poise, she wasn't dumpy like my Mom's other cousins. Tall, thin and sophisticated, she carried her family's money well. Her clothes were the finest, and I used to wait for her hand-me-downs every time she discarded something she grew tired of. During those years, I was the only girl who fit into any of Elizabeth's clothes.

As she came out of the shock room, my mom went to help her. My God, she looked like someone had done brain surgery on her and removed what parts of her brain she had left. Her hair stood fuzzy and high, her eyes looked like they had seen their own death. Mom never should have taken me with her to that place.

Nathan was prancing nervously, searching for the right words to get through to me. "Fine Trish, but they might not be able to treat her here . . . here where it happened. I'll call and stop speculating as to what we can do, okay?"

"Yes, you do that." I vowed to myself that I wouldn't weaken and let anyone take Angel from my safety.

"Trish, I love her too, you know! I'm just thinking of us all."

"No, you're thinking like a doctor. I'm thinking of us all, especially her. She doesn't want to go to a hospital . . . I know." My mind became bright and I found the right side taking over. The twins . . . Patience. Get Patience and take her to Angel. She might respond to Patience.

I was right, Patience was the answer. Angel started to react to her presence, and I had my daughter's crib moved into Angel's room. I thought her recovery was making headway, but . . .

"Sis, can I bathe Patience today?" Angel was talking to me again. Her voice had life, a new brightness to it.

"Sure Sis, she loves the water. How about I get her tub and help you?"

"Okay. Can we move all of her stuff in here, closer to Pete and I?"

"Oh Angel, I don't know about that." Dear God, she still things Pete's in here with her. "She needs to be close to her twin. I'm surprised she falls asleep in here without him next to her."

"She belongs with her *mother*, not her brother." Angel's voice was cold, so unlike her past, soft ways. She sounded vindictive, and now she thought she was Patience's mother. I knew things were worse than I had thought. I hated to admit it, I loved Angel, but I also loved Patience, and found myself caught between my sister's scrambled mind and my daughter's own safety.

Angel was committed on March 9, 1982. Nathan had assured me that it was the best funny farm money could buy. The care was supposed to be above reproach, and he tried to convince me we had done right by her. He wanted me to visit the place, to check it out, but I couldn't bring myself to face reality that much. If it was a mistake, then Nathan had made it, not me. I took the coward's way out—and only time would tell if he had made the right choice.

• • •

The inn had twenty-six bedrooms, and thirteen of them now were occupied by family members, leaving the other half for guests. When we first opened, twenty-one rooms were rentable. If my family kept growing, we could close the inn to the public and rename it "The Full House"! There was Angel's room, the closed off room that Pete hung himself in, Mom's, Tilly's, our room, Tim's, Becky's, John's, Tina's, Tom's and Glady's room, and finally the twins took three more slots, a room for each and a playroom. I wasn't sure if this was what Dad had planned for the inn, but it was the way it was turning out. I contemplated selling the homestead in Nashville, after all, it stood so big and tall only for the purpose of housing someone so small as Bill.

"Mom, I need to sit down with you today and want your

help in thinking some ideas through. Can you help?" I thought about how much I missed Angel—she being my idea sounding board.

"Sure, Trish. Let's get a drink . . . some of that stuff from the cellar that you and Beacher save for your outings. It seems to do wonders for you and him." I could tell she was edging toward a conversation I didn't want to pursue.

"Mom, don't let your imaginative mind drift too far . . . there's nothing going on between Beacher and I." Nip it, I thought!

"Oh, I know. Nathan put those fears to rest a long time ago."

"You discussed Beacher and me with Nathan?" I was appalled at the invasion, and wondered why Nathan hadn't told me about Mom's discussion with him. I saw red when I thought someone was talking about me behind my back. Nathan was my protector, and Mom was trying to remove the shield.

"After one of your cellar trips, yes, I did."

"Why can't everyone around here mind their own damn business? That really upsets me, Mom. You have no right, that's between Nathan, Beacher and I." I was irritated, and scared that she had some secret friendship going with my protector. "You ever do anything like that again, and I swear I'll send you packing back to . . . " the place I want to sell, I thought to myself, as I stopped short before I pre-empted the topic of conversation I wanted to have with her.

"Don't over react, Trish. It was a talk we had a long time ago. It's over with. I'm sorry if I upset you." She thought nothing about invading my rights, my privacy.

"Just don't do it again, ever, understand? Nathan is the best thing that ever happened to me, and I don't want you ruining the relationship like you did Jimmy's and mine."

"You never forget anything, do you?" Her eyes grew defiant, defensively sharp and accusing.

"Not things that hurt so deeply . . . things that you can make believe never happened. You'll just never be able to understand what losing him did to me."

In the beginning, Jimmy's and my relationship went over alright with both my parents. Dad enjoyed having an adopted son that he could proudly watch play football and all the manly sports. The attention he showed Jimmy was what I had been striving to get for so many years, using sports as my tool. Well, Jimmy's highly acclaimed athletic ability was a constant source of conversation around our house. Everyone seemed to marvel at his accomplishments.

I never felt even a twinge of jealousy at the attention he got, because if they accepted Jimmy, then they accepted me and praised me through him. After all, he was mine and I picked him out. I had brought a winner home. For once, I had done something right, and it was the good type of attention that a child likes to get.

But, as we grew closer together, and our high school days drew close to an end, my parent's attitude toward Jimmy changed, and the town's attitude toward us changed as well.

We had been the perfect pair, king and queen of everything, until suddenly my folks seemed down on our relationship. All my mother did was ridicule his mother for being a tramp, which she was, and all I heard was how he was destined to be a nobody in life. "Always shoot for someone one step higher than we are, Trish, or you'll never be happy." Mom's favorite, so often heard words of wisdom.

When I say the town went against us, I mean the whole town tried to break us up. Jimmy's priest talked to him, his coach set his mind to reeling about what a grand future he had planned for him in college, and the principal even persuaded him to repeat his senior year, in order to raise his grades so that college was within his reach. He became a single hero overnight, and I became the scorned girl who was dragging Jimmy down; in the eyes of the town, that is.

At the same time, across the tracks, my parents were making great plans for me to go away to college, find someone equal to our name, someone better than that tramp's son . . . "He'll never make it out of this town, Trish, so you'd better pick yourself up and find someone better." Just like that, throw away four years of love and protection. I remember fighting back, screaming my devotion for him, vowing they would never break us up, and then . . .

Jimmy walked away from me that year, leaving me alone and unprotected once again. He swallowed all their great ideas for him, and believed that without me he could bring himself to great new heights. Mother and her townies had done a great selling job! I often wonder if he ever found out that they all had planned our separation, and if his hurt was as big as mine. I can still feel the pain when my mind envisions him and the coach's daughter holding hands and sharing sodas.

    I left Mom sitting there in her thoughts, as I went to the kitchen and got a bottle of red wine. No cellar proof for her, she had pissed me off again! The memory of Jimmy and I wasn't one I liked to think about. It wasn't only the hurt of losing him that was nightmarish, it was all the things I did to get even with them that creep back into my memories. I tried every ploy that any soap opera star has ever connived to get her man back. The memories are embarrassing; how I ever lowered myself to such schemes I'll never know.

    I tried telling him I was pregnant, and when that didn't work, my false pregnancy just went away. I called his new girlfriend, pleaded with her to give him up. I hounded him, begged him, and then finally gave up. I left for college and left my protector to live his life without me. I dated, fell in love for a couple of months with some poor unlucky dude, and then backed away from him when his intentions got too serious. Again, trust was shattered. Again, I had no protective shield to hide behind. Finally, after four years of trying everything to forget him, I tried my first marriage. Marriage was the only thing I hadn't tried. After all, didn't getting married prove I was over him. My world thought I was finally cured of Jimmy. But, deep down inside of me, I knew I had been hurt by someone that was supposed to have loved me. I had trusted and been burned.

    "I want to talk about selling the homestead, Mom. I see no reason to keep the place, with you and Tilly showing no signs of staying there. I want you both to stay here, to make it your home forever. The place is just a shelter for Bill . . . and that's economically stupid. He has a home with Mary and the kids."

    Mom sat still. That was a good omen, because normally she would have cranked up a squeak and rolled around while she thought up some derogatory answer to my suggestion. "I have such beautiful memories back there. It's the only place left that Dad and I shared anything together." She sat perfectly still, staring at me, casting a look of disbelief at me that went straight to my heart. "I know our money situation is just fine, that the dealings in oil and the utility stocks have made plenty for us—enough to care for all of us the rest of our lives *and* the homestead."

"Well, you haven't been reliving too many of those cherished memories, or if you have, you've been doing it long distance. Since you came here for the open house, you haven't made one trip back there." I wanted to add that Father Daniel seemed to be helping more and more lately to build new memories. I doubted she sat around thinking of Dad when he was here at her side.

"I know . . . but sell it . . . I'm not sure I can handle that yet." She wasn't looking at me, her head was down, staring into her drink. Squeak . . . the chair started to move. "Can we include your sister in this conversation?"

"Why, what she thinks makes no difference." Dad's picture on the video came into my vision. His words I played over again, *"Do as I would, or as you see fit."* I thought of the pact I had made with myself concerning my relationship with Tilly, and said, "Okay, I'll get her."

I made a pact, not a resolution, because I never followed through on resolutions, promising that this year I would crawl our of my hole a little farther and make amends in my heart with Tilly. I didn't know how I was going to accomplish it, but somehow I wanted to help her and myself find peace in our relationship. Tilly wasn't getting any younger, and neither was I. I had a need to become a symbol of righteousness. I wanted to establish stability in the family. I knew I was ready to cross a little further over the bridge that spanned the past thirty years. Maybe this year I could get halfway across; my New Year's pact.

"Well, Tilly, what do you think? Remember, our expenses keep growing . . . I just got the bill for Angel's first month at Grace Landing. Hell, you know the books as well as I do." Mother had been right, our well was deep and I doubted that any of us would ever live long enough to spend all of the money. But, I also felt it was financially uneconomical to just blow thousands off each year just so that Bill could live in his past, in the house that held his security for so long. By selling the place, I also thought maybe Bill would go home to his family, where he belongs.

Much to my surprise, Tilly agreed with my suggestion. "Mom, Trish is right. We don't need to carry the overhead of the homestead just for memories. We won't be in need of the place, and why spend our money on such a big house that only Bill uses to hide away in."

Mom looked shocked at Tilly's proclamation, but said nothing to either one of us. I figured the real reason she didn't want to let the place go was because of Bill, not Dad's memories.

After our talk, Father Daniel came to the house, at my request, and he seemed to be able to help Mom accept my decision. The homestead was vacated of Bill and his empty bottles, and sold one month after we put it on the market. Our bank account took a big jump, and the inn was refurbished with family antiques that we hadn't auctioned off. Tilly took care of all the details, and did a super job of closing that part of our past.

"Thanks, Tilly, for doing such a fine job of settling our affairs with the homestead. I know how you and Mom felt about letting it go. Where did you ship Bill off to?"

"Mary helped me move him back to their house. Trish, we've been neglecting her and the kids. She said it was the loneliest Christmas she has ever lived through . . . and we never even notified them when Pete died."

"Yes, I know. I figured Mom kept them up to date . . . or you." I didn't tell Tilly, but I figured my announcement about her husband, my rapist, had caused Mary to shy away from us.

"No, she's been all alone out there with the kids. She said Bill never even shows up when the check comes in anymore, something about he doesn't want your money or help!"

Maybe there's hope for him, I thought to myself. Maybe I don't hold the key to his cage.

"She read about the double wedding, and had hoped that you would invite them all. We just haven't handled his family right."

"I'll call her and take her and the kids our to dinner, or something. I know it isn't right, but I can't have anything to do with him. The memories are still with me, and probably always will be!"

"I never knew he did those things to you . . . why didn't you come to one of us for help?"

"Please Tilly, I can't discuss it with you. You were part of the reason why I couldn't tell anyone." Tears began to form, and a mist settled on my lower lashes. I didn't want to cry, to show Tilly how badly the past still haunted me.

"Trish, I really didn't know. No matter what I thought of you back then, I certainly would have helped you."

"What you thought about me—now that would be food for thought, wouldn't it? What did you think of me back then, Tilly?" For some reason, I never worried what Tilly had thought of me. I didn't care then, but now my curiosity was piqued.

"You were the pretty one, the one the boys liked. Do you remember Chuck Devens? He used to be kind to me, and I thought he liked me. But, when I found out he was only nice to me because he liked you and wanted to talk about you all of the time, then I hated you! You won at everything. All you did was win! You never failed at anything. I even remember when some of my friends asked why you were so pretty and I was so homely." Tilly started to cry, and I was sorry that my looks caused her pain.

"Tilly, it wasn't my fault that I looked like I did. I know you'll find this hard to believe, but I never felt pretty, never knew I was good looking. I used to think I was dirty, and that everyone knew I was. No matter how many hours I spent primping, the dirt wouldn't come off."

We hugged each other, and let some old tears flow together. "Tilly, I was so envious of you and your ways, because Mom and Dad liked you. They loved everything about you."

"Oh Sis, many a night I could hear them talking about you and how beautiful you were, about the way that you were an achiever and would someday make it big. Dad used to talk about you, bragging about those damn trophies of yours. I remember when the cabinet he had specially made for your trophies arrived. He put it in his room, under lock and key. I was happy that he didn't put it out in the open."

"Jealously is the devil, Tilly. It can stir up a lot of trouble, bring the worst out in anyone. Why were we all so jealous of each other? We should have been proud."

"Honest Sis, I didn't know that Bill hurt you like that. I would have helped you, I think. I can't honestly tell you what I would have done. I know now what I would have done, but back then I hated you so. I'm sorry. Something was terribly wrong with our family."

I believed she hadn't known, but it was her ways as a child I resented, not the fact that I couldn't go to her for help. Her lies and schemes helped make me the vulnerable one.

"Tilly, I don't want to discuss our childhood anymore. Dad's gone, and I can't change things that happened back then. You and Bill won the childhood round, but we'll all win the adult round. We have to!"

"I'm sorry, when I did all those things back then, I was only a kid, too." A cruel one at that, I thought.

"Tilly, we won't gain anything discussing it! I know you weren't all to blame . . . let's try to forget, and go on from here. Okay?" I have to be able to *forgive.*

"Thanks Trish. I want you to be able to forgive me, and I hope someday that you can forgive Bill. I know I can't feel what you must be living every day, but if I was partly to blame for his actions, I'm sorry."

It did make a difference, her telling me what she thought of me back then. I could understand why I thought about her like I did, and it felt like a dark cloud that hung over our heads rose and disappeared. Maybe I could really forgive Tilly for her childhood meanness . . . maybe she could understand why I had to win at everything.

Tilly looked at her watch and reminded me that it was time for her to take the twins for their walk. Tilly loved them, and spent as much time as she could with them. They loved her, too, which I felt must have been one of the reasons Tilly agreed with me on selling the homestead. It was obvious that she and Mom were at the inn to stay, and I was determined more than ever that we would win as a family!

CHAPTER EIGHT

"You aren't considering their offer, are you?" Tilly asked as she continued to push Mom's chair down the garden path to the gazebo Nathan had built in the back yard. Mom cocked her head around to hear my reply.

"Yes, because if we don't, I'm afraid they'll sue us or cause such a ruckus that it'll hurt the inn."

"Did you ask Brad what he thinks? I know his opinions cost a lot, but I've never known him to be wrong. When I checked into the legality . . . " and then Mom caught herself before finishing her sentence.

"Why don't you finish what you started to say, Mom, or do you want me to finish it for you?" My voice took on the defensive tone that I found I was using less and less nowadays. "If you think I don't know that you two tried to get the will thrown out, you're more stupid than I thought!"

"Well, we did try, right after you exploded with all the facts of the past . . . " Tilly paused, then continued, "just because you were so bitter, and we were afraid we'd find ourselves out in the cold."

"God knows you deserved it, if I had rid myself of you all, but I have to live with myself, you know." I thought about how far I had come, and realized I had done the right thing as far as Tilly and Mom were concerned. Bill was another thought, and I closed the door on that one mighty fast. Tilly and I took a seat across from Mom's chair, and Mom started to speak.

"I think the three of us have done remarkably well, considering what we've been through in the last few years. You two girls have adjusted to each other nicely, and as far as I'm concerned, I'm tired of the past . . . I need to live what time I have in the future. I'm tired of taking notes for your father!"

Tilly's head sank down, and I thought I glimpsed a tiny tear running down her cheek as she bowed her head in memory of Dad. "I live every breath thinking he's ready to spray me."

"I know, it's like he never died . . . or like he can reach out anytime he chooses, and shake me like he used to. But, naturally, I feel good about the way things have turned out, and he did give me a chance to right the wrongs. I thank him for that." I reached in my pocket for a cigarette, lit it, and watched the smoke circle and swirl its way toward heaven. "Mom, I agree with you. You're a very attractive woman, and can be fun to be around. I hate to see you let life slip by, just because Dad's gone."

"I don't plan on letting anything slip by. This September I will have the biggest bash to celebrate my birthday, and I plan on using every penny John left me for it." Mom was smiling in self-satisfaction.

"Good, we'll all help you plan it."

"Daniel said he'll do most of the planning," Mom added proudly.

I realized that Daniel was more to her than our family priest, especially since Dad had died. But then the memory of what she had said about if Daniel had been my father crossed my mind. I found myself comparing Tilly and Mom for likeness, and then I tried to visualize Mom and Father Daniel mixing it up, and erased any doubt I had about Tilly's true parentage. Her nose was exactly like Daniel's, and her eyes had his similar squint! But with Tilly sitting so close to us, I knew this wasn't the time to bring up that subject, and wondered if there would ever be a right time to bring up such a subject with Mom.

I was glad to see the cook enter our little gab sesison in the gazebo, interrupting my speculative thoughts. Tom came strolling up the walk, carrying a tray and was followed by the twins nipping at his heels. "Thought you fine ladies would like a cold drink," he attentively said as he put the tray down. Tilly jumped up and passed the drinks around. The twins divided between Aunt Tilly and Mom, refreshing their thirst for love and lemonade from each. "I'd like to ask you ladies something, if I'm not imposing on you right now?" asked Tom politely.

"Sure Tom, what's up?" I asked.

"Have you decided if the KKK can hold their rally here next month, Miss Trish?" The center of his eyes were black as coal, and the whites were more reddish than usual. Tom looked very tired to me.

"No, Tom, we just started to discuss what we should do about that." I felt uneasy talking to Tom about the KKK. In my ignorant mind, the KKK stood for vandalism and the hangings of blacks.

"Well, I need to tell you that if you decide to rent them the place, Gladys and I won't cook for you. We'll move out and return home." Tom had very clearly warned us of his position.

I couldn't blame the black man for feeling like he did, but I never realized how strong his convictions were regarding the Klan.

"Tom, they march here every year, right?" I asked in search of some of the facts surrounding their past appearances in Pulaski. "I know Pulaski claims to be the founding home of the Klan, but never paid much attention to it, until now."

"Yes, Ma'am, Pulaski is where the original Klan started. But it wasn't like today's white supremacy group."

"Has the town experienced any bad scenes when they've marched here over the last few years?" I inquired.

"No, nothing real bad. They always rent some farmer's private land and burn a few crosses before they leave. The police keep everything under control, but it's like living on a powder keg, waiting for the blast to go off." Tom was truly afraid, and he wanted no part in hosting the Klan.

"I understand your concern, Tom. We'll let you know what we decide to do." I offered the strapping friend of the family a cigarette, and he refused. "If we have to let them rent the place as their headquarters, I can assure you that no harm will come to you or Gladys."

"Still won't cook for 'em, Ma'am. Won't ever cook here again . . . respect is it!"

He'd rather not fix their eats, and seemed determined to quit if we rented rooms to them.

"Tom, we don't want to rent the place to them, but it's a free country, and if the mayor gives them a permit to march, I may be forced to let them have rooms—legally forced. Do you understand that?" I wanted Tom to understand the predicament we were in, but I don't think he did.

"I don't know what they can do, but I know Gladys and I won't be here if they come." I decided he didn't want to understand, and that his mind had been made up before he ever told us where he stood on the subject.

"Fine, Tom, we understand." Tom nodded his head of tight, curly white hair and left us thinking as he headed back to the kitchen. Little Patrick ran and grabbed his hand, and Tom bent over and picked up the boy who loved him dearly. Patrick reached into Tom's shirt pocket and pulled out a pack of gum, helping himself to a stick the best he could. Tom's smile was so broad, the corners of his lips shown on each side of his face even though the back of his head was turned to us. I thought of little Patrick and how someone so small never even knew the difference between black and white; Tom wasn't any different than anyone else in his small world.

"Well, this throws a monkey wrench in our plans. We can't afford to lose Tom and Gladys, especially over some dumb group that none of us has anything to do with anyway," I acknowledged my despair to Mom and Tilly.

Mom shook her head, as if she was ashamed for the town. "Daniel told me that last year when the town refused their marching permit, they got a lawyer and sued. the town had to permit the march."

"Well, I'll get Nathan to get with Mayor Stanley and see what options we have." I was afraid of what we were going to find out, and now I was doubly afraid that we'd lose two good friends as well as the best two cooks for miles around.

Tilly surprised Mom and I both, when she disclosed her feelings for the KKK. "I can't see what harm they'll do . . . and I think Tom is just being pragmatic. They don't do the things they used to. It's just a group of whites that want to keep us first in life. I think some of their beliefs are right."

I was shocked by Tilly's admission. "Oh, Tilly, you don't agree with their ideas, do you?" Tilly has shocked me in the past, but her liking the Klan came as the biggest shock of all. Tillman's didn't think like she was thinking, we had been raised better than that.

"I have some literature in my room, and I read it last week. They don't like what is happening to whites, being pushed aside so that blacks can take over. I wouldn't want a black leading me . . . and their right about the Jews sticking together and making all the money and owning banks."

I looked at Mom, and wondered if she was as surprised by her oldest daughter's declaration as I was. Mom actually looked pleased that Tilly spoke up for them. "Well, it doesn't matter what either of you think, does it? For the inn's sake, keep your thoughts to yourself, or we could have trouble with the town's people." My God, Tilly's a bigot, I thought, but why should that surprise me? Wasn't she always jealous of someone or something?

I left the ladies sitting in the gazebo, soaking up the heat of the day. I wanted to call Nathan and catch him before he left for home, so he could contact the mayor and see where we stood. I had to have an answer for the Klan before the week ended. I thought about some of the circumstances surrounding the Klan, and what it could do to the inn, considering the type of clientele we usually housed. I thought of the other help, who were mainly black, and wondered why our help was predominanatly that color. I remembered that a few white people had shown up to answer our help-wanted ad, but for some reason I had selected primarily blacks for employment. I didn't know why, didn't know if it was because I wanted to help the blacks, or if I had exploited them like some good old southerners were still doing.

Nathan came home with the answers we needed, even if we didn't like the results of his meeting with the mayor and the town's legal advisor. It was settled, we had no choice, the Klan was coming to the inn.

It was a beautiful day, and I woke nervous as hell. I had never seen a Klansman before, not up close. I thought about my days as a sign-carrying rebel of the sixties, and the memory of my college years made me smile. The world didn't seem any different because I carried those signs to Washington, so why worry about trying to stand up for my cause now? I felt a bit of excitement come over me, anticipating the Klan's arrival. I envisioned them from books that I had read with pictures of them marching, wearing hoods over their faces, with white gowns covering their shapes, sizes, and sexes. They looked like spooky ghosts who could float with purity anywhere they chose. Then I thoght about our staff, and I was afraid that all of the help would walk out. I was glad Nathan had cancelled his patients for the day in order to stay home with us, and Buggy had promised us his men would patrol the place frequently. Tom and Gladys lived up to their promise and left the day before—I couldn't get them to say they'd be back after the crowd left. We had found new cooks, but no one would replace our appetites for Tom and Gladys. I planned on getting them back as soon as the Klan left town. They were due a raise, and I hoped more money would persuade them to return.

The day had arrived, August 2, 1983. The inn was ready, but we Tillman's weren't prepared for what happened. . . .

I looked out the front door, watching about sixteen cars pulling up the long drive to the inn on the hill. The sides of the cars were donned with big, bold signs, and their antennas waved confederate flags as they parked. I thought how brazen they were, because I knew that if I were a member, I'd hide the fact, not flaunt it!

"Here they come, gang," I excitedly yelled to the family who had gathered in the main room anxiously awaiting their arrival. Then, I saw them . . . shiny and boldly displayed like badges of courage . . . "God, they're bringing guns in here, Nathan." I was scared as hell of guns.

"They can't do that. They'll get arrested." Nathan thought he knew the law.

I opened the front door a small amount, sticking my foot between the door's edge and jamb, and with my right hand held the door partly opened to a big ghost.

"Welcome." I gripped the door tighter, "but you can't bring any guns in here with you. Lock them in your cars, or better yet, hide them." All five-foot, two inches of me was dictating to a ghost with a weapon packed on his hip. Casper the Ghost didn't pack weapons, I recalled. His backup had rifles, and I swore I even caught a glimpse of a machine gun.

The very large, stern looking man without an expression written on his face pulled the door wide open and started to walk in. I played school crossing guard, and put my right hand up in his face and repeated my statement, "No guns in here."

"Lady, where we go, they come," he bullied me gently back from his path's way. Nathan appeared at my side.

"Sir, my wife is right, we can't allow you to bring weapons in here. They'll close the place down, and confiscate your guns." Nathan was always smoother than I in a crises.

"How will "they" know, unless you plan on calling someone." The large man removed his hood and walked over to the desk. Susan's face was white. Nathan and I moved out of the parade's way, watching in amazement and fear as females, as well as males, armed the main room. For some odd reason, I never visualized females as Klansmen.

I whispered to Nathan, "What are we going to do now?"

"Nothing, right now. Let them get settled in their rooms."

Nathan moved from my side and headed to the desk with Susan. I hustled to be by my protector's side. We handed out all the keys we had, and I personally thanked God that I had seen fit not to accept any reservations other than their's. We had agreed on a plan to keep as low a profile as we could while they were here. Their visit was supposed to be for only two days, and most of the rooms were rented by them anyhow. I held a fear of these people, something I didn't understand how I could feel in this day and age. How could a group of people have such an impact on society, I wondered. Now I understood Tom's real concern, and I wished we had taken our chances on a lawsuit.

The head of the Klan approached Nathan around four o'clock, and demanded dinner be served at six.

"It's a restaurant, open to the public as well as guests. You can all eat whenever you want to." I could tell that Nathan was beginning to fear them also, but he remained strong and tried to keep his position of control.

"Close the restaurant to the public. It's ours while we

stay here," demanded the leader.

"I own this place, Sir, and I'll run it like I want to. I can't, or won't close it to the public, for you or anyone else," Nathan said, keeping a firm stand.

I stood next to the piano, and could barely hear Nathan and the leader thrashing back and forth. I wanted to call Buggy, but was afraid I was over alarmed by the situation and might cause soemthing bad to happen because I pushed the panic button too early.

"Do you serve blacks, or do blacks come here to eat?" asked Brady Townstead, the damanding leader.

"It's America, isn't it? Certainly! It's against the law not to serve a specific race. You know that. Now listen, I won't have any trouble around here. My family and I live here, and you'll have to leave if you keep trying to tell me how to run my place." By now the two men were so close to each other that I knew Nathan could feel the man's heat.

"Save your speeches. We'll be here for two days, maybe more if we like you." Brady reached out and grabbed Nathan's tie. "If you want to keep your inn and family in one piece, then do as I tell you. Close this place to the public, and do it now." The leader, and his two side-kicks who had joined the argument, moved real close to Nathan's face. One of the men handed Nathan a sign that said "closed to the public until further notice" and instructed, "Hang this on the door. Do as I say and we'll all be one happy family for a few days."

I watched as Nathan took the sign, and after reading it, went to the front desk and claimed the tape. He did exactly as they wanted. We were now closed to the public.

Somehow I wanted to get the black help we had in the kitchen, plus the ones who were working in the stables and give them the next few days off with pay. I feared for their safety. I feared for our safety as well, and didn't like being kept prisoner in my own home. If this is what white supremecy has to offer us whites, I wanted no part of it.

Tina, the twin's nurse, refused to leave, as did most of the other help. They saw no fear in the situation. The leader had warned us all to stay around the inn, not to leave or place any calls to the outside.

"Trish, we have to do as they say, or something could

happen. I'm not about to play hero and jeopardize everyone's safety. They'll be leaving tomorrow . . . after they burn those damn flags and crosses outside. Did you see the press here this morning?" Nathan was trying to be very calm and logical about the situation.

"Yes, and I can't figure out why Buggy or someone hasn't come up to the house. He promised to patrol the place." But then I realized that to the outside world, the inn probably looked like it always did: busy and full of active people. I hoped the press would come a little closer to the main house, thinking they might see what the real situation was and get us some needed help. They had been taking pictures of their cars with all the brazen signs on them.

Something else seemed odd to me, no one was even trying to come to the inn to dine. I hadn't seen one customer at the front door since the Klan arrived. Could it be possible that everyone was heeding the mayor's editorial and were staying away from the Klan while they were here in Pulaski?

"Fix us a drink, honey. Make mine scotch, okay? They ought to be down to dinner pretty soon," I noticed Nathan requested his before dinner drink with more urgency than usual.

I offered up what plans I had put in place for the evening. "We'll eat in the kitchen, with the help. I already told Mom and Tilly to join us in there, and to use the back stairs when they come down."

"Good, because I saw Brady and Tilly in deep conversation this morning. She had one of their gowns on her arm. It looks like she gets along with them alright. Maybe we ought to have her do our interfacing, what do you think?" Nathan asked.

I moved myself from the stool behind the bar in the kitchen, and walked over to Nathan in order to be within earshot of him. I didn't want the new cooks to hear what I had to say. "Tilly likes the Klan, thinks they're cute!"

"She would," Nathan quipped.

"I'm not sure we want to help promote her friendship with them." I could just visualize Tilly as a ghost instead of a nun.

"What do you say we have a little family gathering and

warn everyone about the situation we're in." Nathan was asking my opinion, not dictating his thoughts to me. That was something I enjoyed about this marriage; my strengths didn't intimidate him one bit.

"Sounds like you have it all planned out, honey." I found it very refreshing that someone else could think and plan around here. At times, I didn't want to have to be strong and lead this family.

"All I care about is them staying away from you and the twins. I'm glad Angel isn't here with us." Nathan left me with the cooks and went to call the others for his little warning talk.

Tina kept the twins out of sight in their playroom, with the door locked from the inside.

I picked up one of their newspapers, and after taking a big mouthful of straight scotch, began to read their propaganda. It held as many negative thoughts about the Jews as it did the Negroes. I found one article about Catholics, and thanked the Lord we were Episcopalians. I secretly hoped that Father Daniel didn't come on his daily visit to see Mom, with his clergy dress so much like the Catholic priests. I never remembered being this afraid before; not even motorcycle gangs scared me this much.

A loud clap, clap, clap came from the dining room. I cautiously opened the swinging door to the dining room and saw the entire group, all twenty-two of them, clapping in unison. I guessed they wanted to be waited on, and motioned for Maryann to start to take their orders. As Sabbie, the young black waitress picked up her order pad, I intervened and told her not to go out to the dining room. I took her pad and followed Maryann, a cute little dark haired townee who was white, needed the work, and was willing to stay on under the circumstances.

"Hey lady, why don't you have a TV in here? I want to see the news while I eat," demanded one of the straggly looking group members. He sounded younger than my Johnny.

"I'll get my husband to bring the set in from the other room." I never knew I could be such a speedy, efficient, and agreeable waitress.

"Well, Sam, here are their orders." I handed the cook the

orders we had taken, and reached for my drink, as Nathan and the rest of the family came down the stairs to join me in the kitchen for our meeting.

"You did what?" asked Nathan, highly disturbed at me for taking Sabbie's place in the dining room.

"I didn't want Sabbie going out there. Why give them the satisfaction . . . they might find some cause to start something," I tried to explain to Nathan why I took the black girl's place. "I did a pretty good job in handling the orders, too."

"Well, Tilly can wait on them, with Maryann." I kept quiet, and let my man run the show. "I think if we play this smart, we can avoid any confrontations with them. Mom, would you mind staying at the desk with Susan. I know she's scared to death, and with you out there they aren't going to pester her as much as they have been. Tilly, you and Maryann can serve them. When they've left the dining room, Trish and I will clean the dishes and tables. Sabbie, I want you to go home . . . leave the back way."

The young black woman immediately removed her apron and picked up her purse from the shelf behind the ktichen door, and never said one word to any of us as she hustled our the door, eagerly leaving for her safety. The cooks, being white, kept at their job, and Mom wheeled her chair out the back way and into the main room to join Susan at the front desk.

Tilly followed Nathan's order, taking the first of the rare T-bones that were ordered, and served her new friends in delight. Nathan handed me the wine cellar keys, and instructed me to lock the doors. Everyone had their orders.

"All we need is for them to start drinking," he added to his orders. "I'm going out and see how everything is with them. Trish, stay in here." I agreed wtih my protector, not opening my mouth and not uttering as much as a peep. I could follow orders nicely, if needed.

"We have to call Buggy," muttered Nathan as he reentered the kitchen. "They're smoking something out there, and it's not plain cigarettes. All we need is for them to get stoned . . . oh, I forgot, they want a TV." I had forgotten to tell him about the TV. I certainly wouldn't be getting a good tip!

Nathan went to the phone on the kitchen wall, and then

we all found out why the thirty-six phones had stopped ringing; the line was dead. As Nathan dropped the receiver, leaving it dangling by the cord, he mumbled something that only I heard the end of . . . "see if I can catch Sabbie."

"Nathan, what's wrong?" I yelled as I picked up the phone's receiver and heard no dial tone. "Oh, no, it's dead!" I ran out the back door to catch Nathan, who was already heading back up the walkway. His look was tight and scared.

"She's gone, and all of our cars have been locked. Where is your second set of keys?" he nervously asked.

"I think they're upstairs in my purse." I stopped talking and ran up the back stairs to our room in search of my keys. When I opened our bedroom door, I stopped in shock.

Our room was a shambles, and after searching for my purse and not finding it anywhere, I knew we had been robbed. Clothes were scattered all over, and our mattress was pulled off the box springs. I knew instantly that someone had found Nathan's .45 under our mattress.

Nathan's .45 was his keepsake from the Korean War, and wherever he slept, it slept with him. I remembered the firsty time we made love, and how he tucked his weapon between the top mattress and the box springs, and I thought about the feeling when I climaxed . . . the pistol contributed to such a beautiful moment: the thrill of making love with a gun ready to go off underneath me drove me over the top!

My jewelry box was on the floor, half open, and some of my less expensive jewels were hanging out of the box. We had been searched and robbed, and the phone lines must have been deafened by them. I found myself in prayer as I ran from our room to the twin's room. Please, Lord, I prayed to myself, let the kids and Tina be okay.

Tina was playing with Patience, having tea and crackers. Patrick was in the playpen, chewing on his own cracker and gave me a big welcoming smile. I thanked the Lord that all three of them were safe. I made sure Tina locked the playroom door after I left, and headed down the stairs to report my findings to Nathan.

"Did you find them?" Nathan's hand was outstretched, waiting for the keys to safety.

"Nope, my purse is gone, and so is your .45. Our room has been torn apart . . . and some of my good jewelry is missing. I did check on the twins, they're fine. God, Nathan, I'm afraid. What's going to happen? How can we get help?" I'll never forget the feeling in the pit of my stomach: it was churning and flipping in circles. My digestive juices were up in my throat, and the constant shivers I was experiencing were a reminder of how afraid I really was.

"I'm not sure we want help . . . let me think this through." I fixed him another drink as my train of thought was trying to figure a way out of this mess.

"Tilly, are they stoned out there?" I asked.

"Oh, some of them are getting a little high, but there's nothing to worry about. You know, they asked me why we don't have blacks for waitresses."

"And what did you tell them?"

"That you gave them the day off, because you didn't want any trouble." She seldom tells the truth, and now she chooses to do so, I thought. "Did they like that answer?"

"They laughed!" Tilly then asked Nathan if he thought we were in any danger.

"Hell, yes, they've robbed our room, and who knows what they'll do next. The phones are dead, and they have locked all of the vehicles so we can't leave."

"Robbed? Who . . . has my room been robbed, too?"

"Our room has been turned over, Tilly . . . it's a mess up there. I didn't have time to check on anyone else's room," I alerted her to our present situation.

"Where are the twins," she asked. I put her worry to rest; the two loves of her life, my twins, were safe.

I came up with a plan to get to town and sounded out with it. "Nathan, I'm going to saddle Sunny and ride the ridge down to Judge Beacher's place. I can use his phone."

"No, I'll go," he commanded.

"No, I'm afraid to stay here without you, and we all can't leave . . . or can we? Why don't we all escape on horseback?" I looked at Nathan, seeking approval for my latest, spontaneous idea.

"I don't think everyone can ride, can they?" he asked with a gleam in his eye, acknowledging to me that my plan might be feasable.

"Let's find out . . ." and I started to run upstairs to check on Tina. But, before I got too far, I remembered that Mom couldn't ride, and I'd never leave her alone with them. I turned around and went back to the kitchen, discouraged by my thought.

"Nathan, you or I will have to go for help. I forgot, Mom can't ride a horse!" I stood thinking about Mom going for help in her wheelchair, flying in high gear across the damn dirt roads in Pulaski. I could just visualize it!

"Oh, I forgot about Mom . . . " One plan dismantled.

Tilly piped in with a good idea, harness up the old winter sleigh and let anyone who can't ride a horse hitch a ride in it. Her seasonal timing was off, but the sleigh was our only hope of getting everyone out of here. We certainly didn't want ayone to be left for their use as a hostage, when they found we'd run out on them. I was glad I had watched so much TV, because it kept me one step ahead of our captives in figuring out what they might do to us. One's imagaination has as a tendency to wander out of fear when they find themselves living a nightmare like all the TV heroes seem to take in stride each week.

"Everyone be ready when I come back from the stables. How many horses do we need?" Nathan was planning.

"Let's see, you, me, Tilly, and," I looked at the two cooks and asked, "how about you two, can you ride?"

"Sure can Ms. Brawn," both cooks answered simultaneously.

"So that's five, no six, because Susan can ride. Mom, Tina and the twins can ride in the sleigh. Have I forgotten anyone else?" I checked, looking at everybody in the room.

Nathan piped in, "Yes, Louis is somewhere around. I'll check the grounds for him when I go to the stables. Okay, everyone get what few things you can take, and be ready for me. They might hear the horses or the sleigh. Trish, how about helping me get them some wine . . . something to keep them busy with."

"You go to the barn, and I'll get the wine. As soon as I serve them, I'll join you. Don't worry, I'll be able to handle them." Maybe the wine will get me a tip. . . .

We all scrambled in different directions, and Tilly took the keys to the cellar from me and went to get the wine. I tended to the twins and Tina, and made our great escape plans known to Mom and Susan.

Susan started to cry and then she grabbed my arm and pleaded with me to save her, in her ungodly high pitched voice. "*Please*, Ms. Brawn, don't let them keep me here," and then with her voice breaking out with even a louder shrill, "*Please* save me!"

I grabbed her and shook the shrilling girl to her senses. "Shut up you fool, do you want them to hear you? Go to the kitchen and wait for Nathan. Stop crying . . ." I looked at serene Mom.

She cranked up the chair, shifted into full speed, and headed to the kitchen, saying, "I knew I wanted to live in the future, not the past!" She was the only person enjoying the excitement.

Susan hustled ahead of Mom, like a scared rabbit, hitting the door like it was her hole of safety. Mom followed her, not stretching or flinching one line of fear on her aged face. She held the door open for me, and motioned for me to help Tina with the twins, which I did as fast as I could. Both of the young kids had selected their favorite stuffed animal, and Tina had their saddle bags crammed full with bottles and diapers ready to ride.

By now the dining idiots were well on their way to a good state of stoneness, and I prayed they would keep laughing it up, staying oblivious to our escpe plans. Tilly made one last stop at their tables, trying to keep them from seeking our service on their own. I heard the horses and Nathan approaching, and opened the back door to find him holding six horse's reins in his mouth, and his hands were steading the team of horses that pulled the sleigh. I couldn't help but crack a smile, it reminded me of a scene from some old cowby movie, and I compared him to "The Lone Ranger," my favorite western as a youth. We were going to make a break like the prisoners of yesteryear!

Everyone but Tilly had left the kitchen and was ready to flee, and while we were waiting for her appearance, the kitchen door flew open and out she came running and screaming, "Get away, Trish! Get the twins to safety!" On her tail was the leader and some terrible-looking woman, dressed in tight, black leather pants and a halter top that barely covered her, and in the confusion and noise, the team jolted and took to galloping across the side yard and down the front hill, with the sleigh in tow. I steadied Sunny, and held on to Peanuts as Tilly tried to jump on her horse, but Brady grabbed her leg from behind and she fell to the ground. She didn't move.

"Tilly, get up!" I screamed at her, but she didn't budge. The big hairy hands of Brady picked her up, and with one arm he threw her heavy weight over his shoulders. He raised his fist at me, and yelled at his companion, "Get that one Gayle, fast, before she makes a break."

I grabbed Peanut's reins tightly and kicked Sunny, taking off after Nathan and the rough riding sleigh. The sleigh flew up in the air and traveled over rocks and grass mounds in the field, across to the pasture on the other side of our road. I could see Judge Beacher's house as I rode faster and faster, trying to catch up with the sleigh. I worried for Mom and the twins, because I could see their heads being thrown up and down as the winter sleigh took the bumps and picked up speed. The bells that flapped in the wind rang out, and then out flew one stuffed monkey: Patience's favorite toy.

"Slow that thing down, Louis, or it will break into pieces," I yelled to be heard above the horse's hooves and the sleigh's bells. I told myself not to fret over the abandoned monkey; I'd buy her the company that makes them if we all got out of this safely! I checked the best I could to see if everyone was still alright in the sleigh, and I saw Mom holding on to Patience, nestled in the hay as deep as she could get between bumps. I didn't see Patrick, or Tina, but assumed they must also be down deep in the hay.

We must have been a sight as we pulled up to Judge Beacher's house, because Nathan was laughing and so was everyone else who was sitting so proudly in their saddles. "Is everyone okay, Trish?" Nathan asked, still wearing that grin he had. I didn't think anything was so funny.

"I don't know, but I have to go back. They have Tilly. . . ." I heard Nathan and Mom protest, as I headed Sunny back in the direction of Galaxy and took off. I prayed one of the laughing fools behind me had called Buggy for help.

"Wait, Trish, let me go. You go back with the twins. I'll

get Tilly." Nathan had ridden hard to catch up with Sunny and I.

"No, she did my job . . . she took the wine to them, it's because of me that she's back there." Nathan pulled up next to me and grabbed Sunny's halter, forcing her to a stop. "You can't go in there with them. They know we've all taken off, and I imagine they know we've called for help." Thank God he took time out from laughing to call for help.

"I can't leave Tilly with them. She fell when Brady grabbed her foot. She didn't move or try to get free when he picked her up. That damn broad shot at me, Nathan. What will they do to Tilly?"

I gave Sunny a nudge in her side, and she reared up ready to fly. But Nathan kept tight hold on my hooves of rescue.

"Wait Trish, think before you do something stupid. We don't know what they'll do, but Buggy will be here soon to help. It doesn't make any sense for you to go in there alone. Then they'll have two of us." I looked at Nathan, and started to shake and cry. I had to know if Tilly was alright. I actually feared for her life . . . I thought about my past, and how it would be better if I was the one that they abused. . . .

"See, buggy is at Beacher's. Let's go see what he thinks we should do." Nathan pulled on Sunny's halter, turning her direction away from the inn and Tilly.

I followed Nathan as he took off back toward the judge's house, taking one last look across the fields surrounding Galaxy, silently praying and promising Tilly that I'd get her out somehow.

As I approached Beacher's house, I saw that everything was out of control, with people coming to the scene as fast as they could. The press finally took an interest . . . and then I saw him, the ghost floating on Beacher's front stoop.

"You! You're damn bigoted ideas! What the hell are you people trying to prove?" I dismounted quickly, and reached for the man's white garment, trying to shake him or tear his pure image into shreds. I wasn't sure what I was capable of doing to him, but I was totally out of control, the thought of those lunatics riling me into a frenzy. Buggy grabbed me, and pulled me back from the ghoul, and I looked up at him as he removed his hood.

It was Judge Beacher!

CHAPTER NINE

"Trish, listen to Buggy and the judge. Let them explain what's going on. Stop crying . . ." Nathan was holding me, but I still kept shaking and trying to get my claws into the judge.

I looked at Nathan with a wild, boar-like charge written across my face, my eyes filled with resentment for the judge whom I thought was a good best friend. Why would he let this happen to me? "Dear God, he's one of them!" I exclaimed in horror and disbelief.

"No, he's not one of them. That's not the Klan up there at Galaxy . . . it's some crazy group hiding in the Klan's shadow." Nathan's sweaty hands closed tighter on my shoulders, his nails digging in and trying to take hold of my senses. "They call themselves 'Baldheads.' "

I heard what he said, and still struggled to get away from his gripping hands. I wanted to look the grand ghost straight in the eyes. I needed to see lot's of hair on his hoodless head.

The judge ambled over to me, very nonchalantly and quite composed, putting his arm around me, and said, "I've got just the right medicine for you, Trish."

"Probably poison, or maybe you want to hand me a torch."

"Let's go in the house and away from this crowd . . ."

"Don't touch me! Why don't you call your smooth buddies and tell them we're friends. Tilly is up there all alone," my voice echoed to the heavens.

We walked into the house and finally I began to feel more calm with the security of free walls around me.

"Here, little one, have some of the good stuff. I've been

saving this for our meeting next month, but what the hell, let's have a taste now." Judge Beacher handed me some imported stuff, and it burned like fire all the way down, but it did break the nervous, overreactive spell I was in.

"What are we going to do about Tilly?" I started to cry again, and then I thought about the twins and Mom. "Are the twins okay? And Mom?"

The judge spoke softly, "Sure, honey, Meg has them in the kitchen. You know, I think Patrick liked the ride. He keeps saying giddy-up, giddy-up!" The judge was smiling pleasantly as he wiped away one of my tears. I looked up to see Nathan watching us, and I felt self-conscious over the judge's attention. I stood up and went to Nathan's side, taking his hand and begging him with my eyes to help; protect me and mine.

"He really isn't one of them?" I asked.

"No, Trish, it's like I said. They're some punks from New York that follow the Klan around stirring up trouble."

"What are you going to do?" Please protect me . . .

"Can we use your study, Judge, to plan our next move?" Nathan asked.

"Sure, Doc, I'll get Buggy and meet you both in there." The judge and Nathan had been friends for years, and whenever anyone called Nathan Doc, I still found myself looking for someone else to answer. Doc wasn't a family label for Nathan.

Nathan closed the door to the study as soon as we entered it, and grabbed me. He planted one of the most sensual kisses he had ever given me on my wet lips. His hold was tight, and I felt his manhood growing against my V-patch. We both pushed our fears and needs against each other. His hand tore at the hair on the back of my head, pulling my mouth tighter to his. The tongue that I so often found stimulating my juices started to mingle with mine. I wanted him, right there, right now! Even if his .45 was missing, I knew the climax would be my best yet! Danger can be very stimulating.

Buggy came barging in, one hand on his revolver, and the other formed in a fist. "Well, folks, we've got a real mess here." Brilliant, I thought, as I watched him strut around the room on his short pegs. He wasn't even aware that he had just spoiled a beautiful memory building time between Nathan and I!

"Brilliant deduction, Buggy," Nathan astounded us all with that comeback.

The good judge entered the room and took over, saying the real Klan members would be here soon, to help. I started to laugh, and when I noticed that no one else saw any humor in the Klan helping us, I halted my mocking. By now, I was totally confused. The memory, the look on Tilly's face as she fell to the ground in front of me, and her captor's ugliness flashed through my mind. I was seeing ghosts, a group of people that someone had called 'Baldheads,' although they had hair as long as my hippie friends in the sixties, and now my protector was trying to tell me that the Klan was coming to save the day! It was too much to comprehend.

"How can the Klan help us, Judge?" asked Nathan as he glared at me, warning me to keep my mouth shut.

I mustn't laugh about grown, intelligent men who want to dress like ghosts and ride white horses to victory, I mocked to myself.

"This particular group has been using us as a cover for too long. The National Guard will be here, too. We need to talk to those fools, and see what they plan on doing. They are violent, and have caused us a lot of embarrassment up North."

The head of the National Guard in Pulaski turned out to be Banker Lilly. Nathan and he cornered themselves, whispering too low for me to hear what plans they were formulating. Soon, I found myself sitting alone on the couch, with the four men huddled in conference across the room. Tilly's safety and my home were now in the hands of these four men: the banker who played Colonel on weekends, Nathan, the Korean Vet who was minus his .45, the town police chief, Buggy, who had just learned to twirl his revolver, and my drinking buddy, the hanging Judge Beacher. I couldn't get any relief from fear, not from them, so I left in search of the bottle that Beacher had offered up as a tranquilizer.

I found Mom was watching TV, so I joined her, handing her the bottle and a glass. I filled her in on the strategic plans taking place in the headquarters in the study, and then the four self-appointed generals made an entrance. In the middle of their speech, the TV posted a bulletin and everyone stayed tuned for the news.

A picture of the inn appeared, and then the winter sleigh raced across the screen. A local newscaster I recognized from Nashville was telling the world of our plight. I thanked God that I was inside, protected by privacy. Mom started to laugh as she watched a video-replay of her gliding over bumps to safety with the twins in the sleigh. Someone had captured our escape scene on camera in its entirety, which the older children had seen on the national news and called the judge's house to announce their plans to come home. Soon, my family would be together. For the first time since Angel's committal, I was happy she was out of harm's way.

It was around ten o'clock when we all settled in for a long night of waiting. Nothing could be done until daylight, according to the four generals. Then, the TBI would show up to help, adding some confidence to Tilly's rescue that was planned for daybreak. At least I thought the Tennessee Bureau of Investigation would know how to handle this type of situation.

Meg fixed us all something to munch on, and after the twins went to sleep, oblivious to all the happenings around them, she put Mom and I to bed in a spare bedroom. Tina escaped the hectic commotion by returning to Pulaski to spend the night with her brother and his wife. She assured me she'd be back at daylight, to care for the twins and help however she could. I was lucky that she was ours.

"I hope you can sleep, Mom . . . I doubt I can."

"We haven't shared a bed before Trish. Do you snore or something?"

"None of the men in my life complained about sharing a bed with me, why are you?"

"I wish Daniel was here. I can't imagine why he hasn't at least called." She's right, where is good Father Daniel and his angels? Aren't people of the cloth supposed to be strong fibers to count on in a time of need? They've been taught the right words to say, and all of the positive thoughts to think . . . maybe he's a 'Baldhead,' nothing would surprise me anymore, I thought.

"Do you love him, Mom? Did you love him a long time ago?" I couldn't believe I asked her that question, but once it slipped out, I couldn't retract it.

"Years ago, before your father came into the picture, I did . . . Daniel wasn't a priest then. He was the star football player at Henderson High. Yes, I did love him once."

"I thought so. Do you love him again, Mom?"

"I'll always feel something for him. He was my first." I thought about Bill, and knew he was definitely Dad's son, so how did Tilly, born later than Bill, get Daniel as a father, I wondered.

"Mom, is Tilly Daniel's daughter?" I held my breath, waiting for Mom to confess. I finally had asked the question.

"You picked up on the clue I gave you . . . why did you wait so long to ask me?"

She wanted me to know, she wanted me to ask about it.

"When Angel was at church with Father Daniel, it struck me like lightning. Tilly looks just like him."

"Yes, she does, and I think she has always wondered why she turned out so homely. She doesn't know, and your father never knew either, but Daniel does."

"Did you ever love Dad?"

"That's a funny question coming from you! Certainly I loved your father. I stayed married to him long enough."

"Would it be too personal of me to ask how Tilly ever happened, considering you must have been married to Dad when she hatched?"

"Don't be sarcastic, Trish . . . I went on a retreat, and I hadn't seen Daniel since we broke up in high school and he joined the missionary. We had a lot of catching up to do . . ." Then, she started laughing hysterically, and her laughter turned to tears, and I could feel her quivering next to me.

At first, I didn't know what to do. I felt restrained, and couldn't bring myself to console her by touch. It took force, but then I reached out for her hand, and took it into mine. "Just as well Dad never found out, or you'd only have the two kids you wanted . . . Angel and I would never have been born." I could just imagine what Dad would have done to her. . . .

"Do you think I should tell Tilly?" Mom asked.

"I think that's up to you and Daniel. Maybe it would help her, maybe it wouldn't. I don't know what to do."

"Think about it for me. I hate to die thinking you know and she doesn't."

"Then why did you hint at it . . . why did you want me to find out?" For the first time in my life, I knew something Tilly didn't.

"Because I thought you could help me decide, and I thought maybe you'd understand why I've been so close to Tilly all these years. I had a need to protect her."

I think what Mom was trying to tell me was that she had been motherless to me because Tilly needed her more . . . that she needed to make up to Tilly for what she had done. She raised me like she did because of the guilt she carried around.

"When your father called her a mold-spore, I thought I'd curl up and die. He never liked her. He protected her because I forced him to. He lived with guilt because he couldn't love her like his own, and didn't know why he couldn't. I'll always wonder if I should have told him . . ."

"He knows now. I wouldn't be so anxious in wanting to join him." Her cover up, her pretending Tilly was his, had cost us all some hell. "You created a monster of a child, Mom."

Silence took over the room. I looked at the ceiling, waiting for Dad to crash through the darkness and bellow his hate for what she had done. Maybe so much wouldn't have happened in our terrible family, if only. . . .

"Mom, I'll think about what you said, but if we can't settle this mess we're in, you might not get a chance to tell her." The bold truth of my statement silenced her whimpers, and she fell asleep. I lay awake all night, perfectly still next to the mother I never had, until now, when she needed me.

Before dawn, I crept out of the bed and knelt by its side. Mother was still sleeping, and I had the need to pray. My prayers were jumbled with thoughts of everything, my mind telling God how confused and scattered it was. My final prayer was one that asked him to try to understand my thoughts and previous prayers.

Mom was ready to get up, and she had managed to sit

herself up on the side of the bed. All these years I had taken for granted the way she maneuvered herself in her chair. I must have thought she slept in it.

"I smell the coffee. Ready to go, Mom?" I pushed her chair next to the bed, and helped her into her security chair for the ensuing day. I thought about Tilly being here, doing her usual job of caring for Mom. I don't think I ever realized how much work Mom really was . . . I had to help her to the bathroom, help her dress, hold her cup under her chin as she brushed her teeth. . . .

We all had coffee, and Nathan's posse was discussing the last minute details of their raid on Galaxy. Ten commandos had been selected, handpicked by the four generals as the rescue squad. I wanted to help, but knew the best way to help was to leave the men to their plans. They didn't need me second guessing them.

The awaited hour came with an even greater surprise than we expected. Brother Bill was standing on the front stoop, knocking to get in, with Father Daniel at his side. Mom wheeled her chair to the front door faster than I had ever seen her move, and welcomed their addition with tears. I sat looking at them, trying to remember if I had ever seen Mom shed a happy tear before. I felt like an outsider, seeing her and Daniel with Bill.

"Trish, I'm so sorry. I was out of town on a retreat with the sisters, and as soon as I heard the news, I came back as fast as I could. Thank you for caring for your mother."

Retreat! But you forgot to take Mother!

"Father Daniel, she needed you last night. I'm glad you're here now. Sorry we interrupted your retreat!" His retreat from priesthood is what I was thinking. So, when they need it, they call it a retreat.

I thought about Tilly, his daughter, caught up in this nightmare, all alone with those crazy people overnight. "I'm sorry I didn't care for Tilly so well . . . she volunteered to serve them, sheltering me from them. I should have done it, not her." I found myself apologizing because she was his daughter.

"Why things happen like they do, no one knows. Don't blame yourself, my child."

Words, just rehearsed words. Words they teach you to

say at times like this. Tilly should have been a nun . . .

"By the way, what happened to Maryann? Her parents called the parish last night because she never made it home. Did they call here?" Father Daniel looked at us all for an answer.

"Oh, my God," and then I yelled across the room to Nathan, "we forgot about Maryann, Nathan. Did you see her escape?" Maryann, the young girl who wasn't afraid to work for us, who actually acted excited because the Klan was coming to Galaxy.

Nathan quickly joined Father Daniel and I, and we looked at each other with neglect. "Where the hell was she when we counted heads?" Nathan asked.

"The last time I saw her she was serving the main meal." I had overlooked the waitress. "Mom, did you see Maryann get out?" My staff work was incomplete.

"No, I forgot she was even there. Didn't she help Tilly get the wine?" Mom's alert mind came through again.

"Yes, maybe you're right. Oh, I don't know, it was all so confusing." I thought about her being in the cellar, the main path of attack that the rescue crew was going to take. "Honey, she may still be in the cellar, if they haven't gotten to her, too."

"We'll soon know." Nathan reached for my arms and pulled me to my feet, close to him, and hugged me tight. He bent over and kissed me, once, then twice, real hard and satisfying. My man was going to war . . . leaving me and the twins behind. I didn't like him going, but I knew I couldn't stop him. Someone had to be our protector.

He left my side, and strolled over to the twins who were playing in Meg's cupboard, pulling out every noisy pot and pan she had. He started to reach out to them, but instead, stood up from his bent over position and turned away. He shook his head and rushed out the back door.

I lowered my head to rest on the kitchen table, and I lost all touch with reality. The tears just gushed from my eyes. I felt Father Daniel's hand touch my head, and Mom's squeaky wheels pulled up next to me. She reached out and stroked my arm. All I needed right then was Father Daniel to start praying out loud.

I stood up and went to the TV, and watched the scenes

of the house as some idiot tried to explain the rescue attempt that was about to take place. I remembered that the captors of Galaxy had requested a TV, and knew that the newscaster was forewarning the gang in the house as well as the public. I screamed, "No, you idiots! You'll get them all killed . . ."

I ran back to the door and whistled for Sunny, but to my surprise deadbeat Bill had mounted my horse and was already galloping across the field toward the inn.

"We heard, Trish. Bill went to warn the guys," Mom hollered across the back yard.

"Jesus, Mom, he'll blow it! Why did you let him go?" I reached the fence and called for Peanuts, mounting her as fast as I could. "Take care of the twins, Mom," I yelled as I sped toward the inn pursuing Bill.

Tilly's horse was so damn slow . . . a lot like her, I thought. No wonder she named this thing Peanuts, because that's all he ever developed to support his manhood; a dud, through and through!

I slowed the pace, which meant we were about crawling now. I couldn't see anyone or any action around the inn, everything looked so peaceful. I dismounted Tilly's horse and turned him loose in the stable. He immediately went to the oats, just as I'd figured, because I had just pushed him to run more than he had ever been since his birth. I don't think Tilly had worked him since the twins were born.

I left the stables, noticing all the drapes in the house were pulled closed. It was too quiet . . . where was Nathan, where was the Pulaski army? I forgot my TV movies, and ran through an open field to the back of the house. I pulled the cellar door open, and listened for voices. Bill was no where in sight. He probably rode right on by the place, I thought.

It was dark, no lights or voices. I cautiously stepped down the stairs, and stood in the dark cellar, scared to hell. I heard nothing. I decided to get on my hands and knees, to crawl my way to the kitchen stairs. (Lower down in case of flying bullets!) Then, just as I reached the bottom of the stairs, I thought I heard something move behind the wine cellar door, so I picked myself up off the damn floor and then froze! Something or someone was holding the top of my head. I was going to faint! The next thing I remember was being carried to the wine cellar with Nathan cursing under his breath all the way. I had fainted. . . ."Someone had my head. . . " I couldn't stop shaking. I clung to my protector.

"Shit Trish, you came up under a coat sleeve, it was cupped, resting on the top of your head before you fell."

"A what? A coat sleeve?" I started to laugh, and Bill told me to hush! Bill telling me anything snapped me to sane attention.

"Maybe they'll just leave after they hold their rally, Nathan. Do you think they will?" I asked.

"No, they sent a list of demands to Nashville. Seems Maryann was their carrier-pigeon. She was a member of their group."

Maryann a member of the group? More confusion.

I sat rubbing my head, still feeling the fear I had when I thought it was someone's hand holding my head before I fainted. Then I remembered why I had raced to the house.

"They know you're down here . . . the press covered your plan in detail on the early morning news. I saw pictures of you as you entered the cellar."

"We know, they used the old dumbwaiter to deliver us an ultimatum; either we leave here by noon, or Tilly will burn on a cross out front!"

"They'll what?" I heard what he had said, but the realization of it didn't register in my brain.

"It's a mess, Honey. I don't know what we're going to do. The FBI should be here soon, the TBI called them in. I guess the leader is wanted for seven murders in Montana. Just thank God we got the others out!"

I groped for his shirt, "Nathan, we have to get Tilly. I don't care what they do to her, but they can't burn her!" Wanted for seven murders. . . .

"Don't worry Sis, I have a plan that will work," interrupted brother Bill. I raised my eyes to meet his, and I wondered if it were me upstairs instead of Tilly, if he would have even come to Pulaski. Not likely, I figured. But I was sort of glad he came for Tilly's and Mom's sake.

"I think they'll prefer to have me as a hostage over Tilly . . . when I tell them that Tilly is dying of cancer, and her death is imminent anyway." Bill wasn't shaking, and his voice sounded sober and strong. I didn't know the Bill that was offering up his life as a trade for his sister.

"She's not dying of cancer! Christ, she'll tell them the truth. She likes them. She doesn't know what they're planning for her."

"You don't know that. Listen to what your brother has to say," Nathan commanded.

"Well, let's hope she doesn't say anything to them. If they buy the story, then they'll gladly take me instead of her." Bill was being very noble. He did have a plan.

"What do you think, Nathan? Does his idea make any sense to you? If it works, they'll still have a Tillman at their disposal." I thought about what I called him, a Tillman . . . and I knew I had been wrong in banishing him from the family. He was a Tillman, and nothing I did would change that. His past wrong to me would never strip his born title.

"Please Trish, let me do this for you. I don't want them to hurt her. They can't hurt me." Bill's voice took on a pathetic tone. He was pleading for a chance to make amends.

"Mom won't like it, Bill." I reached out and touched his hand for the first time in years. It was warm, not cold like I always remembered it to be.

"Doesn't matter what Mom thinks anymore. I'm going to go." He turned to Nathan and searched his face for an agreement.

"Okay, Bill. Let's make them the offer, we'll use the dumbwaiter to send them our deal. I just pray they don't end up with two of you. You know what to do when you get inside, right?" Bill never answered.

Well, the exchange went over without a hitch, and Tilly was returned to us alive. Her glare looked a lot like Angel's when she snapped on us and went bonkers, but she was alive and safe. Her eyes registered fear, with their two brown stones lying inert in reddened whites. I wanted to get her back to Judge Beacher's place and call the doctor.

"Nathan, Tilly and I are going to Beacher's. I need to get her away from here. If you get any news, or if anything happens, please send someone back down to tell us what's going on . . . or I'll come back up here," I threatened.

"Okay, Trish. See that Tilly gets any medical help she needs. We'll help you get away."

Tilly mounted Peanuts, and I snuggled up behind her, holding her tight in the saddle. She still hadn't spoken one word to anyone.

We made it to the house at a remarkably fast speed, certainly faster than I made it going up to Galaxy. Peanuts seemed to like Tilly's familiar butt better than mine, I guessed.

It was eleven o'clock, and I knew Nathan and the guys had to be out of the house by noon, or something terrible was going to happen. I couldn't imagine that the 'Baldheads' would really burn anyone on the cross. I never believed anyone could be capable of doing what they did at exactly noon on that horrid day.

Everyone at Beacher's house was ordered to stay inside, out of the way and view of the house. Someone had shut up the news, and normal soaps were on TV. It was the longest hour I had ever lived; the not knowing what was going on up at Galaxy was driving me crazy.

I took a seat on the floor with the twins, playing drop the clothes pin in the milk bottle, and they were having a ball. I couldn't stop the slow tears that escaped, drop by drop, from my swollen eyes. Patrick would smile up at me, and I'd cry a little harder. Patience cocked her head, dropped a clothes pin in the bottle, and looked up at me in amazement. I don't think either one of them had ever seen their mom cry.

Suddenly, someone's fate was determined . . . I had an urge, and the runs were about to gush out of me again. I ran to the toilet, and when I flushed the toilet, I knew I had just flushed someone's life down the drain again—but whose?

One by one the army returned, entering the back door parading their wounds into Beacher's kitchen. I searched for Nathan and I panicked. I screamed the most important question of my life at Judge Beacher, "Where's Nathan?"

"He's fine, Trish, or will be. He took some flack from a grenade in the dumbwaiter."

"Grenade?" My God, isn't this America, aren't we living in the eighties?

"He's probably already in a soft bed at Hillside with some sexy young nurse licking his wounds."

"Thank God . . . I hope she treats him like royalty! I hope every fantasy he's ever had comes true . . . I hope the double-mint twins give him the ride of his life!" I could visualize the satisfied smile on his face as the two gummy girls licked and popped his bubble! I never even had a twinge of jealousy!

It's over, I sighed to myself. Everyone is safe. The runs were wrong, unless someone else got killed. . . .

"Did anyone get seriously hurt, killed?" I asked of Beacher. Then, before he answered, I saw the vision in my mind's eye. . . .

"Where's Bill? I wanted to thank him for a job well done." Silence.

"Judge, where's Bill?" I saw the judge talking to Father Daniel, and then I knew, something had happened to Bill. "Father Daniel, what's wrong with Bill? Is he with Nathan?" Father Daniel never answered me, so I ran to the judge, and searched his eyes, grabbing his arm and pleading, "No! Not Bill . . ."

"What's wrong, Trish?" Mom was alerted to my fear.

"Come over here, Amanda." Father Daniel reached out to help Mom, puling the chair in front of him. He bent down, and gently took her hands into his. I knew! Bill was dead . . . the judge didn't have to answer . . . Bill was flushed down the drain of death, like Dad and Pete!

I never had a chance to thank him, make peace with him—I only got to touch him once. Now he was facing Dad's wrath, all alone, without Mom there to protect him. He had gone to hell! Now I was overwhelmed and the one caged with guilt.

● ● ●

> Great happenings, we often find,
> On great things depend,
> and very small beginnings,
> have often a mighty end.

A single utterance may goof
    or wrong wish inspire;
One small spark enkindled
    May set a cross on fire.

What volumes may be written
    With many drops of blood!
A small leak, unnoticed,
    A mighty ship will sink!

Our life is made entirely
    Of moments multiplied,
As little brooks, joining,
    From the ocean's tide.

Our hours and days,
    Our weeks and months,
Our years and decades,
    Are in small moments given:
They constitute our time below—
    Eternity in Heaven.

    I sat reading the poem from Dad's book that he left Angel. I didn't know if he was the author, but I found the reading appropriate. How did he know what I would be feeling?

    Somehow, I knew he was looking down and turning the pages for me. The ribbon that marked this page was made of red silk, and was ragged from his use. I retraced where his fingers must have worn the ribbon edges. I prayed. I cried. I mourned the past of my life. I wished I were hidden away like Angel, out of harm's way. I secretly hoped my mind would go blank, erasing every memory and previous wish . . . the wish that Bill would find his death through his own guilt. I felt hate, I felt love. I lived the next month in despair, full of grief that no one could ever begin to explain. I was an empty person. I had no protector.

    I had wished death on my brother last year; it happened. I never had a chance to unwind the hate feelings I held for him, to ask him why he did it to me, or to forgive him for his sin. I'll never know if he was unhappy in life because of his guilt, or if I had done something that forced him to hurt me so badly. Did he do it out of anger?

I've taken my mother's only son from her and added another widow to the world. I've orphaned his children. Maybe Mom knew best, maybe two wrongs never make 'one' right. . . .

It took me six months to pick up the pieces of our family, and only then was I capable of deciding that it wasn't too late in life to change. I had to learn to forgive, and maybe then I could forget.

I nursed Nathan back to health, and then turned my concentration to Angel's recovery. Only four of us third generation Tillmans remained on earth, and I wanted all four to be sound and capable of marching on.

Every day I read a poem from Dad's book, always the same one, as I sat in the hospital with Angel, never knowing if he really had authored it or not.

Crosses are Ts
The sign of the ghost
The home of our host;

All charred and darkened
its shape still tall
A lonely horse's rein in the stall;

As we cross our Ts
He really sees
As we bend to our knees
Only to please;

Soften my load
Remove my burden
Let me walk in a quiet mode
Rid me of my guilt-ridden load;

Forgive and forget
Take his hand
Dig through your sand
Rejoice in our land;

Live for tomorrow
Bury the past
For nothing will last
Now he's given you a chance;

Sow your seeds
Plow your fields
Take his lead
Do good deeds

Mother is land
Treat it well
Whereas you can see
He can always tell.

I had no idea that this poem was getting through to Angel or to me, but it did. Seven months after Bill's horrid death on the cross, Angel and I came home to our inn to rejoin our family in reality once again.

CHAPTER TEN

If the inn hadn't been successful before the "Baldheads" seized it, it certainly was now. The world knew who the Tillmans were, what we were made of, and where we lived. Pulaski was on the map. Tragedy breeds success in our society. The charred, still grassless circle on the front yard was a national shrine, a constant reminder that cremation ends all.

Construction started on the additional twenty-two rooms, and the main house was repaired and enhanced. The grenaded cellar was redone, turning it into a teen club, which Johnny and his friends designed, free of charge. What I would save in cruising gas money by Johnny's being home would pay for the teen hideout in no time. I liked knowing where Johnny was, and until he was ready to go to college, I'd know what he was doing with all of his free time.

We used the stable closest to the house as our new outer lodge. Angel designed the whole decorating concept herself, and coordinated all of the work. She had the old stables completely gutted, with the new rooms occupying the outer walls of the perimeter. The original stone walls were left in place, and the center of the building was turned into a warm paradise with a twenty-by-twenty pool in the center. A domed skylight formed a massive roof directly above the pool, letting the great outdoors shine in. Live palm trees were strategically placed throughout, and the furniture coordinated with the warm, breezy look of South Florida. Angel mixed multiple hues of green and yellow, enhanced by just a touch of bold pink to compliment the glassy green of the featherlike palm leaves. If the trip to the outer lodge weren't so short, I would have thought I had been transported to the tropics.

Soon after "The Paradise Lodge" was christened, I found

myself wondering if history repeats itself; "Hello Ma'am, it's the telephone company." Immediately I thought of Pete, and I looked up and sized the young man, comparing him to the past. Whoever did the hiring locally for telephone men certainly had a mold. She must be a dreamer, I thought to myself.

"Yes, what can we do for you today, young man?" I inquired.

"I have an order for twenty-two new phones, and a center switch board. Can I do the service now?" Again, I was too tired, and now too married to take him up on his offer to be serviced! Time moves on, doesn't it?

"You said twenty-two phones?"

"Yes," and the young man nodded his head in agreement as he double-checked his orders.

Well, I see this time your company got the order right." I flashed a big, agreeable smile at the new telephone jock; Pete's replacement. "Follow me and I'll take you down to paradise."

I was interrupted by a nice surprise. "Mama, let me take him down. I'm going for a swim anyhow, save you the walk," chimed in Becky, who was home on a spring break. This was the first time Becky and Tim had skipped Florida beaches at spring break and had come home instead.

Both were now college seniors, almost ready to venture forward into their own futures. Becky brought home a gorgeous friend who was a second lieutenant in the Marines as well as the son of an admiral. His macho great looks added to the pool's landscape as if he had been designed into the picture: the perfect lifeguard. He was a mother's dream come true for her daughter.

Tim had invited his Sigma Chi friends, six males to be exact. Again, my family was taking up too many rooms, but I was extremely pleased to have them home with me. I needed to know they still loved their mother with her many faults.

"Okay, you can handle it. Call if you run into any trouble." I doubted she'd run into any trouble, and if she did, she was certainly in capable hands. Off went my virgin to paradise . . . maybe if I got lucky, she'd get laid! Then the two of us would have more in common, I thought.

Angel came bounding in, wanting to know what plans I

had for the day. "I'd better stick close to the inn, because the telephone crew is here to install the phones and center switchboard. I saw Patrick go running down there to help, too. I bet'ya he comes back infuriated because he can't help the guys." Little Patrick was more Nathan than me. He also lived with a hammer and nail close by his side, always building something and taking things apart. Every time I watched him proudly display a new object he had built, I would find myself thinking about how proud Nathan was of his son. No matter how busy I was, I always took the time to listen as my little fellow boasted his accomplishments, and I never buried them in some hidden room.

I glanced at Angel and knew she was reflecting on Pete; I knew that look. Nathan and I had tried everything to get her involved romantically with someone else since she had returned home, but she wanted no part of any man: she chose to live in the past with the memories of her first love, Pete, or at least that's what I thought until she shocked me with her new plans.

Angel asked, "How are the reservations looking?"

"Better than we ever projected; booked solid through December. I think we could have added fifty rooms and they'd be all gone, too."

"Good, because I want to ask you something." She hesitated, almost like she was carefully wording her next sentence. "I've been thinking, again, about having a baby."

I gingerly walked over to the antique love seat and plunged into the empty cushion next to her. I looked into her face that reflected deep thought, and reached for her delicate, long fingered hand. "Someone as beautiful as you needs to pretty up this world, Toots." I was pleased to hear that the past was fading from her, and didn't want to dampen her free spirits with any doubts that I might have about her having a baby.

"I think I'll make a good mother, and if we're set financially, then you can hire someone to do my work around here. After my son is born and he's older, I'll resume helping out." She definitely spent some quality time contemplating this move, I thought.

"Well, sounds like you have everything ready to go. Do you want me to go the the 'bank' in Nashville with you?" I had assumed she was going to go through with artificial insemination, but I was wrong again.

"I'm not going to get pregnant that way." She added no details to that statement, and left me wondering what she had planned. I knew she was our angel, but an immaculate conception was far fetched, even for her! Maybe she was going on a retreat. . . .

"Well, have you been sneaking around behind our backs? Who is he? The banker Nathan brought home last week?" I teased.

"No, I haven't made a choice yet. I've decided it will be some stranger that books a room, one that isn't a regular. One that I can visualize as a perfect man—someone who closely resembles Pete." She stood up and danced in swirls in front of me, turning and twirling like a magical top, devilishly happy in her thoughts. Her plans were on the table now. I sat, astounded by her; my Angel sleeping with a one-night-stand was hard to swallow. I wasn't sure she had thought out all the circumstances surrounding her decision, and wished Nathan were there to help me talk it through with her. She went on, clarifying her plan to me.

"I think I'll move down to paradise, and use a room there. Any man I would want would definitely be the type to want to use the pool." A girlish grin came across her face, and I could tell she was visualizing her perfect stranger. "I can size him up better if he's wearing swim trunks. . . ."

"Angel, you little devil!" I thought about my Angel being a devil, and somehow, now, neither angel nor devil suitably titled my younger sister. I held an image of her that took thirty years to build, and that was slowly fading, being replaced with one that I couldn't define yet.

"I'm going to have to stop calling you Angel, you know," I kidded with her.

"Try Mama!" Angel proudly offered up a new tag for herself.

"Oh, I forgot about Mom . . . what will she think about this?" I interjected.

"I've already told her. Guess what she said to me?" It must have been good, because she was still wearing that girlish grin.

"Can't imagine!" I knew Mom was still alive, so the shock

must not have been that hard on her system.

"She said to pick out someone not as handsome as Pete. She said good looking daughters seem to find more trouble in life than homely ones."

"Well, she might be right. She was probably comparing Tilly with you and me, although I wonder what her definition of trouble is."

"She also said she was afraid of what Tilly's reaction would be to my getting pregnant." Angel's smile turned vindictive. "I told her I'd kill her if she told Tilly what my plans were." She looked at me defiantly and added, "And I will, Trish, if Mom says one word to her favorite, like she always does, even after I explicitly asked her not to, there will be hell to pay around here," she vowed.

As a mother, I prided myself on my ability to keep a child's secret. I set the goal early on in my career as a mother, because I wanted to be a better mom than mine had been in that category. Granted, there were times that the secret had to come out, for everyone's sake, but I smartly asked permission before divulging it to anyone. I understood Angel's request, and hoped that Mom understood the importance of keeping this one from Tilly.

"I'll warn Mom not to, but I don't know if that will stop her. I've threatened her before, but it never did any good. And of course, Tilly waits in the background for just the right time to divulge she already knows, Mom already told her. Sometimes I think it kills her trying to keep the secret quiet for as short a time as she does; she just has to let us know that she knows, too!"

I thought about Tilly's relationship with me while Angel was in the hospital, and it did seem to be a better one when it was just she and I around the house. Maybe the old saying that two is company and three is a crowd is close to the truth. I decided that Tilly and I had made too much progress in straightening out our differences, and I reminded myself that I didn't want to regress back to what it had been like in the past. Who she was and what she did when we were kids wasn't her fault, not entirely.

"Angel, it's your life, and you can tell anyone you want, but I think it would be nice if you told Tilly before Mom did. Can't you see the look on Mom's face when Tilly tells her she already knows!" Angel gleamed in delight at the prospect, and agreed to tell Tilly immediately. She left me standing alone, wishing I could be present when Tilly and Mom tried to tell each other the latest family secret.

Two hours later, I asked Angel how Tilly took it, and wanted to know if I could tell Nathan about her sperm selection process.

"I think I gave her ideas," replied Angel, obviously still disturbed over her conversation with Tilly.

"You have to be kidding. . . ."

"No, she started planning some crazy beautification plan. She grabbed her keys and went to town to join some thinning salon." Angel wasn't kidding, and i could tell by the look in her starry blue eyes that she didn't like Tilly's idea one bit.

"I'm sorry I suggested that you tell her, but when she heard what you were planning, she'd probably do the same thing, anyway. Can I talk to Nathan about your decision?" I couldn't wait for Nathan to get home and tell him about our new family venture.

"Sure . . . when it happens, the whole world will know," she paused for a second, then reflected further, "I hate to say this Trish, but I've never thought it was right that people who are so homely in life should be able to bring children into this world. The cruelty that society bestows on ugly children is terrible. Look what Tilly has gone through because of her looks." I wanted to tell Angel that her homeliness wasn't the only reason she was so mean. I wanted to tell her who her real father was, and tell her why Mom was motherless to us, but I didn't.

I handed Angel a cup of fresh brewed coffee, and settled in for one of our long debatable conversations; the type we used to have when we were teens. I had missed our talks, and couldn't wait to get started on this particular topic, which Angel's shared thought had just jolted my memory to recollect.

"Brooks was picking on Tilly, saying she looked like some ape's child. She described Tilly's looks to a tee, but it roused ire in me. Tilly was trying to get into that snobby clique that Gayle Dawes was the leader of." Angel was leaning closer to me, using the bar's counter in the kitchen to prop one elbow, getting good and comfortable. I didn't want to leave out any of the details, because this was a good story and I had a good listener, so when Angel was all settled in for story hour, I continued reliving a memory of hurt.

"I can still see Tilly sitting up on the bleachers, at the far end, all by herself. She was watching as the club gathered into one of their little gossip sessions, and they were going to either vote her in or out, depending on the results of their debate. They didn't see me, and Tilly never knew I was around. I hid behind the football dummy, and listened as they discussed her. They also raked our whole family over the coals."

I took a drink of coffee, and took a deep breath, which allowed Angel to butt in with a question, "Why did they discuss all of us?"

"It was their way. The whole town was that way. If their parents accepted our parents, then they liked us. If not, and kids do listen to their parent's gossip, then we weren't considered good enough by their standards. Remember, back then Dad was just getting started in his won business, and our folks were trying to climb the town's status ladder."

"Yeah, that's true. We stopped getting hand-me-downs when I was a freshman in high school. I remember having to tear my old sneakers beyond repair in order to get a new pair." Angel looked at me, and realizing I was chomping at the bit to get on with the story, apologized, "Sis, I'll shut up and you can go on."

I was used to both of our interruptions when we got deeply involved in a discussion that focused on our teen years: the interruptions were usually timely and only added to the whole scenario. I started in again, "Well, Tilly sat there while they said terrible things. I prayed that she would get up and leave. I hated to see her succumbing to their tactics. Actually, I guess I was ashamed for her."

I stopped talking long enough to try to capture the feeling I had that day, and it came back to me very quickly. "I wanted her to have more pride than that, but she didn't! Then that bossy Gayle walked over to the bleachers, followed by the crowd of worshippers that clung to her throughout high school, and they climbed to where Tilly awaited her election results. Little Miss Leader began to speak, "We tried to accept you, Tilly, but for these reasons we can't have you in our sorority." She listed several reasons, but one really made me choke: they told her that she was so ugly, that even if she had all new clothes, she'd never get a date to the prom and every member had an obligation to be at that dance. She said they thought maybe her brother could bribe someone to take her, but if anyone outside the group found out that's how she got a date, they'd be shamed by the whole school."

I waited for Angel's reaction. She was speechless and appalled, and I noticed her eyes were tearing. Mine were, too. Our family loyalty was showing . . . "I wanted to run to her, and take her home, but then I thought about her knowing that I had heard, and figured that would only make her feel embarrassed and add to her hurt. But Angel, Tilly handled it pretty well, better than I would have, considering that Bill *had* bribed Tom Toury into taking her to the prom. She doesn't know that I know Bill did that, no one knows I know. Mom and Dad planned the whole thing and got Bill to pay Tom fifty dollars, plus Dad let the kid use the Lincoln that night. Jimmy told me the guys laughed about it in gym class."

"Gee, Trish, I never knew all of this. How come you never told me?"

"I don't know. I remember being tempted, because Tilly acted so smug about her date that it killed me. She carried the whole plan off like he really asked her. It just amazed me how well she could cover up her real feelings."

Angel looked sad, obviously pitying her sister's position. "It must have been terrible for her."

"It should have been, but she didn't act like it was."

Angel prompted me on, "Well, what happened to her on the bleachers?"

I started in again, "She picked herself up, and never shed one tear, until she got to the end of the football field, then she ran to Grandma's crying her eyes out. I felt sorry and very proud for her. I was afraid she would beg them, and if she had, I was ready to stop her."

"Did the group ever find out you were there?" Angel asked.

"Yeah, because I sneaked up behind them when their laughing covered my arrival. They turned around, shocked to find me standing there, especially since I was smiling from ear to ear. You see, I didn't want them to know that I had heard, figured they would bury themselves by trying to justify what they had just done to my sister."

"Did they?"

"You know they did. I should have been invited to the meeting, after all, I was the vice-president of the sorority. I remember asking, 'Are we having a meeting today?' Gayle responded, after looking to each member for help, 'Didn't you get the word? We had a new member vote today. I left the note on your locker." I told her, 'No, someone must have pulled it off the locker.' Then I continued to play dumb and asked her who they voted on."

"What did she say?" Angel's mouth was open in awe.

"She didn't, Cheryl Lawler answered, 'Your sister, Tilly, wanted in.' I played it dumb, like I didn't know that Tilly had petitioned membership, then asked them the results and the whereabouts of Tilly.

Angel slapped her opened palm on the bar, and exclaimed, "You didn't!"

"Yes, and I couldn't wait for one of them to try and tell me about the results."

"Who told you?"

"None other than dear Gayle . . . 'Your sister isn't suitable Trish. We're sorry, but she isn't our type.' All of the other fools nodded their heads in agreement, and I tightened my fist for a blow."

"You didn't hit her, did you?"

My memory of my reaction to Gayle's speech surged me forward, proudly plowing further into the story, "I knocked that damn fluky so hard that she fell on the bleacher steps and rolled clear to the ground between the seats. Everyone started to scream, crying and running toward the school. I ran down to Gayle, and helped her up. A shiner was already puffing up on her sneaky face, and I threatened to blacken her other eye if she didn't get the group to change their vote and let Tilly in."

"Is that how she finally got in?"

"Well, I'll finish telling you what happened, if you get us a bottle of wine." I pushed the cold stale coffee mug away from me, and suggested, "Coffee just doesn't seem suitable for this finish." I lit a cigarette and waited for Angel to get us something more stimulating to drink.

"Sure, but don't you go running off." I didn't, Angel returned, and after wetting our dry mouths with some good wine, I started in.

"Gayle promised to get Tilly in, and went running after the other girls. I followed her to the school, and Mrs. Green was still in the gym with the senior girls' basketball team. The other girls were crying and telling her what I did, and she was ready for me when I followed Gayle into the gym. She pulled me off to the side. I remember making a fist and shaking it at Gayle as I was cornered by our gym teacher. Gayle came running over to us, and told Mrs. Green that it was all her fault, and not to do anything to me. I kept my fist doubled, just in case. I figured I was going to get it anyhow, so if Gayle was going to win with Mrs. Green, I was going to puff her other eye." And lowering my voice to emphasize my disappointment, I added, "It never came to that, though. Mrs. Green let us go, telling us to get some ice from the school nurse for Gayle's eye. We promised to care for her before we left the school grounds, and ran out of the gym. As soon as we got outside, Gayle let the others know that she had reconsidered her vote, and if I had come to the meeting and voted, that Tilly would have had enough yes votes to be elected in. So unknown to Tilly, she was now a new member of the elite female group in school."

A phone call interrupted us momentarily, and then I finally got to finish the story. "When I got home, Tilly wasn't there yet. She was still at Gram's, I guess, because she didn't come home till late that night. I waited up for her, and as soon as she came in I delivered the good news to her."

"I bet she was happy, huh?"

"Well, she turned in circles and jumped like a ninny around the room. She was so loud that she woke Mom and Dad, and they called us to their room."

"What did you tell her the reason was, you know, why did the club suddenly change their minds?" Angel inquired.

"She told Mom and Dad that she just got the news from me that she was accepted into the sorority. She said nothing about being rejected at first. She made up some crazy story about waiting at Gram's for the answer, and how nervous she had been."

One look at Angel and I could tell she was flabbergasted. "She never told them the real story?"

"Not that I know of, because I never told her or them how I got her in, but two days later Dad cornered me when he picked me up after cheerleading practice. Seems Gayle's mother called him at the office about my hitting her, and he learned the real story. He thanked me for helping Tilly and made me promise never to tell Mom how Tilly got in. He also had a proud gleam in his eye, although he did lecture me about still being a bully at my age."

"Wasn't that sweet, he didn't want to hurt Mom I guess . . . did Tilly ever find out that Dad knew? . . . " and then she stopped her question and answered it herself, "No, guess not, because she never knew the truth either, did she?"

"Oh, I'm sure she found out, it was all over school for the next week, but she never said one word to me about it. Everyone called me slugger, and Gayle's eye was a mess for a month or so. I remember that I shined a nice ladylike smile every time I passed Gayle in the hallway."

"Tilly never thanked you?"

"Hell no, she acted like it never happened, and that she actually did get voted in legitimately, and when Mom heard from Gayle's mother how I beat her, I caught hell again." Before I finished telling the story, I sat quietly in thought about the outcome. Then, I sadly picked up my thoughts where I had left off, and finished the true story.

"I couldn't understand why Dad hit me so hard, because he knew the reason why I did it. He even thanked me before Mom found out the whole story. I can still hear Tilly and Mom egging him on—saying that I had caused Tilly embarrassment in school and almost ruined her chances of getting into the sorority by being such a bully. So, I came away from that incident thinking I caught a beating to satisfy Tilly's and Mom's demands put on Dad. . . ." My head sank, to cover the fresh tears that came to my eyes.

"I remember him telling me he had to do it for Mom and Tilly, and then said something about it was wrong to hit Gayle anyhow! You know, Sis, all three knew the real truth, but they covered it up and let me get a beating just so Tilly wouldn't have to admit how she got in. She needed to tell everyone in school how much hell I caught for hitting Gayle."

I was going to cry over the memory, but I choked it back and funned my way out of tears, "Tune in tomorrow for the next exciting episode of Trish Tillman Brawn's escapades of the past, folks." I removed my fanny from the bar stool, and decided I'd better get back into the 'now' before anything more from my past came creeping into my mind. Angel came around from her seat and hugged me tightly, squeezing into me every ounce of knowing and love she held for me.

"I hope I didn't cause you such heartache as a kid, Trish."

"No way, Toots, you were my escape route to sanity and love!"

• • •

Tilly came bounding in with packages under her arm and wearing a smile that was a dead giveaway . . . she was elated about her future: her decision to get beautiful overnight and have a child of her own.

"Trish, come see all the stuff I bought for myself today, and I joined the health club and Weight Watchers. Meetings are on Thursday at five, so we'll need to get someone to help Susan at the desk for two hours each day. Oh, I got the twins a toy, where are they?" I had never heard Tilly talk so fast, never knew her brain could formulate thoughts that quickly.

"You shouldn't spend your money on the kids, Tilly. They're so spoiled as it is, and Nathan gets a little disturbed at me for indulging them like I do."

"So, that's you . . . he never says anything to me when I get them something." She was right, he only seemed indifferent to me when I spent on them.

"What's all this stuff about getting fixed up?" I asked.

"I've hidden under this terrible layer of fat long enough! At least I can do something about the fat, and I have an appointment with a reconstructive surgeon in Nashville next week! Maybe he can get rid of this ugly nose, and I read where it is possible to fix my eyes. . . . " Her excitement was contagious, and I found myself caught up in it. It was the first time I had ever seen Tilly care what she looked like.

"Can I help you with anything? I want to go to the doctor with you when you go. And I can talk to the cook about some diet recipes for you. I just might join you in a few of those light meals."

"Would you really go to the doctor with me?" Tilly just stared at me, like she was having a hard time believing that I would ever offer to help her.

"Sure, maybe I can help you decide what look you want to achieve."

Tilly's head slowly bowed, and then timidly she said, "I want to look like you."

"No you don't, Tilly. After you look at some of the shapes and sizes he shows you, you'll want to look like one of them." I felt a slightly embarrassed for her and myself. I knew all she had ever needed was the same father.

"I've always wanted to look like you!"

"It's hard for me to understand why, Tilly. Now that you want to better yourself, go for the limit, kiddo!" I thought to myself, by yourself!

"Well, we'll see next week. Thanks for offering to go with me."

I wondered why it took so long for Tilly to change, and thought about what Angel had said about ugly people having babies. People usually go through reconstructive surgery after an accident . . . but then I realized she was an accident, wasn't she?

"Sis, it's good to see that you care. I'll do anything I can to help you out."

"Won't it be fun to have your two sisters pregnant? You'll finally be an aunt."

"I don't know about that decision of yours. Imagine what the town folks will think about we Tillmans! Two unmarried girls pregnant! Shit, I thought I set this town to talking, hell, you two will make headlines for years to come!"

"I thought what people think never bothers you . . . you, the could-give-a-damn sister!"

"It always bothered me, Tilly, but not enough to make me *not* do what I wanted. I used to test the waters, and if the flack wasn't going to be too big, then I took the plunge. I guess you could say my happiness meant more to me than to them!" I thought to myself, no one cared what I did anyhow, unless I got caught and shamed them somehow, so why not do what I wanted. Anyhow, I never did anything that terrible.

"I know what you felt, and used to wish I had the guts to pull some of the things you did. You were always having fun, raising hell and enjoying it, while I sat around wishing! Well, no more, I'm going to have some fun and live like a queen for a change, before it's too late."

"Good for you. I'll back you up, but it will be harder for you, because you're a lot older than I was when I had all my fun. People will expect you to be mature . . . you can't count on youth to cover for you."

She proudly boasted, "Watch out Pulaski, Nashville, and the world, a new Tilly Tillman is ready to shock you all."

I remember telling Nathan that night, after we had dined and retreated to our room—the only place of privacy that the inn afforded us—that Tilly and Angel had decided to get pregnant by some one nighter at the inn. We laid in bed, indulging ourselves with bits of chocolate, watching TV as we ended the day with our 'wrap it up' conversation, something that had become a habit for the two of us. I enjoyed our peaceful times together, and no matter what urgency needed discussing, I always knew that within any twenty-four hour period, I'd have Nathan's undivided attention and be able to discuss anything with him, alone and close in our bed.

"I know that comes as a shock to you, but I want to know what you're thinking." His hand was twiddling my left breast, and he suddenly removed it. I rolled over toward him and pulled myself up on one elbow, above his chest, in order to see his eyes. Nathan's eyes always said more than his mouth: they were the gate to his heart and soul.

"You must be thinking something, honey, so let's hear it." I rubbed his belly which was his own rounded stock yard of gin. My hand traveled the road it always took, lower, beneath the gin mill, down to my staff of life. "Come on, Buddah, talk to me."

Early in our marriage, I found that if I rubbed Buddah (Nathan's belly), that something good was going to happen between us, something that I couldn't seem to get enough of. My rubbing made his manhood throb and wink at me as it bobbed up and down like a flag waving proudly, signifying his patriotism of love at its greatest height.

He started talking very slowly, "I'm thinking about the twins. They'll be five this year, and starting school." I noticed my rubbing didn't seem to be working this time; Buddah was still limp!

"Yes, I think they've been ready for two years. I probably should have put them in some school sooner, but I hadn't wanted to part with our babies. I wanted to keep them home with me as long as I could." The twins were more than ready for school, and everyone's constant waiting on them would probably cause us a few headaches with their behavior in school, but I knew they knew what the meaning of love was. I never believed too much love could do anyone real harm. They'd get used to their peers in school, and how the real world treated people soon enough, I thought.

"Are you worried about what people will think? Is that it? Do you think it will cause the twins some kind of embarrassment?" I asked.

"Well, it's sort of unique, you know? Not everybody thinks like you Tillmans do." His tone was rare, almost bordering on sarcastic. I removed my hand from unfriendly Buddah.

"Well, I'm sorry if it bothers you . . . the way I think! But at least I think. Half of this town never thinks . . . just gossips its way through each week, year, and life. I'll never be like them. My family's happiness is more important than what a small town thinks."

"But you're not thinking of the twins, or me . . . we all aren't as hard as you . . . and we all weren't raised as Tillmans."

I moved myself from the closeness of Nathan's chest. How dare he challenge my feelings for the twins? I'd never do anything to hurt them, or cause them any shame. I wasn't the one getting pregnant. My twins were my second chance at parenting, my continuing youth, my reason for being around the next twenty years. I held such plans for each one of them.

How could he say I was cold . . . Buddah wasn't exactly heated up!

I turned my back to Nathan, and lay quietly in thought for a few minutes, then said, "Good night. I love you, I'm sorry you don't like my ways." And on one of those rare occasions, I went to sleep without my man holding me. Nathan never spoke one word, or moved one inch, and Buddah remained dead cold.

CHAPTER ELEVEN

Reformation can take many paths, some inside and some outside. In Tilly's case, it took both avenues and was remarkable. The old Tilly was gone. The bandages had been removed, and the world found itself getting acquainted with a new being. Gone were the squinting eyes with the ever possessed glare of hate. The old, rarely gleaming smile was replaced with lips like a small birds, ready to chirp and sing out. The crevices on both sides of her cheeks were large, very similar to Angel's blushing dimples. She was poised, confident and happy. I still laugh when I think what Patrick said to me, after he greeted his new Aunt Tilly..."Mama, why did Aunt Tilly throw away her old face?"

The doctor had truly worked wonders, although it's amazing he didn't throw her case out after the first two appointments. Tilly drove him and his staff wild, changing the sketches constantly, replacing one nose with another, mixing eyes and shapes like they were a set of grammar school blocks that she had just found for the first time during playbreak. She sat for hours, jumbling the pieces of the puzzle, until one day she unveiled the future Tilly to all of us.

"Well, what do you think? Mom, do you like what I have picked?" Tilly asked with enthusiasm.

"Yes, but can he do that with your face?" Her words sounded horrible, the way they came out, and even though Tilly was used to those insinuations when it came to her appearance, she was shocked because they came from Mom. She tried to cover her hurt, thinking it didn't matter anymore, because in six months, she'd have a new face. She ignored Mom completely, and turned to me waiting for my opinion.

"I like it, Tilly. It sort of reminds me of someone, but I can't place who." I turned to Angel, to see if she could give me a clue to Tilly's prospective new look. "Doesn't it look like someone we know, Angel?" I asked.

"Sort of, but I don't know who. I like it, too. Do you think the doctor can remove my dimples?" she giggled as she pulled at her cheeks, trying to straighten her folds. We all laughed.

"Yeah, think of the things they can do. Someone could commit a crime, and then get redone and never be caught," I mused.

"I'd expect you to think like that." I didn't like Nathan's tone. I didn't like a lot about Nathan lately. He had withdrawn himself from all of us, and although I felt sure it was because of my sisters' pregnancy plan, I didn't like it and didn't think his attitude was fair. He had picked fights over everything lately, and I tried to just ignore his comments. But, I knew he was getting more unhappy by the day, and figured sooner or later he'd blow up and tell me the real reason why he was being so nasty. We all ignored his comment, and went on discussing Tilly's new deal.

Weight Watchers had worked for Tilly. I think any diet would have worked, because she had been determined to lose weight for the first time in her life. She was a lithe success: now weighing one hundred and twenty pounds, and with her height, she looked like a model. I wished she'd had the notion to change a long time ago. With her new looks, her whole personality seemed to change for the better; softer and caring , almost fluffy-like.

"You're gorgeous, Tilly. No one will know it's you." I complimented her on the results of hard work by both she and her doctor.

"Good, I've said good-bye to the old Tilly. I wish I were moving, going some place where folks would think I always looked like this." I could feel the apprehension that she was coping with. The change had been so dramatic, so severe, that people were bound to discuss it for weeks. I had an idea.

"Maybe we should plan a coming out party for you. That way they won't see your hidden fears about being accepted as the new you. I always believed Dad when he said, 'Meet 'em head on.' "

"Oh, I don't think I could do that. I'll just show up in church Sunday and surprise the hell out of them. Father Daniel said he'd help me. You know, he seems as proud of my new looks as I do. Said something about writing the sermon around it."

I bet he does, I thought to myself. I glanced at Mom quickly and then back to Tilly. "Well, good luck in your new life, Sis. Knock 'em dead!"

I wouldn't be joining them in church this Sunday. I wasn't going to heed my own advice and meet them head on with Tilly. Church had taken a back seat with me lately, ever since Bill's death. I was uncomfortable sitting in church, and didn't know if it was because of my death wish for Bill, the guilt of it, or if my little walks of prayer around Galaxy each morning and evening had replaced my religious house. In church, I felt smothered—forced into thinking about Father Daniel's Sunday topics. Ever since Mom told me about their retreat, Father Daniel had lost his collar as far as I was concerned. When I was outside amongst nature's beauty I felt wide open and capable of any topic of conversation with my God, with no one sitting across from me, peering into my thoughts as they surveyed what I wore or how loudly I sang out of tune. I gave Tilly a lot of credit for even thinking about going to church, and didn't envy her first Sunday on the town.

Angel asked if Tilly knew when her next high school reunion was, and they continued giggling about the prospect of showing up at the next one with Tilly's new looks.

"Wouldn't that Gayle somebody be shocked," she said. I looked at Angel, and knew we both were thinking about the same thing. Angel spoke the picture in her mind, "Gayle, that mean girl in high school, that's who you look like Tilly!" She was right, Tilly had taken on the look of her past rival.

Nathan shook his head and left the room that was full of cheer for Tilly. He took his bottle of gin and disappeared outside. I excused myself and followed him. I was beginning to get angry with him and his attitude, and wanted him to act like he did before all of this transformation took place. I needed for him to be happy. After all, I hadn't changed—Tilly had.

We met in the gazebo. "I think it's time we talked, Nathan, don't you?" I paused, looking at him for his reaction. "Everyone is beginning to see that you've done some changing, too, and I hate for them to be curious about you." Like my parents before me, I wanted to tote an air of satisfaction in front of everyone. I hated for the family to think I was having marital problems, again. Now, if it had been something good that pivoted me to the pedestal of glory for awhile, then that would have been an unusual, and cherished mood. Seeing the root of the problem in this case, I didn't want anyone's attention to be focused on me.

"I thought what people think doesn't bother you," he said sarcastically. His eyes held contempt, and I had trouble seeing why Tilly's attempts to better herself could have caused his ire. I was getting tired of people telling me that what others thought about me didn't matter.

"What outsiders think, doesn't! But what insiders, what you think, does. You know that. Please, let's not fight, let's talk this through." It wasn't like Nathan to keep his feelings inside, not with me at least. I walked over and took his hand. I placed it on my cheek, and looked up into his clear blue eyes. I said nothing, waiting for him to follow up on my start of the conversation and my touching.

He withdrew his hand abruptly. "I don't mind her changing her looks, but this pregnancy thing is wrong. No one is thinking about the child—no father, no real family to love it."

"Then why don't you tell the girls what you think? Why take their decision out on me? They'll listen to you, they all love you."

"Don't you see? They are doing exactly what you have done in the past . . . well, almost. They just won't have to go through divorces."

I saw red. I hadn't planned on dumping the first two husbands. I didn't marry them because I was pregnant, or wanted kids. At the time, my first two marriages were right. I just stood back from him and stared at him and his thoughts.

"I know how this town will react. The town's been good to you all. Look how they helped with Bill's death. Why do you treat them as fools . . . why do you laugh at them? They have feelings, too."

This isn't the man I married, I thought, not the one that

planned our marriage and our wedding ceremony. Not the one who liked my different ways . . . what's gotten into him? Silence hung over us both. I wasn't sure what to say to him, but somehow my feelings just came pouring out.

"I never thought we were laughing at them. I'm sorry if that's what you think. Yes, you're right, they have been good to us, but at the same time they have been guarded also. No one moves here and really gets accepted. You have to be born here. They gossip about us all of the time, and when I play into their stories, it's my way of covering my hurt."

He may not have liked my words, but I wasn't about to hold my feelings back any longer, either.

"That's not true. Look at the way Johnny has been accepted . . . and the way the teen club was accepted. If they didn't like you all, they would never have supported this place like they have. My folks and their folks before them worked hard to make this town, and I get the feeling that you work hard at irritating them."

I thought about what Nathan was saying, and about the way everyone helped us over our grief of Bill's death. Then a warm feeling came over me as I visualized my buddy, the judge. He was a friend, always would be, even if he was grand dragon or something of the Klan in Tennessee. Our relationship was the way two friends *should* think of each other; no matter what one disliked about the other, they still cherished the strengths and nurtured the good points of their friendship more than the bad ones.

Nathan gave me a knowing glance, and spoke of the judge. "Why, I think Judge Beacher would kill for you. I think he loves you."

"Don't be ridiculous, we're good friends, and you know there's nothing else between us."

"If he had a clear shot at you, he'd take it!"

"Please Nathan, let's not throw shit into this argument. I want to discuss what's what's really eating at you . . . I know what you're trying to get at, but if the two girls want a baby, then how do you think it will hurt this town? I can't tell them what to do with their lives." Dad's words played through my mind; he was expecting me to coach them, to guide them through life, to make all the final decisions in his place . . . Nathan's next words broke my thought pattern.

"This place is famous now. Everyone is proud of what you've done for their town, and when it gets out that two of the owners stalked the guests, picking out studs to father them a child, it will be embarrassing and shameful. We'll all be the laughing stock of the town . . . remember, everyone here goes to church."

I didn't know it at the time, but Nathan was asking me to choose between him and my family. I was angry and defensive, and my answer reflected those feelings.

"Oh, I know they go to church, but that's just a perfect example of how hypocritical they are. This town doesn't serve liquor, either, but I'll bet you Giles County sells more booze than any other one in Tennessee! They just don't want to legalize it because then the whole world would know how much booze runs through their veins . . . I call that ludicrous! Dad used to say only the sinners went to church."

"Your dad said a lot, didn't he? But he never lived here, either." Lately, whenever I threw something up at Nathan that dear old Dad had said to me, he seemed to grow angrier. I should never have mentioned anything concerning what Dad had taught me, but it was too late now.

"That's right, he'd never live in a town without liquor. How could he entertain his business associates in the style they were accustomed to? Until this place gets some mixed drinks, it'll never grow. No good restaurants will ever come here."

"You may be right, but they choose to stay this way for many reasons."

"And I suppose that's why they hire some Canadian to the tune of seventy thousand dollars a year, to find new businesses to come in here . . . because they don't want to grow? On one hand they entertain the idea of growing and prospering, and on the other hand they put obstacles so large in the way that the two concepts conflict," I tried to debate my position.

"They want to grow, but not grow because of the wrong reasons, and not change for the worse, either."

He doesn't see it, I confirmed to myself. "Well, they'll be crowded right off the map before they even know what's happened to them. Huntsville will grow to the north, and Nashville keeps growing to the south. Mark my words, in less than ten years, this place will be full of strangers with more progressive ideas than Mayor Gaylord has, and all of the new people will eventually vote liquor in."

"You may be right, but why do *you* have to be the one to tell them? I don't like hearing the things I hear all week . . . the way they already talk about you and our family. That idea of your's to push for liquor by the glass has them all up in arms."

"Are you ashamed of us, Nathan? Is that what's wrong? Is that why we're fighting?" I felt tears rush to my eyes, and I tried desperately to hold them back. I've had many fights with men before, and never cried in front of any of them. I was determined this time would be different.

"Yes, that's some of it. Some of my friends even shy away from me . . . why, last week alone I had three good patients cancel out and go to Ardmore for help."

"Well now, I can't help that we've been both a success, and a source of embarrassment to you, and find it very small of you . . . " I couldn't finish my sentence. I was sick inside. My husband of six years didn't like his wife or her family. I knew Nathan loved me, but while we were expanding and growing, he wasn't. He didn't like growth, and would have preferred things to remain like they were in his past.

I wanted to feel for him, to understand, but I couldn't understand anyone that never greeted change with enthusiasm. Sure, at times in one's life, you slowed down and took it easy. It was like each person's life holds peaks and valleys, quiet times, pacing times and growing times. Myself and my family were getting ready to grow and expand, having rested and lulled long enough after Bill's death. Our grieving time was over, and no one, not even Nathan's wanting it to be different, would slow our pace.

"I'm sorry that it's taken you six years to find this out. I love you, Nathan. You're very important to me and our family. But, you need to see and understand my side of it. If I try to be more like the way you want me to be, then I'll be miserable. The family will be miserable. Our marriage will be miserable. I can try to slow my ways down some, but I don't want to live the life you want me to. I'd go crazy without some type of change and excitement." I heard myself crying.

"I know you would. That's why I haven't voiced my opinion until now. I hate the prospects of what all this means to you and me." Then Nathan's eyes watered, and I could tell he wasn't quite finished with his say, as his lips parted, ready to strike out again. "I want you to leave me in my past, Trish. I like my past . . . and I can't change or keep up with your crazy family. I have nightmares about the twins being raised like this."

I snapped, defensively, "Fine, you can go to your little town and its hypercritical people. But you'll never get the twins . . . never! The children I bore will be somebodies . . . the best they can be. No stupid little town will dictate their future every Sunday in church. It's my obligation to our world—to foster better and bigger human beings."

"Maybe they don't want to be pushed. Patience isn't like you. She's quiet and meek. She's lovely."

"Patience is a Tillman. She'll grow more independent now that she is separated from Patrick in school. Being a twin has shielded her, but she'll get her wings. You'll see."

"Like Angel did? You nearly destroyed her, too." I slapped him hard. I heard the smack, and my heart broke into peices.

"How dare you say that! I have always cared for her because we had to stick together . . . "

"That's the way you see it, through blinder's of the past."

I stormed off, crying. I was hurt, and furious. I wondered how he could make love to me like he did, not liking me, but taking me so eagerly. I thought back to Bill, and then to Jimmy. I wondered if all men were the same . . . I wondered why they didn't believe love was a prerequisite to sex!

I woke the next morning to find Nathan gone. His closet was cleaned out, and I hadn't heard him disappear into the night. I desperately called his office, and there was no answer. The recorder said the office was closed until further notice.

I had too much pride to call around to find him, and it took all my courage to tell the family over breakfast that Nathan had left me. I had nowhere to run, no D&R like before. It looked like number three was on the rocks! A three time loser . . . and like before, I got two more Tillman's out of the deal.

I was glad I was forty-eight, too old to have any more

loves and children. Yet, as often as I had spoken the words "I love you, Nathan," I never really knew how desperately strong my love was for him. Now, realizing that he was really gone made me sick. Mom and the rest of the family couldn't understand why Nathan had left, and that didn't offer me any help. I didn't go into detail as to why he fled our sides, and I should have known they'd blame me for his leaving.

"Why do you drive them all off? He was the best one yet, and you toss them out like they mean nothing to you or anyone around you," Mom questioned my habits with men.

"Mom, you just don't understand what went wrong. Does it matter to you anyway, he was *my* husband."

"He was good to me and your sisters. We all loved him, still do. You seem to think that you can bring husbands into this family, demanding that we accept them, and when we do just that, learning to love them like family, you toss them aside and expect us to hate them, too." I thought about what Mom had just said, and from her prospective, it probably seemed like that's just what I had done. But from my slant, it wasn't that open and shut. Family loyalty should come first: I was her daughter. No matter if I was the single cause of my three marriages falling apart, the bottom line was blood: family blood that *should* bind.

I became defensive. "Good, keep on loving him then. It shouldn't matter to you how much he hurt me, or your grandchildren, for that fact. I know what happens to me doesn't matter. . . just like back when Bill screwed up my mind so badly. You never once said one word to him about the terrible things he did to me, did you?" I changed the subject back to our pasts.

"What sense would it have made to talk to Bill about it . . . it was over."

"No, Mom, it was never over. It will never be over until I die."

"Did you say something to Nathan to make him leave? Something about your past? That's it, you told him about Bill, didn't you?"

"Christ, Mom, I told him about that years ago."

"Why can't you have loyalty to your family and its name? You never did care what embarrassment you caused us all. Who else did you tell?"

"You're one to talk . . . what you did with a priest would have made this town lynch you both. But then, no matter what hurt you caused Tilly, you never did give her a chance in life and tell her the truth, did you?" I challenged back at her.

"It didn't hurt her, keeping it from her. I did just the opposite, we protected her."

"I'd think about that, Mom. Tell me why she grew up so bitter . . . not having any identity but a mean one. You're protection buried her. Your guilt gave her a way to be so mean . . . and I know you knew all along that she was lying and stirring up trouble for Angel and I. You did nothing, you let her! You were very vulnerable because of the mistake you made. You let her get away with anything, as long as she never found out about who her real father was. You let her hurt Angel and I," my voice echoed loudly.

Mom sat still, thinking about what I had just said. I wasn't finished yet, and I began to speak before she took her turn. "If it matters to you, he left because he doesn't like me . . . or my famiy and our creative ideas. He doesn't want to share in the way I want to bring his children up."

"I don't believe that . . . not Nathan. He would have talked it over with me. Did you do something with Judge Beacher?" I expected that final blow would come!

"God, Mom, don't make matters worse. Will you ever believe me? Just once? Why do you always think I'm messing around?"

She said nothing, and left the room with her damn squeaky chair moving at quite a quip. I was tired of squeaks, and more tired of being to blame for everything that happens around here. I found it very hard to accept; she liked her son-in-law better than her own daughter.

Of course, Tilly agreed with Mom, assuming I had just tired of Nathan. Angel and I confided in each other, and once again I found myself finding comfort only with her: just having someone to talk to was therapy enough.

I spent months pondering what I would do without my man, my protector. I knew I had finally found a love that I thought would never fade, and wondered why this was happening to me. I tried to see what had changed, what made Nathan want to leave me and his children. I attempted to joke about it to the kids, but the hurt was so deep I didn't think I'd ever love again. I began to think Becky's way was better; never love and never be hurt!

Since a man stood for protection to me, I struggled inwardly to become stronger and shed that past trait and need. I beefed up my conviction daily, trying to make myself believe that I was strong enought to go on as a single woman and mother of two very young children. I kept trying to reinforce that thought, but inside I kept telling myself that Nathan would return any day, begging for me to forgive him and take him back.

• • •

While I barely survived, my two sisters put their plans for their futures into high gear. Angel kept a notebook about different men's capabilities. She was very organized, and I had to give her credit for her studious ways. On one page of the ntoebook, labeled "Mate's Credentials" she listed every feature of mankind: eyes, brows, smile, weight, hair color, texture, and length, height, build, and penis size.

She spent evey moment checking out guests, and never ventured far from her source, practically living in her swim suit by the pool, sizing up every possible candidate. I wondered what the men would have thought if they knew what she was writing in her notebook, putting check marks in the good, maybe, and definetly no sections, as she categorized each candidate methodically.

Now Tilly went about her hunt differently. She didn't want to know who the father was, and figured if she just slept around enough, then she'd get pregnant and not know which one was the lucky father. She wasn't as picky as Angel was over her choices, and this I had trouble understanding because of her past. I figured she would have cared the most what her child might look like. I worried about her getting some disease, but said nothing to her.

"Trish, come quick!" Angel was running in from the outer lodge, and was obviously bubling over with joy. "I've found the perfect one!"

"Calm down, Angel. Let's see what looks so good to you." I took the outstretched notebook from her hand, and peered down the yes column immediately. I just had to see the man that scored so well. I followed her out the kitchen door and down to the lodge in the new golf cart that she purchased the previous month. (She got the thing because it made her trips back and forth quicker, and she didn't want to miss a single male as he strutted his stuff around the pool.) We opened the doors to paradise, and the humidity was overwhelming. I wasn't dressed for cruising, as Johnny called it. I looked around, waiting for Angel to point out her Mr. Right. She looked scared, and then ran to room sixteen, and knocked on the door. I couldn't imagine what she was going to say when he answered.

"Hello, Mr. Jackson, I wanted to check if everything is alright, your room and the service?" He smiled a big cheesy grin, and looked her over from her bare feet to her face, her suit covering very little.

"Things are perfect. I love it here. The sights around here are gorgeous." He had the right words, I thought.

"We're serving some lemonade by the pool, would you like to join my sister and I?"

"Sure, let me grab my robe and I'll join you."

"You don't need your robe, come join us, now!" Angel reached for his arm, and pulled him clear of the doorway. She wasn't about to let this man go. She led him over to me, and there we all sat. I found my eyes staring at the bulge in his tight little trunks, and I guess I embarrassed Angel, because she interrupted my surveillance with a shame-on-you look.

"Trish," in a real loud voice, "this is Mr. Jackson. He's from Los Angeles, and just passing through. He was nice enough to join us for a drink."

"Nice to meet you, Mr. Jackson. How long will you be with us?" I think Angel thought I was going to ask him how long his penis was.

"Two more nights, although I may be back through here next month. I don't get to the east coast very often." Angel nodded her head quickly in agreement to me, quick enough so Mr. Jackson couldn't see her delight in his answers. I could see that she was mentally rechecking the categories in her bright red notebook.

"Nice to have you here. I hope everything has been satisfactory." I didn't know what to say to some man that was about to be propositioned by an angel. If the tables had been turned, I would have been furious if anyone was eyeing me like Angel and I were him.

"More than satisfactory. I was wondering if the town has any nightlife?" He seemed educated and pleasant enough for the cause.

"No, not much. It's just starting to grow." Angel took over the conversation from there, and offered to take him to the ELKS club that night. He jumped at the invitation, and I just sat there gawking at her forwardness. I never remember picking up any male . . . never. They just seemed to show up and stay around. And the thought of Angel picking up srays for this purpose brought a smile to my face.

"Those two little look-alikes, are they yours?" he asked as he looked me over real good.

"Oh, you've met the twins? Yes, they're mine. That reminds me, the bus should be dropping them off soon, and I need to go see how their day went. Little Patrick needs his cookies as soon as I can put the plate in front of him. He eats like his fath——," I caught the word father and stopped. "It was nice to meet you. Sure I'll be seeing you around."

I had made my excuses for leaving, because I couldn't help myself and knew that at any moment I was going to start crying. I left the two of them sitting next to the pool, and went back up to the house.

Meanwhile, I wondered how Tilly was doing in her sleeping around tactic. When I asked her, she looked dismayed, and announced, "The doctor said I can't get pregnant. I've been wasting my time."

"Oh, Tilly," and I rushed and swept my arms around her. I held her tight, and she cried. I think I sighed with relief.

"No one will ever know how badly I'd like a family of my own," she resolved.

"I think I understand how you feel Tilly, but you do have us, you know, we're you family."

"Yes, but I wanted a child just like Patrick. Someone to share these last years with. I had such plans for him. . . "

I felt terrible for her, but I couldn't offer up my own son to her. She truly loved the little fellow, had ever since he was born. Patrick relished her care and love, and they were much closer than I thought Tilly could ever get with anyone. "Tilly, why don't you look into adoption?" I'll never know how I came up with that idea, but after I spoke it, I knew I had a good solution. "And tell me why the doctor said you can't ever get pregnant?" Not being able to get pregnant was never a problem I seemed to have.

Tilly's crying mood ceased, and I could tell she was thinking about adoption. She wiped the last tear from her stained cheek, and ran her finger under her eye to remove her smudged mascara. "He said something about a lining buildup in my uterus, and that it had gone too far into my tubes . . . " she paused, then went on with the real thought that was now racing through her head, "will they let a single lady adopt a child Trish? Do you think?"

"We can't find out standing around here. I'll call Judge Beacher and see if he can short-cut our way to the facts. I have no idea who to talk to. Want me to call?" I double checked with her.

"Please, do it now. Maybe I can still have my own family." Tilly was lost in hopeful delight.

I wondered what Nathan would have thought about adoption for the two girls' answer to their lack of children, as I made my way to the closest phone. Maybe if he had stuck this out with me, instead of deserting us all, then he could have seen that everything would have worked out for the best. Inside, I was sort of relieved that Tilly couldn't have any children, especially at her ripe age of forty-nine. And then the thought of all those guys she had slept with over the last three months made me giggle inside. She certainly had gained experience in the field of sex; at least she wouldn't die without ever knowing how good the physical side of it can be. I was dying to go into more detail with her about her little one-night stands, but couldn't bring myself to question her.

I imagined her lying perfectly still, letting the man of her choice do all the work. I bet she never moaned, or twitched her hips, or clung to his back as she pulled him further in. I fugured her the type to run to the bathroom and tidy up immediately afterwards.

I called Judge Beacher, and we decided to go to Nashville

for dinner together that night. Meg was at her sister's in Chattanooga for the week, and he had some business to tend to in the city the next day. He offered to go to the local adoption agency with me, after he completed his business.

I readied myself for an evening out with my best male friend. It had been ages since I had been out, my last outing was to the races in Birmingham with jolly Nathan; God how I missed my man. My every thought centered around him, and no matter how hard I tried to push them back over to the right side of my brain, the thoughts kept forcing themselves out.

Nathan was always happy when we were alone and none of the children were around. Sometimes, during our brief time together as man and wife, I felt like he resented the older children, my children, and the time I spent with them. He knew it was the right thing to do, to love them, so he tried very hard to do just that. I don't think he ever faced the reality that he wasn't truly capable of loving my children, through no fault of his own. He was never mean to them, never intentionally shunning them or provoking them into ire against him, but he also never really showed the same type love that a natural father could have for his own children. It was as plain as that, his love wasn't natural.

My first three children grew up with no one loving them but their mother. My biggest worry now was that they, the older children, had given their hearts to Nathan, and our split would cause them a lot of grief. I could see it in their eyes, when I told them that Nathan had left me and went away somewhere to forget us all. I assumed they thought I had failed them again, and as far as providing them with a father, they were right, I had failed. The twins were still too young to cope with the reasons why, but they, too, missed their father. Maybe it was the sadness that caused them to be melancholy, but their usual bounce had disappeared along with their father.

My favorite dining place in Nashville was "Boots Randolph's." Sometimes, Boots himself showed up to entertain the dining crowd. When we pulled up in front of the place, I was delighted the judge had chosen the right spot.

"I see our taste buds run the same, Judge? Nathan used to take me here once a month. It's such a nice change from the ways back home."

"Yes, I think you told me about this place some time ago. I remembered the gleam in your eye when you related your night on the town with him." He paused, and then asked, "Have you heard from the Doc yet?"

"No, not one word. The part of not knowing where he is, and why he left, is torturing me." I turned my head toward my side window and watched the valet approach our car as we waited in line, hoping my tearing eyes weren't apparent to the judge.

"I'm sure he's okay, Trish, and I think he'll be back. Pulaski is his home."

The valet opened my door, and I willingly jumped at the chance to change the subject and got out of the car. I didn't want the night to be ruined by conversation of Nathan and his whereabouts. The judge joined me and we entered the dining place that held many memories of Nathan and I.

The judge ordered us two drinks, and that alone seemed to change my mood to a happier one. Just the capability of being able to order a mixed drink was a nice change from the ways in Pulaski; beer just doesn't go with certain foods.

"Judge, do you think it's wrong of me to force the issue at the next election? You know, liquor by the glass?" It felt good to have another's ear to fill and question. I wanted to know his opinion, so that I could compare his thoughts with those of Nathan's. I'd do anything to understand why Nathan thought like he did.

"Many people have tried before you, Trish. But, I must tell you that none of them stuck around Pulaski after the vote failed."

"Were they town folks, or outsiders trying to move Pulaski into the times?" I wanted to know about the last attempts, especially who originated the change.

"I have to admit that having a drink before dinner is a nice custom." He swirled his scotch and water, and then tightened his lips and sipped from the glass rim. "Really nice." Then he answered my question, "Mostly big business people tried to get the law passed."

"It's very relaxing. Seems to set the mood before the main course, doesn't it?" I agreed with his opinion, enjoying my drink to its last drop.

"That mood is what stops the vote from passing. . . ." He didn't elaborate, something I disliked about people, the way they prompted your mind to think, and then dropped the issue before your mind had captured all of their thoughts on the subject.

"Well, what do you mean, the mood?" I wasn't about to speculate on his meaning.

"People are afraid if they pass that law in Giles County, that less desirable places will spring up, and things happen when people get high on this stuff."

I laughed at the reasoning . . . certainly, I knew things happen when one has too many before dinner drinks. But things happen as often in people's homes where they sit around sharing friendship and drinks; only the setting is different, not the outcome. "I know what you mean, but everyone brown bags it in Pulaski anyway. I remember discussing that with Standfords right-hand lady when we first moved here. I told her I wished Pulaski had some decent restarurants, ones that serve booze. She told me that everyone puts their bottle in their purse and just buys the mixer."

"Yeah, a lot of them do that."

"Well, isn't that being a lttle hypercritical? Almost like going to church every Sunday, confessing one's sins, and then starting to sin all over again on Monday."

He smiled at me, knowing my arguments were valid. "Yes, but if they vote it in, then their ways are made public. What they do behind their own doors is privy information to only the ones they *want* to share it with."

"But surely they know that Pulaski won't grow if they don't allow liquor by the glass?"

"They don't look at it like that."

"So I hear." I tried not to hear Nathan's words on the subject pass through my memory, but I couldn't forget the day he walked out on me, and the reasons why.

"Trish, aren't you ready to dig in? It looks and smells absolutely delicious, doesn't it?" checked the stately judge. I thought back to our first meeting, and his coveralls, at how I had mis-judged the judge.

"Oh, I'm sorry. Sometimes I get lost in thought and become oblivious to anything and anyone around me, even good food and friends. I promise it won't happen agian."

We had a lovely dinner, and then went to the dance floor area and secured a table up front. I loved to dance and hear live music, and the judge couldn't have pleased me more wtih his choice of nightly entertainment spots.

We talked of Meg, and her family. We discussed the twins, and how the inn was doing with the new addition. He inquired about Tilly and Angel, and Mom. We discussed Tilly's hopeful adoption plans, and our visit to the adoption agency the next day. It was a nice evening out, and I hated to see it come to an end.

"I got you a room next to mine, Trish. I hope you like the arrangements. The Mid-South is supposed to be the nicest place in town."

"Oh, don't worry about the place. I'm rather tired and any place without bed bugs suits me."

I watched the agile man of fifty pay the waiter with a gold American Express card, and found it odd that anyone else in Pulaski even had one. Nathan used to boast that he was the only person in Giles County with one.

"Sometime, Judge, you'll have to tell me how you became grand something or other in the Klan. I sure was shocked that day when I saw you standing there in your white robe.

"Next time we go out, okay?" The way he said it, sort of alarmed me, because this was a rare occasion, the two of us out on the town, and I didn't think it would be repeated very soon in the future.

"Maybe we'll visit your cellar sometime soon, huh?" I kidded with him about our little getaways. They hadn't been so frequent lately, and I did hold those indulging times we shared with a bottle very dear.

"Let's hit the road, girl. I'm ready to call it a night, too." I look up at the judge, directly into his deep brown eyes that were shadowed with bushy eyebrows and long lashes. Few men I knew had such long, thick lashes. Any woman would kill for them.

Everything remained as it should: the judge went directly to his room and I to mine, after we exchanged "thank-yous" and "see you in the mornings." As I closed my door, I wondered what Mom would say about this little outing of mine. She'd never believe that we didn't even share a dance together.

I couldn't fall asleep, and decided to read for a while—to enjoy the peace that fresh, unfamiliar surroundings sometimes brought me. I pined inside with an ache that physically hurt because I missed Natahn at my side. I wondered if he missed me, and prayed that he was safe and finding whatever type happiness he longed for when he left me and the twins. I closed the book and my eyes, but sleep didn't come.

I thought about the way he left, the things he said; they made no sense to me at all. We only talked for a few minutes, and never really tried to solve our problems . . . then he left like a sneaky cat in the still of the night, shunning his patients and practice of thirty years, going to some place unknown to all. It just didn't add up, and I wasn't sure how to stop my mind from reliving the past the two of us had shared. Maybe if he had said he had to get away, that he needed some time to himself, anything other than what he did. The unknown always drove me crazy.

I began to twitch, down there where women get that funny feeling. I hated that feeling, and thought about my youth and how I had asked Mom what that funny feeling was. She shooed me off, telling me she didn't know. I left thinking some worm was growing in me, and was scared because I was different from other females. I wondered, back then, if my brother had infested me with pin-worms of the pussy. . . .

I fell asleep to the tune of my body aching for his, still questioning why he so mysteriously deserted me and his children. My twitch went unsatisfied.

CHAPTER TWELVE

From time to time, I had been known to take up a cause that no one else in the family really believed in. During the sixties, I paraded proudly in Washington, carrying my handmade signs up and down Pennsylvania Avenue with the best of them. It was amazing that Dad's video-displayed will hadn't captured the pictures of me that ran in the *Times*. I believed that social change was important, and being caught up in the fury was just another part of my lively past. Back then, I never thought about the embarrassment those pictures had caused my folks. I was a Bobby Kennedy advocate, as strong as they came. Well, even though I had mellowed some by the age of forty-eight, I still picked up some causes and fought gingerly for them; liquor by the glass being one.

I called a family meeting to discuss my campaign, and found that not everyone believed in my cause as strongly as I did.

"Here you go again," said Tilly, "just when final word on my adoption is expected, and if you ruin it for me, I'll die."

Mom piped in with her agreement of Tilly's thoughts, and surprisingly so did Angel.

"Trish," Angel tried to reason with me, "why don't you give up on this thing. It's obvious that this county wants to stay dry."

"It's not dry...."

"Well, you know what I mean. I don't think it's a wise idea to push it any longer," Angel added, not giving me one concrete reason for her negativeness.

"Will someone explain to me the valid reasons behind your opposition—something besides just your feelings?" People who operate only on their feelings, without any logic, irritated and annoyed the hell out of me. What I needed were some good sound reasons behind their opinions, so I could understand their positions and maybe accept them.

"Tell us why you think it's the right thing," Mom suggested.

"Haven't you all been listening to the radio, my speeches and propaganda?" I asked.

"Sure, Trish, but it's difficult to lay facts out against it. All I know is that Father Daniel says it will be the downfall of the county. More bars will spring up and less church goers. . . ." Mom resolved. Sure, I thought, whatever Father Daniel thinks. I wondered if they served drinks at retreats.

"Hogwash, everyone goes to either Nashville or Huntsville on weekends to enjoy a few drinks and dinner now, so why not let some decent restaurant come here and save us the trip. It's not like we don't have bars here already, you know, and they're such shabby places, just plain old beer joints! Wouldn't it be nice to have a Steak and Ale here, or one of the better run of restaurant chains?"

"Sure, but think of the business we'll lose, the competition we'll have," injected Tilly.

"I'd welcome it, besides we'd serve liquor, too." At least Tilly was thinking along the lines of credible reasons, I thought.

Angel injected some more of her thoughts, "We'd have to close the Teen Club. Now that's something that did good for this place. God only knows it must have saved the teenagers a lot of money, not driving around all night for the lack of anything better to do."

"Yeah, I'm surprised the kids took to it so well. Maybe having just teens and no adults hanging over their shoulders made a difference," I said. "There, that's a perfect example: the people were all up in arms about no chaperones in the club, until their kids proved they could handle a little privacy. At first, they didn't like that, either."

"Trish, we all know it's who promotes what in this town that gets accepted or rejected. They don't like it and will never accept it."

"Well, do you all mind if I continue trying, or do you want me to hang up the cause?" I wasn't sure what I would do if they asked me to halt my efforts, but I wanted to know how they felt. That was growth for me, finding out I actually cared what they thought.

The final family vote was against liquor by the glass, my cause. I went off pouting over their decision, now knowing what I would do, until Patrick came running in from school bawling his eyes out and gasping for breath as he tried to repeat what had happened to his ragged self. "They sat on me and called us names."

"Patrick, please stop crying and tell Mama what happened. Here, drink this milk and let me get a wash rag so I can take a look at that cut."

"Mama, they don't like us here. They said I was a bastard child . . . and that Dad left because you are crazy."

I put my arm around my wounded son, and checked the cut above his eye. I summoned Tilly, who called Dr. Nashe and asked about stitches, if they were needed. It took the two of us to hold him down on the table, while the doctor closed his wound; seven stitches total. The scar would be permanent, but would fade over a time. I wondered if the words that they hurt him with would fade in time.

Patrick was a strong-willed little fellow, and after our talk that night, he held his pride high, and eagerly marched out to the school bus the next day. I worried all day about him, and even though I promised him that I wouldn't call the school, I did. The gall of that principal, to tell me that it wasn't their fault, that it was mine; me and my crazy ideas.

The more this damn town fought me, the more I wanted to fight back, but for the first time in my life, I began to think of the repercussions my actions had on others. I felt for my children's safety, and thought about Tilly's adoption and Angel's budding belly. She was three months pregnant, and that in itself caused the family enough grief with all the gossip it had stirred up.

Pete had been a local, and his memory still lingered in most of the town's heart. They didn't know how she could have done what she did, and turned against her immediately when the fact became well know around town that she was an unwed mother-to-be, widow to boot. I tried to warn her, but she didn't care. Her Mr. Jackson had done the trick, and all she did was bathe in the expectation.

Tilly got her news that the adoption was refused, and all

hell broke out around Galaxy, until she began a new crusade, applying for a foster care license, which probably was a better idea than the adoption. She had been turned down by the adoption authorities because of her age and the fact that she would be a single parent. She kept busy fixing a room for her new charges, and we all celebrated the day that one battered little boy named David arrived. I now started worrying about the day he would have to leave.

I was glad I gave up the fight for liquor by the glass, and bowed to Pulaski's old fashioned ways. I was beginning to think I was growing old, too old to fight for better ways. I was secretly relieved that Tilly's adoption refusal wasn't my fault. I did get the last one in with the smug town, though.

Two large manufacturing contractors made their decision not to settle in Pulaski for numerous reasons, one being lack of culture and good entertainment outlets. I told them so, and took every opportunity to throw it in their faces every chance I got. I even went as far as writing the local gossip sheet and pointing out their foolish ways to them. Now, their children would leave Pulaski in search of a future and careers, probably going to a bigger city that undoubtedly served mixed drinks. What had they gained? I asked.

• • •

"He's coming here this Thursday and he's reserved a room for two weeks . . . what will I do, Trish?" Angel nervously asked.

"Stay away from paradise! Go away or assume he won't know that it's his."

"Maybe he won't count, although I have to think he's coming here because we hit it off so, and he'll expect me to be available like before." We both looked at her belly and burst out in laughter, so hard that we had tears running down our cheeks. I was going to wet my pants, and she *did.*

"Wait until he sees how you've blossomed since his last trip here!" I had to say it!

"Guess I'd better pack my bags and hit the hills in hiding, Huh? I never thought about him coming back so soon. I thought he said he doesn't get away very often."

"Yes, he said that. But maybe he has a reason to come here more often. You must have shown him a good time, Kiddo," I teased with her.

"Hell, after he left last time, I soaked it for days. I could barely walk . . . stamina he has." Her eyes reflected the pleasure she had shared with him.

"See, you overdid it! He liked it, and wants more southern Tillman hospitality."

"We could offer up Tilly this time. No danger where she's concerned."

"Angel, what a thing to say . . . besides, if he's that good maybe I'll visit room sixteen this time—armed with protection, though."

It had been so long since a man held me and desired me, that I wondered if I would ever make love again. I'd had some good opportunities to romp in the hay, but something wasn't the same with me anymore . . . it wasn't Nathan throwing me down and loving me like there was no tomorrow. I looked at those latest chances with an attitude of "It's nice that you want me, but no thanks." I didn't know if the scare of AIDS or the lack of Nathan kept me celibate, but I did know it had been a very long time since I had made love.

"Well, make your decision soon, Sis, because he checks in tomorrow," I warned her.

"Let's see what Mom thinks. Where is she, anyway? I haven't heard her squeak this morning."

"She's out back with Father Daniel. And you won't hear anymore squeaks from her . . . I oiled the hell out of that chair yesterday!"

"Trish, why did you do that? After all these years, why now?" My sudden urge to quiet Mom's announcement of arrival had shocked Angel. I really don't know why I did it, but at the moment it made me feel very good.

"I don't know, I just felt like it and did it! Frustrated or something, I guess."

Angel looked at me and I could tell by her eyes that she was sorry for my husbandless state. "I know it's been hard on you since Nathan took off, but he'll come back, you just wait and see. Why is it that when someone really falls in true love, something happens to ruin it for us?"

Angel was right, I never felt like this after I shed myself and the children of the first two losers. Actually, I couldn't get rid of them fast enough, once I had made up my mind that I couldn't continue to live with them. But now, instead of me leaving him, Nathan had left me, and that made things different for me this time around. Somehow, it made me feel like I was the one at fault, although I didn't know what I had done.

"Those little words of encouragement mean nothing to me any longer . . . I doubt that I'd take the fool back, It's been almost a year, Angel, and not as much as a card. He never even sent the twins anything for their birthday, or mine either. If he was ever going to return, he would have shown up for Tim's and Becky's graduation." The hurt of it all was overwhelming, and almost hard to talk about, even with Angel. I knew I was about to give up on him, and started thinking about filing for divorce.

"I still can't believe he left like he did. I know you've told me everything about your argument, but it just doesn't add up. Does he have family anywhere, Trish?" Angel inquired.

"Yes, his brother is still alive . . . somewhere in Arizona or Mexico. He's only a half-brother, but that's all I know."

"Did he talk about them much, his parents?"

"Nope, just that his mother was married five times, and her last husband adopted Nathan when he was around twelve. He learned to love the man. He was born here in Pulaski, somewhere."

"I didn't know that his mom was married five times . . . no one in town had leaked that fact about his family."

"Amazing that they didn't, but for some reason everyone seems to think pretty highly of them and what they did for this place. Sometime I'll dig deeper into his parent's heritage, for the twins, when they're older and want to know. Right now I need to forget him and his town. . . ."

"I told Mom that you really did love this husband." Her telling me that made me wonder what else was discussed about my latest failure.

"How fathers could sell their kids, like Tim's and

Becky's did, or abuse them like the second one did, or just walk out of their lives like they never existed, like Nathan did, is beyond any reasoning to me. All three were rotten fathers! They would have been better off not having any father from day one . . . like you're doing," I declared with belief to Angel.

"You have a point. I'm glad mine is mine and no one else's. I don't care what people think, only what my child will think. It can't fall in love with a parent they'll never know. I plan on telling it exactly what I did to get pregnant. It will know how badly I wanted it. . . .", Angel believed what she had just vowed.

"I guess I'll go talk this over with the squelched, flying nun and her guardian out back. Somehow I'll have to get Father Daniel to leave Mom and I alone for a while," she said as I heard the back door slam shut.

Angel left the inn that evening, going to Mary's place on the outskirts of Nashville. Since Bill's death, their family pride had been restored and to good standing because everyone believed Bill was the hero of the eighties, sacrificing his life to save his sister. Mary welcomed any of us into her home, and often frequented us at Galaxy. The subject of incest and what Bill had done to me was never mentioned in their presence, as if it was buried with Bill. I still sent the monthly checks to Mary, who was always very appreciative. Ironically, the one sum of money he could have capitalized on legitimately, he never did; he had no life insurance policy.

Mr. Jackson checked in promptly at six the next evening, and after seeing his things disposed of in his room, he approached me in the main room. "Where is that lovely sister of yours," he asked with his overly masculine voice. His eyes weren't focused on me, he was trying to catch a glance of Angel as he searched the room for her.

"Oh, Mr. Jackson, she's on a little vacation. Won't be home for two weeks."

His face contorted a look of disappointment. "She left in a hurry, didn't she?"

I wondered why he thought that, and if Angel had forgotten to tell me if he called her earlier in the week, or something. "No, actually, she's had this planned for some time." My acting wasn't at its best.

He heard my words and turned quickly from me and left me standing next to the piano, pondering his thoughts. I twinkled at the ivory keys, fingering a couple of low notes. Guess he was in need, I mused.

Before too long, Angel's good looking stud reappeared at the piano and took a seat next to me on the bench. He acted confident, and determined about something. "Do you mind if I play? I'm a little rusty, but I don't think the people will mind." He slid his bottom over in the center of the bench, nudging me to the side. I stood up and told him to go ahead, play it.

Rusty, hell, he was an accomplished musician . . . the keys emitting the sound of perfection and many obvious hours of practice. I watched his manly, dark haired hands glide, and saw his eyes closed as he weaved with the beat. I remembered Angel saying how good he was at lovemaking, and mused over the thought that he had more than one thing going for him; he certainly did have the beat. I wondered just how much Angel really knew about this man, and if they even talked before they jumped into the sack.

"I understand you're staying with us for two weeks this time, Mr. Jackson," I asked, making small talk.

"Thought I was, but things have changed. I'm leaving in the morning," and after flashing a devious smile at me, "but I'll be back. Don't know when, but soon, I hope."

"Sorry to hear you've had a change of plans, but do come again when you can, and feel free to use the piano whenever you need some practice time."

He never looked up, or even opened his eyes as he began to speak, "I'll be transferring to the east branch next month, and you'll see me a lot. I like this place and the people here." Then, after finishing his words, he lifted his head. I noticed his eyes looked devilishly cunning, and I felt an uneasiness creep over me. Angel wouldn't like this news, I thought, and I hurriedly left Mr. Jackson at the piano and called Angel. Something was up, but I didn't know what. . . .

Trust your *instincts*, look into the *future*, use your *powers*—all words Dad had willed I should use. My instincts read trouble with Angel's little plan, and Mr. Jackson seemed very familiar to me, even though his name or appearance never rang a bell. But, something about that determined young man's mannerisms reeked of familiarity, and I tried to use my powers to grasp the meaning behind my feelings. My so-called powers evaded me, so I let my suspicious hunches rest.

Angel returned to the inn after a three day get-away, and after we discussed my thoughts on Mr. Jackson, she decided not to worry the situation to death. She kindly told me that it wasn't good for the baby, and flew off into her own little pattern of life. If she wasn't going to worry, then neither was I, I thought at the time.

But, we should have worried, because her Mr. Jackson greeted us at the breakfast table the next morning. He must have staked out somewhere, waited to see if Angel came running home after he left.

"If I didn't know better, I'd think you deliberately left because I was coming, my dear," boldly challenged Mr. Jackson as he helped himself to a seat at our table, without even being asked. Neither Angel nor I answered him, and I felt like getting up and letting her handle this challenge all by herself, but she reached under the table and grabbed my hand and squeezed it. Her teeth were gritting, and she was shaking slightly.

I tried to help her. "Well, Mr. Jackson, back so soon? I had to call Angel home because we're surprisingly booked solid for the week, and I needed her." I made an excuse for her, and as I did, she must have welcomed the help because she squeezed my hand, signaling for me to go on, to continue talking to him; please, the harder squeeze asked.

"See how unexpectedly plans change," he said, and then continued, "call me Hal, will you?" His attitude was almost daring, and I had a feeling he knew about the baby, but how? I asked my self. I knew her belly was growing, but if you weren't looking for a bulge in that area, you'd never be able to tell.

"Sure, Hal. Glad you could make it back so soon, and it's a miracle that you got your room back."

"I never let it go."

"But you told me four days ago that you were leaving

because your business plans had changed," I said, trying to assure Angel I hadn't misunderstood when I gave her the green light to return home. He confirmed that he had said that, but let us both know that he hadn't meant it. He then asked to be alone with Angel, and after getting her nod of assurance that she could handle him, I left.

They sat at the table for what seemed like hours to me. I was going crazy with curiosity, and even thought I'd make up some excuse and interrupt them. Just as I started over to the table, I saw him take Angel's hand in his and help her up from the table. They walked out of the dining room, and headed out back to the gazebo. At least she wasn't crying, and they did look civil to each other. I decided I wouldn't offer my help, because she seemed to be handling him alright. I decided to peek out the back door at them. I saw her thin arm raise and then she slapped his face and turned and ran toward the house. I ran outside to her and saw him following her toward the house.

"Are you okay, Sis?" I asked, doubling up my tomboyish fist, ready to protect my little sister like I always had. She ran into my outstretched arms, sobbing and muttering incoherent words. "What did he do?"

"I did nothing but put the facts on the table to your scheming little sister, head honcho!" His tone matched his eyes: bitter and angry. So, he had figured out her little scheme, and she must have admitted it to him.

"What do you want, can't you see you've upset her? Go away and leave her alone, or I'll call the police and have you thrown out." I threatened in defense for Angel.

"I don't think you'll do anything like that, Mrs. Brawn, because I have my rights, too."

"Angel, we need to talk." I didn't know what this young man knew, or how much he knew either, and I didn't feel free to discuss anything with him concerning Angel. I needed to get her away from him, somehow. "Let me take her to her room, so she can calm down."

He sarcastically snapped back at the two of us, "Oh, did she move back into the big house again, now that the pool room is of no further use to her?"

It sounded like he knew everything, and I opened the back door and pushed Angel into the kitchen, after I let him know that he wasn't welcome. I closed the door as he started down to his room. Angel and I hurried to her room, seeking the privacy we needed to talk.

"Okay, Sis, so he knows. So what? You don't have to marry him. Please stop crying."

"I can't. It's all so bad. . . . "

"I can't help you get rid of him if you don't tell me everything he knows. Don't tell me what he feels or what you feel, tell me the facts . . . how much does he know?"

"Go away, Trish. I've made a mess of everything. I'll call for you after I settle down some. Please leave me alone."

"Sure thing, I only wanted to help. But you rest up, and if you need me, call down." I tucked the quilt over her legs, and turned to leave. She reached out one hand, begging me to take it.

"Sis, everything is my fault, and Tilly's, too. Nathan left you and the kids because of us, didn't he?"

"What makes you think that? Does that guy know something about Nathan?" I couldn't understand why that subject came up now, and had trouble trying to figure everything out.

"Wait, Sis, don't leave, come sit down and let's talk. I'm so sorry, but I wish you had said something about Nathan being so upset with us girls having babies out of wedlock. I thought he acted funny when I asked him to be the father, especially when I told him you said that it was his choice."

"I said what? Nathan the father of your child? Are you crazy? I never said he could father your kid." I was furious at the thought, and was lost in anger mixed with bewilderment.

"No, no! You don't understand." That, I didn't!

"So, what is that guy doing here, then?"

"He knows he got me pregnant, knows that I picked him and he came here to confront me with the facts." Angel could tell that I was very confused, and slowed down and started from the beginning, before I got the chance to butt in. "Trish, I'm the one with a story for a change, so let me tell it without you interrupting me."

"Okay, Toots, I'll shut up and you do the telling, but you'd better not leave me dangling or I'll butt in." I tried to smile at her, but smiling at this point didn't come easy to either of us. I got comfortable, and she told the most important story of her life and mine.

"I asked Nathan to be the father, but he refused. He actually acted like I was crazy, and he sure had trouble believing that you went along with the idea."

I had to interrupt. "When did you ask him?"

"Right after you left him in the gazebo, after Tilly revealed what she wanted to look like. Why?"

I remember losing my breath, feeling sick at what she had just disclosed, but she started in again and I couldn't get a word in between her thoughts as they came pouring out.

"So, after Nathan refused our idea, I decided to get a man on my own. Shit, all I needed was one little fishy, at least that's what Mom always threatened me or warned me about for years." She was knotting the quilt up between her shaky little hands, and started to bite on her lower lip, between the startling words that she spoke. "You know the rest, how I hooked my fishy, but what you don't know is that Nathan sent him here to be the fish!"

"Oh my God, he didn't!" So Nathan left that night because she asked him to father her child . . . he had a counter plan of his own, did he, I thought. My anger grew with each word Angel related to me.

"Yes, it was his plan to give this baby a father, and seeing as he couldn't do it, he figured his brother would if he paid him enough. He gave Hal twenty thousand dollars to get me pregnant . . . no wonder he had so much stamina!"

How could she add those puns, I thought to myself . . . this isn't a funny story at all! It was all a misunderstanding, he shouldn't have left me. Deserted me!

Angel took a breather, and I took the queue and delved in with questions, "You really asked Nathan to father your child?" I didn't hesitate, "His brother? I don't know how you could do that to me, Angel. He's mine . . . or was mine." I had too many questions, and couldn't seem to organize them in any logical order.

She looked directly into my big startled eyes, and challenged me on that point, "I asked you, and you said to ask him. And you even said something about the kids being together all the time anyway, so they all could share him as their father."

"Oh, Angel, do you know what you've . . . we've done? I can just imagine how Nathan felt when you told him I didn't care if he fathered your kid."

"Well, you said you didn't."

"No, that's not what I said. We were talking about artificial insemination, not Nathan's making love to you! I never would have gone along with that plan, dearie. He's mine. The thought of it drives me crazy! Him with you or anybody else makes me sick all over!"

"I thought that's what you agreed to, so he must have thought you really didn't care about him. Now I see what I've done." Her hands moved to cover her face. "Oh, God, I didn't mean to hurt you both. I'm so sorry, Trish."

I thrashed all the known facts around to myself, forcing myself to play Nathan's role, to think like he might have, when her heard what Angel proposed. No wonder he didn't go along with their new plan, because he couldn't bring himself to impregnate Angel, and he probably thought he was letting the family down, or something. Maybe he thought I didn't love him for him, just his ability to father more Tillmans. I thought about calling his children Tillmans, which wasn't fair, either. Oh, how I must have hurt the man, I concluded sadly to myself. To him, I had made my choice and picked my family first.

"Sis, please believe me that I didn't know you wouldn't let him get me pregnant."

"Angel, how could you ever think I would let my husband do that?"

"Well, you do everything for your family first . . . and I just thought this went along with everything else."

"My God, did Tilly ask him to do it, too?"

"I don't think so. I never told her about that part of my plan." Thank God!

"Well, what does his brother want?"

"He said it's his, so he plans on staying around here and seeing it. He even asked me to marry him!"

"How much more money did Nathan offer him for that deal?"

"Sis, I don't think Nathan did it to be mean. Hal said something about us getting in over our heads, and didn't want my child to be fatherless like his."

"That's nice, considering he's the one that left them that way! He deserted them."

"Maybe he wouldn't have, if I didn't plan such a foolish thing. I should have tried them all, like Tilly did. Then, no one could claim my child."

"I don't know about anything Angel. I need to see the judge and get his opinion, a legal one. I can just visualize all of this coming out. . . ."

"I suppose if I try to keep the baby to myself, he could cause us some problems, huh?"

"I've got to go, Sis. I can't think straight . . . did Hal tell you where Nathan is?"

"No. I hit him when he said something about getting paid for such pleasure."

"I hope you decked him good, Sis." I bent down and placed a soft kiss on her cheek, and tried to say good-bye as my mind raced with thoughts that were all jumbled. I needed time to think and plan, to sort out everything that had just come to light. I needed the ear of Judge Beacher, and my ears needed the familiar pop of a well soaked cork!

CHAPTER THIRTEEN

Time to think and gather my confused thoughts into something coherent—something I could understand, that's what I needed . . . time, I decided as I strolled across the field toward Judge Beacher's cellar. Our cellar was gone to the teens, and the farther I got away from the scene of our latest folly, the better I felt. As Galaxy faded behind me, I prayed the judge was home, and thankfully found him peacefully sitting on the front porch with his wife, Meg.

"Thought that was you walking over, Trish," greeted Meg. She was such a tiny person, with her "Alice in Wonderland" structure standing about four feet-nine inches tall at its peak. But her personality wasn't tiny, and I envied her inner strength of calmness in a crisis. No matter how big a problem was dumped on her lap, she never missed a stitch while darning it.

"Yup, in need of that great listener that you corralled years ago, Meg. Do you mind sharing him with me for a few minutes, for a few legal questions that I need some quick answers to," I explained only one of my immediate needs to her.

Meg turned to her husband, and they both gave each other the knowing look that only they shared and understood the meaning of for the past twenty years. They had such a dream-like marriage.

"Sure, Trish," and she added a wishful thought to her approval, "I hope you haven't got bad problems to worry about again. You didn't hear anything bad about Doc, did you?"

"No, nothing any worse than our past troubles," I owned up to her in a sad way. The judge and I disappeared around the back of *their* home and down into *our* working cellar.

The judge's den was different. He used it to hold some Klan meetings, and the decorating was appropriate as a musty hiding place. The color scheme was dark, and almost bordered on dingy and dismal; all browns and dark greens. There was a speaking podium, and a microphone, with speakers in each corner of the room. One wall had bookshelves, which were crammed full with knowledge of some sort. Another wall was a bar, rail and all, with at least twenty stools. His stock was plentiful, and I helped myself to my choice as we readied to start our conversation. The judge took a seat in an overstuffed chair, as I plunked myself down on the old used couch across from him. Only a dim bulb behind the bar reflected any light in the room. The setting was perfect for any confessional, I thought, as I started telling him about the mess Angel had gotten herself into.

About three hours later and with fresh tears, I found myself composed enough to drift back to Galaxy. Now I knew legally where we stood, but didn't know where we all stood emotionally. Hal had been right, he does have some rights, if he can prove that the baby is his. I knew my next move was to sit down with Angel and develop our counter-plan against Nathan and his newly introduced brother, Hal Jackson.

I knew I had very little time—we needed to spin our web fast, because Hal was ready to take control and I couldn't let that happen. I can't let my Angel down now, I thought to myself as I entered my lonely bedroom.

I walked directly to Nathan's picture on my nightstand, and picked up the lovely cloth frame that I needle-pointed during the last two months of my final pregnancy. As my hand glided over the stitches, I thought about my present situation, and succored to a gush of tears that just had to come out. I let the rain pour, and just when I thought a let up was in sight, I forced my mind deeper into my saddened emotions and seeded the clouds so a bigger burst of relief would continue. As I licked at the salty tears cascading over my upper lip, I thought how right it had been that the Lord added salt to our tears. Salt on any wound causes some additional pain at first, but also aids in a faster healing process.

A knock on my door interrupted my immediate affairs, and I resented the intrusion. "Who the hell is it, and what do you want?" Guilt came over me, and mellowed my next words, "I'm sorry, but I want to be alone."

A meek little voice announced that Becky was home again from school, and even though I hadn't expected her, I found myself delighted with her arrival and briskly stepped to my door, greeting her alarmed face with a big welcome home smile. I grabbed her, and pulled her into my room, hugging her tightly out of need. Her timing couldn't have been better, and I knew at that moment that she was going to play some part in my future plans to save Angel and our family from the predicament we had gotten ourselves into this time.

"God, girl, it's wonderful to see you . . . thank you for coming home."

She broke my embrace and stood back, freeing her closeness to me so she could look at her mother in astonishment, and with that look, she opened her mouth in a gasp and asked, "What do I owe this happy greeting to?" I took her hand and pulled her over to the sitting area in my room and down on the couch we fell.

Becky had come home to personally congratulate Angel on her pregnancy, and had hoped to find some peaceful place to study for her finals which were two weeks away. She was now attending graduate school at Vanderbilt. I told her that this house was anything but peaceful, and when I finished the story that was taking precedence over everything else in my life, she announced that she was more than willing to help in any way she could. I knew before I had asked her that she would comply and scheme as hard as any of us Tillmans to get the still undecided plan in motion.

It took the three of us four long days to iron out the minute details, but I thought the plan that evolved was brilliant. We had to flush the two brothers out of hiding. I needed to see Nathan and talk to him.

Unknown to the mischievous Tillman planners, Nathan and Hal were also putting the final touches on their plan as they sat sharing drinks and swapping the incidents that led to their preconceived idea that they had scored a victory against us, their *foes*.

"You should have seen the look on Angel's face when I asked Trish to leave us alone. You were right, brother, she tried to get Trish to protect her. Every time she squeezed Trish's hand, some words of defense came spouting out of your wife's mouth." Hal lit a cigarette, and the way the smoke rolled toward the ceiling you could tell it was a confident exhale.

Nathan nudged Hal's elbow, and then entered the barroom discussion, after mixing his brown-bagged drink of gin and tonic. "I know Trish went to see Donald Beacher about their legal rights, and they have been burning the midnight oil planning something . . . and I'm afraid to guess what. This battle isn't over yet, Hal, especially since she called in her kids as reinforcement. Those older children have minds that no one who knows them would willingly choose to take on."

"Didn't you get along with her kids?"

"Yes, I love them all, and was about to approach the subject of legal adoption before this all happened." Hal could tell that his brother was deep in love with the family he had left. Nathan reached for more popcorn which the flirtatious waitress had so kindly placed in front of him.

"Well, we'll have many years to catch up on your past with the Tillman family, but right now we need to settle our own plans. I'm all moved into our place, and eager to get my hands on those girls."

Both men had opened the door to their past when they decided to hibernate in their old farm house on the south side of Pulaski. Their parent's had followed family tradition since his great-grandparent's time and lived their entire life in the old, restored log home. The boys hadn't remained true to tradition, staying on only until they reached manhood, and ventured from the old place to secure their heritage and fend for themselves. Neither one ever thought of disposing of their birthplace, and they still shared joint ownership of it.

Ever since Nathan had disappeared on that dark night over a year ago, he had remained lost to me, ironically hiding out only twenty miles from the inn. The cabin in the hollow had proved to be a good sanctuary, and he opened up the boarded windows and the more peaceful doors of his past with enthusiasm. The refreshing change of pace, the quiet of nature, and the happy memories of his past, helped him to abide his loneliness for me and his children. The secrecy that the hollow afforded him allowed him all the freedom he needed from peering, nosy eyes as he planned his scheme to reunite us as one.

Brother Hal's occupancy fed his lonely fires of rehabilitation, and although he missed the times we had shared in our brief, but good marriage, he found the absence from us and his work somewhat energizing. This was Nathan's home, not some place that his wife had inherited and handed over to him when they married. It had no strange faces every day, popping up and surprising your train of thought or requesting this and that whenever you wanted to be alone. It was Brawns' house, Brawns' fields, Brawns' way of life.

"Tomorrow we'll see Brad and Lilly and set the plan in motion. I know Angel and Trish will mellow, and eventually accept the idea. Once they get a look at those girls, they'll do the right thing. Then, we'll sit back and plant that family garden we've talked about. I wonder if Ma and Pop know we're working the fields again," Nathan said.

"I hope dead people can't see what we're doing! From what you've told me, Trish's father isn't one to tangle with either. I'd hate for him to join their side."

Nathan laughed, and nodded his head in agreement, as he thought about the many words that I had used to describe my father. "Shit, Hal, if he could see us, he'd strike us down right here. I doubt if he'd even let you finish that good Tennessee water that you're drinking." Then he finished up with a good one, "And, since Trish lost her battle against liquor, this brown-bag I'm hiding would burst into flames and smoke us out!" They both enjoyed a chuckle and watered their lips again.

"Well, he certainly trained his flock to stick together. When Angel slapped my face, it felt like the two girls were behind the force of the hit." Hal could still feel the exact place where Angel's blow had landed.

"The only soft blow dealt in that household is by Mom every once in a while. I regret not having taken her into my confidence before I left. She and I hit it off right from the start."

"Who would believe you'd ever get along with a mother-in-law?"

Nathan thought of me and of all the stories of my past. Amanda Tillman was a wife—first, last and nothing more, certainly not a mother! "Maybe she's not a mother-in-law . . . don't you have to be a mother before you can earn that title?"

"It helps. Ready for another warmer?" Hal asked as he pushed his empty glass to the rim of the bar.

"No, I think I'll hit the road south. Are you coming . . . it's your turn to cook dinner, you know."

"Yeah, I'd better leave now, or you'll get no dinner other than what the can opener unlocks tonight."

Back at Galaxy, I sat huddled in the kitchen, retracing the day's events in my mind. I've taught so many IBM staffies to be good staffs, that detail rarely escaped my plans. I sat satisfied that all the loose ends had been covered, and grabbed my keys and headed to town. Once the rumor was planted in the right person's mind, I knew it wouldn't take long for it to coast through the air to wherever Nathan and Hal were hiding out. We had almost caught them, I thought, as I picked up speed on the road toward town, if only Tilly hadn't let Hal escape her tail when he moved out of the inn.

My habit of checking every parking lot for Nathan's red jeep was almost mechanical to me by then, and after seeing it wasn't parked around the church, I entered Father Daniel's abode next to the church safely and unannounced. I found Daniel in his den, and surprised him with my unexpected presence. We had a good talk, and he offered to help Angel and I keep our real plan a secret. We had to tell him that Angel really wasn't getting an abortion, just to put his righteous beliefs at ease before the fact became known around town.

Next, I went to see Dr. Nashe, and made the necessary appointment for Angel's "pretend abortion." Of course, the doctor couldn't be let in on our scheme, because he would never have gone along with our plan. His friendship with Nathan went back to childhood, and after being neighbors for twenty years, they had a boyhood bond that could not be broken. If anyone knew where Nathan was watching our every move from, he did. I felt certain of that fact, and found his friend's occupation a perfect carrier pigeon for our hoax.

The good doctor's oath wouldn't get in the way, either, because the small town doctor had taken a different oath, the one that all cliquey doctors take in small towns; "I hereby promise to keep everyone informed with my patients' latest illnesses, doing my part in the community to spread good will and cheer to the best of my ability. If I fail to tell you important citizens the latest, then my nurse has taken an oath to back me up!"

I sped back to the inn, eager to tell Angel that it was her turn to flaunt her condition and her impending date of hospitalization. She and Becky were planning a shopping spree, and knew how to follow up on the rumor that was serenely hopping from lip to lip on the square by then. After all, she needed a new bed jacket and some fresh undies for her stay in the hospital, and was only doing her community good will by shopping uptown.

The most stylish women's shop was run by a well known contractor's wife, Linda Lou Buckly. Linda Lou acted and looked like a post-bellum bride, and her southern drawl was definitely a carry over from those times. I always figured she rehearsed that slow twang every night with the aid of a diskette labeled, "How to Learn to Speak Like Your Ancestors."

Angel and Becky entered the shop, after rehearsing their parts to perfection.

"No, she needs something frilly, something in pink should do nicely," Becky suggested to Linda Lou.

"When are you going into the hospital, Angel?" Linda Lou started her fact finding questions sooner than expected by the two shoppers.

"Next Thursday. I'll only be in for two days, unless something goes wrong. . . ." recited Angel in her pre-staged sad tone.

"Just what type of operation are you having? I know

that Clara told me, but Pete's mom gets carried away sometimes and she's hard to understand. Was it your appendix?" Linda Lou's glasses slipped from habit down her nose, and her peering, challenging eyes eagerly awaited Angel's answer.

"Hardly, Mrs. Buckly. Those things come out unplanned"

Angel and Becky avoided answering any more of her direct questions, leaving the poor unfed gossip with no news to pass on, other than her personal confirmation that Angel was expecting a hospital stay in the near future, and that the poor dear was surely pregnant. This she could verify by her own eyes, because Angel had made sure the fitting woman had seen her budding belly during changes.

So, the girls returned to Galaxy, reporting to me that the rumor's back up mill had started to churn.

On the other end of town, Dr. Nashe had reported Angel's surgery schedule to Nathan and Hal. Both brothers were aghast! She wouldn't, she couldn't do such a thing!"

"Well, it was only about two hours ago when Trish came in and made all the arrangements for her. She said Angel was too embarrassed to make her own plans." The good doctor and friend was attempting to make them believe the truth of the situation.

Hal questioned his brother first, after lighting a fresh cigarette and gathering his scared thoughts together into something coherent. "Nate, would Trish really coax Angel into an abortion?"

At first, Nathan was disturbed that Hal thought it was Trish's fault that Angel was going to have the abortion, but then he, too, had grown used to everyone automatically assuming Trish was behind every move any of the Tillmans made. "I hardly think Trish can be held responsible for Angel's abortion decision. Sounds more like they feel trapped, and think it's better to rid themselves of the baby than have you around as its father . . . this wasn't the reaction I planned on, or paid for."

Even wtihout me there, he was still my protector. I know that now, but before this all uncoiled, before he related his side of this story, I would have guessed that he was far away, still in hiding some place, probably in some other woman's arms.

"I didn't plan on falling in love with your wife's puppet, either. I wish I never came here."

Nathan turned to his brother with a defiant look, and asked, "I thought you said Angel was in love with you? It looks to me like she only fell in love with how you did it . . . not you!"

"Well, I won't stand for it . . . I have some rights, don't I?" Hal's face was white, peaked looking and tight with fear, and then it turned crimson red. "That's my child, too!" he added, searching for sympathy and agreement from both his brother and Dr. Nashe.

"Calm down, Hal. We need to think this move through. Let's go sit on the porch and come up with a plan, or figure out what legal rights we have to stop it." Nathan turned to the doctor, and verified the date of Angel's pending operation.

Long into the night the brothers, aided by their boyhood friend, planned and worked on the latest turn of events, until they felt they had a counter-attack to add to their previous plan of action.

Unknown to me, the brothers had decided to publicize their plan in a big way. Their plan finally came out in the open two days later.

The bus load arrived before the press did, so we all got the shock of our lives when all of those chubby bellied girls walked into the inn. The brothers had obtained state approval for the inn to become a house for unwed mothers, and the first bus load of young victims had arrived, and were standing around, waiting on some kind of celebration to break out.

The flashing cameras of the accompanying news reporters kept blinking, adding rays of light to the scene. A TV anchorman held the microphone close to my face, as he announced to the world that the Tillmans were sharing their good fortune with those less fortunate by opening a home for unwed mothers and fatherless children. An adoption agency had been approved by the state, and would be located in paradise. The inn was closed to the public. Three qualified nurses would live-in, and a staff of doctors would be on call at all times. A transport vehicle had been donated by Smith's Chevy, and the Bank of Pulaski had so graciously offered to start a savings account for each new arrival. As I stood listening to all those ridiculous claims, I knew Nathan and Hal had come up with a better plan than ours. I sure had them flushed out. . . .

I can still hear him laughing, and see his cunning smile of victory, as he followed the last press camera into the main room.

He quickly stepped up to my side, and joined in on the announcement, taking the microphone in one hand, mine in the other, and saying, "This is a happy day for Pulaski. We all are so delighted that we found a way to help this community, our home, and hope that this little venture will show you all how much your friendship has meant to my wife, myself, and our family. After working with Banker Lilly and Judge Beacher, my brother and the local state officials, our proud day has finally arrived. Please join us all in our opening," and then, turning to the young, pregnant mothers, he told everyone to make themselves at home while the last of the paid guests checked out.

As I watched him smothering in delight with his victory, I must have counted at least twenty unfortunate girls. What the hell was I going to do with twenty pregnant women, and what about all the reservations still to be honored on the books? What I had hoped looked like tears of joy to the uninvited guests, started to pour out, and I fled to my room, locking the door behind me. I heard no footsteps behind me, and I fell, shocked and exhausted across my bed.

I must have fallen asleep, because the next thing I heard was the hinges coming off my door and the hall light invading my darkness as Nathan entered our room of old with door in hand. He propped the door up against the opening, and then walked very slowly over to our bed. He was followed by the twins, holding on to his pant legs as tight as they could. I knew the deck was stacked against me.

I looked up at him, and started to laugh, then cry. "You miserable bastard, look what you have done to this place! You leave me alone for a year, and then you have the gall to come tramping home with twenty pregnant women in tote. I see you and your brother have had a very productive year! Sowed many a seed, have you?" I caught my breath, and continued to shred him verbally.

"Well, I don't plan on taking care of your children, or your wanton little hussies either. I'll go kick them out right now." I rose from the bed and didn't give him the satisfaction of looking in his direction. "How could you?" is all that I managed to say before he grabbed me. He held me tight, so tight that I couldn't break his hold and get away.

"Just calm down, Trish. Hal and I thought Angel might like some company . . . look-alikes need to be together, don't they?" He looked me straight in the eyes, and then elaborated on what they had done to our inn, why they had done it, and what I could expect in the future if I didn't go along with their little scheme.

Nathan and Hal had planned the whole thing in order to close down the inn. They didn't want Angel and Tilly stalking the guests for planned sex any longer, and he let me know that he was good and tired of me running such a demanding business. They both had figured that Angel and I would be able to see what the consequences were when we looked twenty young girls in the belly, and just maybe we would think about bringing more fatherless children into this world.

Two hours into explaining their motives, he told me that Hal loved Angel and no way was she getting an abortion. Hal was supposedly going to ask Angel to marry him again, and he hoped for her sake and mine that she accepted his offer. Then, he told the impatient twins to put their jackets on, because Mommy and Daddy were going to take them for a ride.

As I left the inn, I caught a glimpse of Mom and Father Daniel doting over the young ladies. Tilly wasn't around, or at least I didn't get a chance to see her before we left.

The inn was hustling, but instead of energetic guests, it was filled to the rafters with slow moving mothers-to-be and nurses, doctors, and state adoption officials. It looked like everyone was quickly making themselves at home, and I was left out—not needed.

As we drove down into the hollow, the kids screamed in delight at the sight of two deer ambling over the pasture.

The deer stopped, and so did we, admiring the doe and her new fawn. The fawn still had black spots, and was unsure of its stand, Nowhere in sight was daddy buck.

"Isn't that a lonely and scared look on the doe, Trish? She has no mate, I guess." Nathan reached across the car seat and touched my hand, then he pulled it to his lips and kissed it lightly, once, then twice. "No children should be deprived of their father. No mother should be deprived of her mate."

"Where are we going, Nathan? Isn't this someone's land?"

"To our home, my home, the Brawns' homestead, which you're a part of. It's where we've belonged since the day we were married. This isn't Tillman land, and never will be!"

"You bought this hidden place? Is this where you've been hiding?" His disappearance still agitated me, and I was not about to be coyed into forgiving him of desertion so easily.

"Yes, this is where I kept track of your every move. This is where I planned our future as a reunited Brawn family. I would leave here every morning, and watch you drop the kids off at school, and then wait for the bus to drop them off. I'd watch as you'd meet them by the road.

"I've worked hard out here, finishing the restoration of the old place before I brought you and my children home. This is our home. Milky Way is now the home of new stars. It's serving a better cause, and we don't need the money, Trish."

I was stunned. I was silent. He really didn't know me.

"Nathan, Milky Way Bed and Breakfast is my home, my business. Dad left me that place, and I have my family back there to care for. We need to talk this through."

The car stopped in front of a log home, big and rambling with a huge front porch. He opened my door and let the children out, telling them to go play while Mommy and Daddy talked. He warned them about the lake, "Now don't go getting wet, your mama and I will be up on the front porch if you need us."

We talked, we touched, we talked some more. I watched as the twins got wet, wading and playing in the lake. The bounce that had left them had returned.

"Nathan, I don't think I'll be content down here, all alone in this hollow . . . I need to work, or I'll smother you and the twins."

"I know it will be hard for you to learn how to relax, but if we have any future together Trish, it won't be out at Galaxy. All those people interrupting us all the time . . . I hated it."

"Sorry, but I think I'll hate this, too. What will I do all day when the kids are in school and you're at work? I have to keep busy, so that I don't think of the past."

Nathan stood up, leaving me on the porch swing. He went inside the cabin and returned with a big box. "Here, see what I bought you."

The box was full of knitting needles, cloth, yarn, quilt blocks and such. I started to laugh, and then he disappeared again. When he returned this time, he held a set of keys out to me.

"We are now the proud owners of a fishing boat. And I bought us a small old house in the Keys, for our winters. By the time we restore it, and you knit and sew quilts for us all, you'll be ready to draw social security. The house in Florida is large enough for Mom, all of our kids, and maybe someday our grandchildren, too." He watched for my reaction, the boat keys jingling in the breeze.

"Trish, think it over before you say anything. I want you to have a chance to be a mother and a wife. Let me give you that, please?"

I rose and stepped into my man's protective and caring arms. I let the tears flow, and noticed they weren't salty tasting anymore. I was healed. I had finally found the true meaning of love.

I vowed to myself that I would find a way to bring the Tillmans and Brawns back under the same roof, someday soon. But for now, I agreed that Nathan was right: I needed to let my mother and sister Tilly live a life that they wanted; not one that the dead had dealt them. Angel needed time with her new husband, and for now, they would have to stay on at the Galaxy Inn and run things back there for me. I was taking another departure, and God only knows what I will return with this time. Maybe love will make it the best return yet!